# A NEW SPEAR

## THE FIRST BOOK OF SPEARS

### SPEARS

#### BOOK ONE

## DOUGLAS OWEN

Science Fiction and Fantasy Publications

**A NEW SPEAR**
**DOUGLAS OWEN**

## Science Fiction and Fantasy Publications

https://scififantasypublications.com
A division of DAOwen Publications




A New Spear / Douglas Owen

ISBN - 978-1-998029-21-1
EISBN - 978-1-998029-22-8



Jacket Art commissioned by MMT Productions

10 9 8 7 6 5 4 3 2 1

*For my father*
*May he be at rest in the Grand Lodge above*

# ONE

Christine cried out in agony once again as her body convulsed with pain. She had been in labour for over a day, and yet the child still would not come out of her. She laid on the bed in the back room of the brothel with sweat beading on her brow. Flashes of lightning lit the room through the only window.

"You must push when your body tells you to," Lattice said, the midwife Madam Kateryn had called in. "If you do not push, the child will not come out." Shaking her head, Lattice looked up at Kateryn. "Is the girl deaf or just stupid from the birthing?"

"Mind your tongue," Kateryn said. She had never called on Lattice to help with the birthing of children in the brothel before, but the last few days had been unusually dank and a storm had rolled in. Today, the clouds had erupted with lightning and sleet, making it a truly dreary day. Midwife Polis would not come when called on, saying the weather was evil, so she settled on Lattice for the birthing of this child. "She is young and does not know the ways of birthing."

It was true, Christine was only sixteen years. She had no siblings, being orphaned at the age of eight. Kateryn had taken her in then, promising to care for her. She had cooked and cleaned, and when her body had flowered, Christine was put to work with her ankles in the air, making the men feel special as only a woman can. Kateryn had made a lot of money off the auction of Christine's maidenhood. She told the girl the money would pay for any problems she would have, even if she grew large with child.

"She sleeps again. Maybe we can get a little rest as well. This child is so stubborn; it does not want to come out on such a night as this. May that I did not have to either," Lattice slurred. "Can I get a cup of mead or even wine before she awakes, just to help steady me, if you mind?"

"No," Kateryn said flatly. "I will have one of the girls bring you some tea. That will help you stay awake for this child when it comes."

"Be as you may. Mead would taste better, though."

Christine's eyes opened slowly, squinting as a flash of lightning lit up the room. She caught a flicker of something just over by the door. There was a figure standing there watching, waiting. She tried to look closer, but could not focus on it.

"Who... Who are you - AAAAAA!" Her body wracked with a spasm of pain and she arched her back.

"It looks like the little one is trying to stay inside her," Lattice said. "And she is seeing things as well. Have you slipped her something while I was not watching?"

"It would be best you watch your charge till she brings forth her child, instead of making wild accusations."

Lattice frowned. She would rather have had the mead; the chill of the night from the storm was getting into the bones of her hands, making them ache. She flexed her fingers into fists and then relaxed them, a lightning strike of pain shot up into her arms this time.

"The storm is what's keeping this child in her. It's scared of the lightning, and the thunder's not helping much either." Lattice wiped her nose on her sleeve to remove a drop of sweat that had formed there. Kateryn wondered why Lattice was sweating so profusely. Kateryn was the brothel owner and madam, just like her mother and her mother's mother before her. It was said her family had always owned the brothel, putting the first-born girl in charge of it after she had spent a year on her back once she flowered. Her maiden hood was auctioned off, and she was put to work so she would know what it was like to be a working girl in the brothel, thus never forgetting where she came from. Once Kateryn gave birth to a girl, she was trained in running the brothel. It gives each of the owners through their lineage a good understanding of what the girls go through who work there.

"She's back asleep now." Lattice looked about, and as her eyes drifted to the door she saw him, standing tall and proud in a grey cloak, his hood pulled up over his head, cast a shadow across his face. "A Wooder!" she said, making the protective sign. "What are you doing here?"

Kateryn looked towards the door and gasped. She had not seen a Wooder for years. The ancient order of healers only seemed to come when there was hurt or death about, always looking for children newly born to take for service as either Spears or Wooders themselves.

The Wooder stood, not moving. He appeared willing to wait for the inevitable. He was tall, standing well over six feet, a dark complexion and appeared comely, from what the women could see. His face had a shadow of a beard, flecked with salt and pepper. He was mid age, possibly around forty. He looked fit, in fine physical shape. He filled out the shoulders of the cloak and stood with his arms crossed. Scars covered what showed of his forearms, signs of training when he was first taken as a child. It is said a Wooder trains first as a Spear, but when any of the tests are failed, the child forfeits the privilege of serving the Realm as a protector, and instead became a servant of healing. They also searched for those children who will become Spears.

He waited, with the knowledge the girl in front of him would die tonight in child birth. He did not know how he knew, he just did. He waited.

Christine woke. She focused on the Wooder.

"I will not survive this night, will I?" she asked of him.

"No," he said, emotion starting to show as his voice softened. His mind thought of the mother he had never known.

"My child?"

"He will come with me," the Wooder said. "He is destined for greatness. He will become a Spear. He will serve the Realm and bring you honour. All mothers of Spears are honoured, no matter their walk in life." He stepped forward, walking between the bed and Kateryn.

"One can accept what happens if one knows great good will come of it." He knelt, taking Christine's hand in his.

She felt the calluses from years of long training with weapons, the muscles from many days exercising to the point of dropping. Her eyes searched the shadows of his cloak to see what he looked like, but his face was still hidden in shadows.

"I will see the one who comforts my soul…" she started, but her body was hit with another bout of pain from the birthing.

"The baby finally comes!" exclaimed Lattice.

The room lit up from the flash of a massive bolt of lightning. The illumination showed Christine the face of the Wooder, and she calmed. He was a handsome man, with a kind face. His eyes told her he was sincere with his claim. They also showed great sorrow, knowing she would not be long in this world.

"Will you look after him?" she asked, gasping with the pain.

"I will not, but there will be many who will love him. He will train hard, and he will gain heart. He will know much love from his companions and friends. He will be a just and fair man who will have the love of the Realm at his feet. He will save many lives and be a great man. You will be proud as you see him from the seat of the Great Protector, the one brother of the Five who looks over us. Be at peace, mother of Spear, bring forth your child. I will be here for you and guide you to the afterlife."

Her body shook again. Teeth gritting with a force that made her wonder if they would shatter. Christine pushed with all her remaining strength. The Wooder kept a firm grip on her hand with his and reached behind the woman's back, elevating her shoulders and whispering into her ear. He recited the ancient sayings to assure her all would be well. It was a beautiful sound, his voice, as he sang the ancient lyrics:

> *To be a Spear is to protect the Realm*
> *From those who mean it ill.*
> *To be a Spear is to protect the people*
> *From those who will do them harm.*
> *To be a Spear is to give up everything*
> *For the good of the Realm.*

*To be a Spear is to be the one*
*Who stands between the Darkness and the Light*
*To be a Spear is to be a weapon*
*Wielded for good against evil.*

The litany seemed to comfort Christine, as Lattice pulled the child from between her thighs. It was pink and covered with blood spots from the birthing. With a great effort, the child coughed out the fluid from its lungs and let out a wailing cry.

"He is born," said the Wooder. "A Spear is born. Show him your love before you pass, child. Show him how much the world will love him."

The Wooder reached and took the child from Lattice's hands, bringing him to Christine's breast. She took him, kissed him, and loved him. The child found her breast and latched on to the nipple. He sucked his first meal from his mother's breast, the last meal she would be able to give him. It was full of all the love she could give and he took it gladly.

"She still bleeds," Kateryn cried, looking down at the bedcovers.

"She bleeds all her blood for the child," Lattice said. "She will not survive this birth. The healing is beyond me."

The Wooder pulled back his hood and Christine looked from her child to see his eyes. They were full of compassion and love. She knew she was dying. She felt herself emptying from the birth. It was peaceful, seeing his eyes looking at her with respect. She did not know a man could look at her that way. She was a whore. Men only saw her for what she was; but this man, this Wooder, he seemed to look into her soul. He saw what others did not. He saw she was the mother of a Spear.

He bent forward and kissed her on the forehead. "Sleep now, mother of Spear, your child will be taken care of, he will be loved, he will be fed, he will be clothed, and he will save us all."

Christine closed her eyes as the world grew dark. Moments later, the last of her lifeblood flowed out from between her legs, and her existence slipped out of her body.

The Wooder said a prayer to the Five Gods who created the world and asked them to take Christine into their care. When he finished, he took the child from her breast and wrapped it in a cloth produced from inside his cloak. He stood and turned to face Kateryn.

"Take care to inter the body of the mother of this Spear with honour. The Five Gods will be watching," he said, voice full of sorrow.

The Wooder then lifted his hood over his head, cradled the child close to his chest and wrapped his cloak about them both to stave off the storm. He paused for a second, head bowed in contemplation.

"His name is Thomasyn Saye, and he will be a Great Spear. Remember him for her, and if the Five smile, he will save us all." With that, he opened the door just as silently as he had before, leaving the two women with the body of the mother of a Spear.

# Two

The rain beat down on the Wooder as he made his way out of the town of Fishily. The small charge he carried was held securely in a swathing cloth against his breast and covered by his cloak against the driving rain. He moved deftly, with a silence that masked his true size; the muscles of his legs, having been trained for long endurance running, were not taxed in the slightest by his pace.

The whole of the town was dark from the overcast sky that released the storm; rain beat down on the street, making it muddy for those who dared to challenge it. The Wooder did not concern himself with walking softly or with stealth, for he knew his footfalls would be washed away just as quickly as he left them. He lifted his head just enough to see the sky, feeling the coldness of the rain wash away the tears he shed for the newest mother of a Spear.

His was a lonely life, having served as a Wooder for well over two decades. He remembered when he was young, living with the other Spears in Flight. He had trained. He had fought. And he had failed. His failure was not in fighting or running; no, he was in perfect condition. His body was muscle and strength, just like anyone who trained their whole life to be one who enforces the King's justice. No, in the end, it was one of the poison tests that made his body fail. He had reacted badly to the test at the age of eight, disqualifying him from serving as the Spear he had been training to be since he had been born and brought to the capital.

But alas, his training had continued, for failing as a Spear did not stop you from serving the Realm. He was taken in for training as a Wooder, and given a second chance to bring honour to the mother who had died when birthing him. He had taken to the training fast, with the knowledge of how important it was. As a Wooder, a healer, and a person who served the needs of others, he would wander the Realm. If he was lucky, he would find possible Spears, and if he was good at it, he could be named as a Great Searcher, the highest accolade a Wooder could achieve.

He still remembered all the long hours of training, the leagues of forced runs, and the feeling of regret when he was told, "Sorry lad, but your body has reacted poorly to the cathale poison. I'm afraid you can only serve as a Wooder".

But being a Wooder did not mean he would not get any rewards. No, he was welcome where he travelled. People would seek his aid to help heal the sick, help with their livestock or even give council when disputes happened. And he would give the advice, directing them to a Spear if necessary. He had been taught the Realm's justice; he only lacked the mark of a Spear. He was to serve, to help, to keep the common knowledge of the world for those who needed it, and he was to find Spears.

Today was a good day, even though the heavens beat down on him with the torrent of rain trying to deter him from his path. Today he had been called to collect a Spear at birth. When he had arrived, the Spear had not yet been born, but was still in his mother's belly. He knew right away the child to be born would be a Spear, a boy Spear, a protector of the Realm. The ache from his arm told him so, even though the child had not passed the proving. The mother was unwed, with not one man nearby to claim the child as their own. He was a lucky Wooder today, for he was able to comfort the mother of the Spear, and pray for her acceptance into the afterlife.

Yes, he felt blessed. He was able to hold her hand, he was able to comfort her, and he was able to tell her the honour her child would bring the Realm as a Spear. Most mothers of Spears did not live long enough for a Wooder to explain this to them. Usually the Wooder was just entering the birthing chamber when the mother passed away, only able to offer a prayer for them.

The child gurgled and fell back asleep against his chest.

He would have to secure some goat's milk for the Spear as soon as possible. The child would wake hungry soon, and he had a responsibility to make sure the new Spear made it to the Realm's castle safely for training. But in order to do such, he would either have to secure passage on a boat to cross the small salt sea, or travel by foot. He knew the weather would continue to drive down for at least a few more days, delaying the departure of any ships. So he travelled by foot, that being the only way left to him.

The mud on the ground was slippery, but he was surefooted. He trudged through it, bending to keep the young Spear in his arms from getting a chill.

The two of them travelled for twenty minutes, passing small farm homes until he found one with goats. He moved towards the home, cautious of any dangers.

A door to the small farmhouse stood in his way. It was little more than planks held together with twine and hinges made of rope, but it kept out the cold wind due to the cloths having been stuffed between the planks. He knocked on the door, hoping someone was home. A shuffling sound from inside was all he heard, and then a rough coughing voice cried out to him.

"Watcha want?" a grumbling sound came from inside the structure.

"I am in need of goat's milk for a child. I can repay kindness. I can help with your cough," he called out.

"Who are you?" another voice from within responded, a woman's voice with a horse sound to it as well.

"A Wooder, with a newly born Spear in his charge," he replied.

"Get the door open for 'im, Drake," the woman's voice sounded as she coughed.

The door opened to reveal a small room with a cooking fire in the centre. The smell of bacon and bread met his nose as he entered, reminding him of how long it had been since he had eaten.

The two occupants of the hut were old, near seventy years, if not more. He bowed to them before he entered their home, taking his hood down for them to see his face. He took two long strides forward and stopped right after entering the hut, allowing the older man to close the makeshift door.

"I thank you both for this hospitality. The boy is new to the world and I must make sure he survives the road. I need a skin of goat's milk for him, and I have something for your cough," he said to them both.

"Can I see 'im?" asked the woman as she got to her feet. "I've never seen a new Spear before." She had a gentle look to her face that told the Wooder he could trust her. She stood with her arms out and a wanting expression on her face.

He opened his cloak and brought forth Thomasyn, who was still sleeping soundly. The woman took the child in her arms as he surrendered it to her charge, knowing from the soft look in her eyes, she would not injure the child.

"Do you have a skin to carry the milk? I have one if you need it," Drake said, under a cough.

"I do, here." He handed over his empty skin. The old man took it, opened it and sniffed to make sure what it had held would not spoil the milk.

"Good and clean. I would have guessed, but I wanted ta make sure," he said, while clearing his throat. "Give me a moment, I can get some from Bessy. She's just outside there under the eaves." He pointed to a door at the other side of the home.

The old man turned to the door at the back of the room and exited the house. The Wooder watched as Drake left, pulling the door shut behind him. The bleating sound of a goat being milked could be heard above the sound of the rain that beat down on the roof.

The Wooder turned his attention to the makeshift oven of stones in the centre of the room, with coals glowing red under it. They blazed fiercely in the dim light of the room, casting shadows against the walls. A bucket of what looked like fresh rain water was beside the stones, and a few clay pots over to the side accompanied it.

"I will need a pot that can boil water," he said to the old woman. "I will make a potion to clear your coughs."

She motioned to a medium pot fired red in colour.

"This one can hold the water and heat. The water in the pail is clean from the sky," she said with a sniffle.

He gathered the pot and half filled it with water. From his cloak, he produced a small leather pouch with some writing on it. The contents he smelled and then emptied into the water. The pouch went back into his cloak.

"This will help ward off the cough," he said, putting the pot on top of the rocks. "It must boil to bring out the right essence. Once it is done you will need to add this." He produced another pouch from his cloak and from it he drew out a small folded square of paper. "Make sure the water is boiled before you add this in it. Let it sit till the paper is gone. Portion half to each of you, no more, no less, and drink it down while it is still hot. Do not drink it if it is cold, for it will be spoiled and harm you. Tomorrow you will feel better, but stay out of the rain for three days."

She looked at the folded paper, surprised he was truly about to rid her of the cough. Her face lit up, and she reached out for it and he allowed her to take it.

"Remember, you need to drink all of it, and make sure he takes only half. If he has too much, he will be sick and you will not be healed."

"I promise, I will make him take half, and only half."

"It has a foul taste to it, like that of bitter root, so be warned," he said, looking sternly at her.

Drake entered the room with two skins bulging. He had a smile on his face as water dripped from his hair and wet clothes.

"I give ya back yours and I offer ya mine as well. It is a long journey to the capital, Wooder friend, and you need strength as much as your charge does. Be with peace, and may the Five Gods protect ya."

The Wooder gathered the child into his arms again, nodding to the old man and slinging the skins over his shoulder. He then took a small cloth and put some of the goat milk on it. Thomasyn seemed to smell what was happening and started to cry. He put the cloth into the child's mouth and Thomasyn suckled at it.

"He will grow fast and strong. I will let him know of the kindness you have shown, and if the Gods are willing, he will return one day to thank you for your kindness." He folded his cloak around the child and himself, reached up and pulled the hood back over his head. "I must leave now. I thank you once again."

"Wait!" the old woman exclaimed. Her hands worked quickly over the fire as she opened a round of bread and put it over the coals to warm. Once lightly toasted, she put some churned goat's milk on it with a few pieces of the bacon that had sat getting black on the flat stone. She handed it to him with a smile. "A finder of Spears needs more than just milk to build his strength," she said.

He bowed to her, knowing they had given to him a great deal of their food.

They watched as he left, knowing they had saved two lives that night, but worrying if the storm was too much for the two travelers to survive.

# THREE

Tess stood in the line to the anti-room of the Spears, not knowing why she was doing this. It was three days ago that her child had passed away from the bad cough and Tess still felt emptiness in her heart.

Gregory, her husband, had also died five months earlier from a mugging, leaving her alone and pregnant with a large belly in a room she could not afford to pay for. They had been wed just a day after meeting and had moved to the capital afterwards. She had not known him very well, the marriage having been arranged by her father just before he died. It had caused her concern that she would end up on the streets before giving birth; it had also worried her she would be alone during the birthing of her child, the only reminder she had of her late husband. If any complications happened, Tess would be in real trouble of dying herself.

But the birth had gone easier than she would have hoped; her child had come forth within minutes, not the hours Tess had been told could happen. Her body handled the pain well and her boy had entered the world screaming, being small and sickly looking. She named him Denis, and once cleaned, she brought him to her chest so he could latch onto her, drinking his full. Though his size had worried her, he had a healthy appetite, and she showed him her love.

Not two days after his birth, Denis had started to cough. It would not stop and Tess did not have enough coin to go to a healer. She was told by others the Wooders would want a lot of coin as well, coin she did not have, and that was just to look at her child, not heal him.

So her child had coughed, small little puffs at first, and then more frequently. Soon Denis was coughing hard and mucus, spotted with blood, coloured his lips. She tried her best to comfort him, wrapping him and keeping him warm. Her heart ached, and she had tried to find help, but her landlord was sullen and unresponsive to her need. Denis stopped taking her breast and soon after the coughing took his breath away, he died. Tess spent that night crying all alone.

Now, with no money left, the owner of the building was threatening to remove her from the room she had shared with her husband. The home she knew would no longer be hers to live in. With that, she took all the clothes she owned, along with the body of her child and the silver points it would cost to have him buried.

She had accomplished the one task, burying her child, and had struck off to submit for testing to be a wet nurse for the newly born Spears. She had heard a great number of newborns were making their way into the capital and though the payment was not much, she would have enough to live.

***

Con's eyes opened to the morning light that streamed into his bed chamber. There was still no noise from outside the door, and his thoughts went to his morning duties. Today was different, for it was the start of the gathering of wet nurses, the event that happened only one week out of every thirty days. It will be the day that reminds him of what he does not have.

The basin on the small table was empty, but the pitcher beside it was not. He rose from his bed, moved to the table, and poured the cold water into the basin. Once it was full, he took out a small wash cloth and proceeded to clean himself. He rubbed furiously at his skin to remove the feeling of sleep, but when he came to between his legs, he only patted softly. The space there was still tender, even after twenty years. Con felt a slight tingling from the scar that stood out in place of where his manhood had been. He wondered why it was so, maybe a phantom pain or healing that had never truly taken.

He could still remember the day it had been taken from his body, but fortunately, he had been young at the time. The western lands had always been full of deviants, and the practice of cutting small boys for the elite class was commonplace. The memory of the pain was clouded and hard to bring forth. With a quick dabbing motion, he cleaned the vacant area and returned to scrubbing the rest of this body.

A slight knock alerted him that someone was waiting outside his chambers. He pulled a robe around himself and tightened the drawstring.

"Come," he said to the person on the other side of the door.

"I have clean linens for your bed and hot water for your basin, sir," the young child who entered said. She was maybe ten years old and limped terribly on her left leg. She was a child who had succumbed to an injury during her training as a Spear. Unfortunately, the injury was severe enough that she did not make it through the training, nor could she join the Wooders. She was given the choice of employment in the service of the Spears, and she had accepted for what else could she do other than beg on the streets. The Realm never wastes talent.

"Put the linens on the bed, child; I will attend to them shortly," he said, taking the pitcher from her. She did as she was told, then reached out, drained the basin into the cold pitcher, took it and left Con in the room.

He looked around for a second, the linens sitting folded at the foot of the bed, and decided to put the pitcher on the table. He adjusted his robe, placing the clasp of his office on the sash he tied around his waist, straightened up his back and walked out of the room.

Con made his way down the corridor and into the kitchen. He took a bread ball and cheese to eat for his morning meal, and on his way out, he picked up a cup of water from the end table to wash it down.

The chamber he would be meeting the hopefuls in was close to the entrance of the training grounds. His walk took him through the square where Spears were already training for the morning. The clutch of Spears from this batch had only three more years before they would no longer be in flight. He was concerned they would still not make much, for most of them had failed, and now their number was only seven from the initial twenty-three ten years ago.

His feet walked steadily and silently as he crossed over and entered the anti-chamber. It was just outside the nursery, and he knew he would be seeing a number of women who needed employment.

Con waited outside the doors of the nursery, anxious to complete the task assigned to him each month. It lasted only a week, but it bothered the eunuch tremendously, for it reminded him of what he did not have: sex.

He gathered himself, straightening his robes, making sure he was without spot or stain, and opened the doors.

His was taken aback by the sheer number of women who had been lining up since daybreak, looking for the privilege to become wet nurses for the newly arriving Spears. Their eyes shone with sadness, for they all had lost children within the last few days.

It was the way of things. Those who lost could gain a feeling of worth that would fill the void in their hearts. It was important to the Spears to have a mother's milk supplied to each and every child until they reached the age of two. But with such need came rules. A woman whose child is still alive could not be accepted as a wet nurse. The Spears would not allow it. They would not take that which belongs to another, no matter how much the woman needed the coin she would receive, or the shelter that would be supplied.

No, it was Con who had to make sure the women were truly without child, and their milk was pure.

He had become an expert at judging breast milk over the last several years. The amount of breasts he had seen was enough to make even a sailor blush. Each month it was always the same. Several hundred women presented themselves and he would judge which one to accept. He would open the doors and the women would shuffle in and present themselves. He would record their names and ask when their child had passed, and of what. Once recorded, he would have them bare their breasts. His examination of them was thorough. He would make sure the nipple was of a sufficient size with no signs of being suckled by a babe in the last day or so.

If he was satisfied, he would have the woman produce milk on a swath of cloth. The effort would show how easily the milk came from the woman's breast and what the colour was, for all milk was not the same. He would smell the milk, making sure it was not sour, and examine the look of it. He had been told good, nutritious milk would have an off white colour, and that was what he was looking for.

The first group of women who came to him he dismissed out of hand. They were too old, breasts sagging. Children would have a hard time latching on and he already knew their milk would be sour.

The next few women who came through appeared younger than the last group, but not as healthy as the older ones. He did not even look at their breasts and dismissed them out of hand as well. He reminded himself once again to talk to the criers to have them add "Young and in good health" to their calls.

The next woman was healthy, with ample breasts and a good colour to her milk. The sample she squeezed out was sweet smelling, with a wholesome colour to it.

"That is good, Tess. Please, could you go through the door over there? A Wooder will take you to the children."

"Yes, me lord."

"Oh, I'm not a lord, just a humble servant of the Realm. But thank you for the courtesy."

She curtsied and blushed for a second, putting an arm across her breasts. Con had returned to writing on a sheet of paper and did not notice her still standing there.

"Ahm," she said, clearing her throat.

Con looked up at her, surprised she had not left, and then realized why.

"Oh, please cover yourself. The door over there," he pointed to the door at the other side of the room. "Go through there and the Wooder will show you where to go next."

The next four days saw the same type of women. Some old, some young, some small breasted, some large breasted, some with sour milk and a few with good sweet milk. He would always choose the sweet milk ones; that was the way it had always been, and the way it will always be.

Foremost in his mind he remembered Tess, the sweet young thing. She reminded him of a woman who had owned his life before he came to serve the Spears. The thoughts of her brought a pang of sorrow for the land that had been his home before he came to the Realm, and for the loss of his manhood when he encountered such a sweet and pretty young thing.

He sought out Tess after the last round of women had come through. She was in the nursery with a child to her breast. He smiled just as she looked up and she smiled back, and then turned her attention back to the babe in her arms.

THE WOODERS BROUGHT THE CHILDREN INTO THE NURSING chamber as they arrived. A total of thirty-seven had been found this gathering, and more seemed to be on their way. The wailing was predominant in the room, and the constant changing of the children was the norm. The wet nurses who had been picked from the city took up the challenge, for like their charges not having parents to take care of them, they had no children to miss the milk the Spears needed. There were almost as many wet nurses as there was newly born Spears this year.

Tess moved about the children, changing bottom cloths and making sure all the children were healthy. She kept busy, sleeping only for short periods of time. Tess knew she would have time to sleep when the children aged more than five months.

The wet nurses were watched by the Wooders, who marked down on the crib list who had fed the child over the last few days. Tess wondered why they recorded and asked one of the Wooders about it.

"We do not want the children to become dependent on any one woman. You need to feed different children so one does not grow accustomed to another," replied one of the Wooders. He directed Tess to another child who needed her attention, pointing out she had fed Bethany already that day.

Tess watched as the trainers came in on the third day. Forty-three children in this one gathering and the women felt the need of every one of them. Each child had their own crib, each fed by a different wet nurse every time they needed to be fed. The trainers started the stretching on the fourth day, and Tess noticed they would keep the wet nurses away during the training. She watched as each trainer took a child for an hour, moving limbs and contorting bodies to increase flexibility. When they finished with the first group, the trainers moved to the next, stretching and manipulating each one.

"Why do you do that to the children?" Tess asked.

"It is important for a Spear to be able to move any way they need to," Master Chail, the head trainer, replied.

At the beginning of the second week, the trainers started to numb the children against being scared or startled. Tess watched as they would duck down, out of sight of the infant and shake the crib, growling and trying the scare them. The sound of the children howling was ferocious at the start of the week, and Tess noticed the crying lessen as the training continued. They also kept stretching the children, manipulating their little limbs and training them not to be shocked. The training continued for the whole week, even during feeding times. It caused much concern for many of the wet nurses whom had never seen anything like it before.


## Month One

The month moved on for Tess and the other wet nurses as they kept the feeding of the new Spears as frequent as possible. Changing of the soiled bottom cloths happened as if on a routine. Each trainer worked with five children, doing stretches and exercises while trying to surprise the children to desensitize them to fright. They strapped small stones to the children's wrists, ankles and foreheads to encourage muscle growth and to teach them to strive to survive. It was the ancient way of training that had been passed down from generation to generation, and it was a proven technique. Furthermore, they needed to encourage strength, for the children would need it in adulthood.

The trainers kept the weights on the children for an hour each day during the first week of the training. Steadily they increased the time until, at the end of the month, the children could lift their arms and legs with ease. Not one child cried or complained about the weight they carried, even when it had been left on them all day.

Every one of the children became used to the adults surrounding them, picking them up and moving about with them in their arms. The touch of the wet nurses comforted the children, teaching them love was in the harsh world they lived in. The Spears encouraged the wet nurses to show affection, but to never grow attached to any one child.

At the end of the first month, the Holders of the Staffs started to come into the nursing chamber, examining each child in turn. The girls first, making sure they were fit and unburdened by any flaws. One was marked as rejected, for they found deformations in her arms and legs. That child would be handed over to the Wooders, her training to begin at the age of three months and continue unless her malformed limbs kept her from serving.

The boys were then examined as meticulously as the girls. After the examination, each boy was circumcised, wrapped and treated by the Holders of the Staffs with reverence. Two children were marked to be trained as Wooders, for there was found to be a defect in those two as well.

The wet nurses seemed taken aback by what was happening to the children, concerned with the inspection and circumcision done to them during the ceremony. Out of them, Tess was the most vocal, having come to love all the children, even the ones rejected from being accepted as a Spear.

"What is the reason for that?" Tess demanded of Chail.

"For what?" Chail responded, turning from Bethan, another trainer whom he had been talking with.

"The cutting of the boys. Why do such?"

"We cut the men to keep infection from settling in. It is an ancient custom for Spears, to be cut down there in order to show they are men of strength and with honour," replied Bethan.

"How does cutting a child show they are strong or honourable?"

"You will have to ask the Five Gods. They are the ones who tell us a Spear needs to be cut. I am just a lonely trainer and have no knowledge of such things," Bethan remarked. Chail put his hand to his mouth to stifle a laugh. Bethan usually did that to people, making them laugh with a deadpan remark to them during a possible argument.

The wet nurses fawned over the boys, knowing they had just suffered tremendously for what they would be. The women would coo at them, hold them and rock them until they settled. Each child calmed from the trauma to become sated with the attention they received. The next day, the training continued as it always did, according to ancient custom.

## Month Two

The trainers increased the weight they put on the children. They encouraged the children to crawl as best they could, trying to teach them how to move when other children the same age would just be learning to lift their heads. The stretching still continued every day, helping with flexibility and maneuverability. Tess noticed the children were continually placed on the ground to see if they would crawl. Some would turn and others did nothing, but the trainers moved about them and encouraged them to keep trying. The wet nurses were kept busy as they struggled to remember who had been fed and who had not. Weights were removed and added to the children to get them accustomed to changing levels of comfort.

Each day, for two hours, the Holders of the Staffs would walk among the children, reading from the Holy Books of the Five Gods. The children would gurgle and respond to the sound of the voices as if they understood what was being said.

## Month Three

The trainers continued the stretching and weighing down of the limbs to keep the flexibility each child had gained. The Holders of the Staffs continued their reading of the Holy Books of the Five Gods, and having exhausted the first twelve volumes, they started on the last three.

Tess and the other wet nurses still fed the children, and the trainers continued to desensitize the children from being scared.

"Chail? I think there is a problem with this child," Tess said with concern in her voice.

"What is it, Tess?" Chail asked.

"This child is very warm, and appears to have marks coming up on his body," Tess said.

"Let me see. Are those the marks you're speaking of?" Chail asked. He was pointing at the reddened area of the child's belly, a reddening he had never seen in the decade he had been a trainer.

"Yes, I think I have seen something like this before. Should we call a Wooder?"

"Yes. I will get one," Chail said.

Chail strode out of the nursery, heading toward the barracks that housed the Wooders in training. His throat tightened at the thought of a possible infection spreading through the children.

"Master of the Wooders, are you there?" Chail called as he approached the barracks.

"Yes, the Master is here. He is sleeping and I would not want to disturb him. Can I help you, Master Chail?" a Wooder asked, not more than seventeen years. He was young, but still had useful training.

"Your master is the one I want to see, but you will do if you are familiar with what is happening to one of the children. He is warm and has red blotches on his body."

"Take me to him. If it is what I believe, we will have to act fast, or this group of children could be in danger of losing their lives," he said, rising from his chair.

Chail was surprised, but shielded it from his face. However, he did have concerns that he kept to himself. Without hesitation, he turned and motioned for the young Wooder to follow him. They made their way back to the nursery to find Tess had pulled four children aside.

"Master Chail, I noticed these four children have the same marks. I can tell you they all nursed from the same woman over the last day," Tess said, her brow furrowed with concern, for she was one of the few wet nurses who had nursed all the children.

"Let me see them," said the young Wooder, as he reached past Tess. He bent over and picked up a child. The reddened areas showed bright and angry, having intensified in just a few minutes. The temperature of the children was high compared to what it normally would be.

"They have the poxs. They will need to be taken away. Their training is over," the young Wooder said. "This one... and this one, the same. Yes, they all have the poxs. The pain they will suffer early in life if they continue training will be unbearable. They will be taken by the Wooders. We will continue with the training after they have passed the time of affliction." He shook his head. "I was afflicted by the same sickness when I was eleven, during my training to be a Spear. The pain from the pox was almost unbearable. To this day, I still have pain in my legs from it. These children will survive, and we will make sure they are taken care of, knowing full well what they have gone through at a young age."

"I understand your pain, for I see it in your eyes. You were only three years from joining the ranks. But we are lucky you were here today. What about the women who nursed them?" asked Chail.

"They need to be cleaned. Scrubbed. They would not be carrying the sickness, for it does not afflict those older than sixteen years. But since their nipples have been exposed, as well as their clothes, we have to do something about it." He motioned to the women. "Please, come with me," he said, as he moved the cribs over to the side. "I need two of you to take on the feeding of these children while they recover. You will be there for them till they finish suckling and the fever has broken." The young one wiped a tear from his eye as he watched the women move about. "We need to remove them from the others now."

Chail reached out to the young man to put a comforting hand on his shoulder, but the Wooder pulled back.

"I'll be well. It just brings back painful memories. At least they will not remember what they have lost."

They moved quickly, following the directions of the young Wooder. He took two children and two of the wet nurses agreed to accompany him. They also took a child as they walked out. The other two wet nurses went with Chail to dispose of their clothes and wash themselves clean of the infection.

## Month Five

Chail walked into the nursery, pacing and trying to decide which one of the children would be tested first. It was the first testing. The most important testing. It would be the one that separates and disqualifies those who do not pass.

The test itself would not disqualify the child from serving; it would just take them away from being a Spear. It was not one of the most rewarding tests he would have to perform, and Chail was not looking forward to it.

He decided he would just pace around the nursery and take the first child, who made a noise. It would not take long. Usually the children made some type of noise at any given time.

There, in the corner, he heard a noise and walked quickly towards it. One of the four in this group, that's the group that had emitted a sound. Chail puzzled over the four, looking and finding that they all appeared to be asleep. Such confusion was unbecoming a man of his stature. He never had this much of a problem before. Usually Chail just picked a child and went through the batch, but something about this clutch told him to be cautious. He spun just in time to notice one of the children pushing himself up, moving as if to escape the cradle he slept in. The child is actually pulling itself up to a sitting position, even with the stone weights on him! Chail thought, believing that would be a sign if there ever was one.

He approached the crib, reached down, and took the child out gently. Chail moved to the foot of the bed to check the name - Thomasyn Saye was written on the clay.

"Well, Thomasyn Saye, you are about to be measured to see if we continue to train you," he said, as he took the child out of the nursery.

---

It was not a long distance to the testing area, but it seemed as if it was leagues. Thomasyn did not make a sound, but looked about with wide eyes. Chail found himself surprised by the awareness of this child. Unlike others, this one appeared to be watching what direction he was being taken.

"You seem to have a curiosity about you, Thomasyn. That is good. In the future, if you survive long enough, it will show you wonders most can only dream of."

They came upon a chamber located several rooms over from the nursery and entered it. The trainers of the clutch were there, including Con, Falon, Natail, Bethan and Dress. Con did not have to be there, but the rest of the group thought it best if he was. The eunuch was dressed in the usual robes of his station, while the remainder wore the clothing of their choice. Falon with a skiff that reached to his ankles, Natail with her usual light dress, Bethan with his leather jerkin and Dress in a strange outfit she found across the seas.

"Well, here is the first one. He is in good shape, stronger than most. I think we should test him first," Chail said.

"He was the one Tess went to right away," Con said. "I have seen her coo over that one quite often."

Falon shook his head, making his skiff open a little. The man was the tallest of the group, with a sour-looking mouth that he hardly used.

"Tess has not been the only one attached to this one. He has been the favourite of a number of them. You know that this child was brought in by him," Dress said.

"Him?" Bethan asked. "You mean the Great Seeker of the Wooders?"

"Yes, that Wooder," Con said.

"Hopefully he passes," Chail said.

They fell silent, looking at the child. Thomasyn just lay there, lifting his arms and legs and putting them down again. Chail showed the others Thomasyn had full mobility of his legs, as well. He then took off the stones that weighed down the child's limbs.

Thomasyn wiggled about on the table, trying to turn on his side. Con looked at Chail with a raised eyebrow.

"Have you seen him do this before?" Con asked.

"Not this, but he did use the side of the crib to sit up before I brought him in here," Chail replied.

They all watched as Thomasyn rolled to his stomach and started pulling himself towards Chail. He found it interesting for such a young and small child to move so deftly.

Chail reached out and moved Thomasyn back to the center of the table and placed him on his back. He gently held the child in that spot and looked towards Bethan.

"Well, it looks like I will have to administer the first test," Bethan said.

He turned and picked up a bundle wrapped in cloth. It was the standard testing package used for centuries to ensure each Spear can endure. The group watched, somewhat shamed they needed to administer it.

Bethan unwrapped the cloth and removed two silver forks. They looked at each other, the five of them. The whole of the operation would take just a few minutes.

Bethan took hold of Thomasyn's right arm, holding it gently but firmly. He did not want the child to move, but he did not want to hurt him. The first instrument was placed against the inside of the child's arm. He took a deep breath and pushed the silver point so it poked through the skin.

Thomasyn screamed.

Blood erupted from the wound, but Bethan moved quickly, taking one of the small silver discs from the package and forcing it on the wound. It has a strange etching on its flat surface and appeared to glow as it came in contact with the child's blood. He looked at the others, turning the arm upwards for them to see that he had completed the task.

They all waited.

It took five minutes before the silver disc seemed to meld with the skin, the metal joining with the child and sealing the wound. Another minute and Bethan took his hands away, smiling. The etching on the disc was now a complete red glyph that slowly spread out over its entire surface, and skin formed over it. Thomasyn had stopped crying as if nothing had happened.

"He has passed, the disc has accepted him," Natail said, with a great sigh of relief.

They all smiled down at Thomasyn, happy he had passed the test. It was something that would be with him for the rest of his life, being a

Spear. The disk helped all Spears know if one of them was nearby and in mortal danger.

Chail let his breath out.

"I am glad he passed. I could hardly bear to face Tess if I had to tell her he had to be removed from the nursery," Chail said.

"Yes, it is good," Con agreed, imagining what that heartbreak would do to Tess.

---

The rest of the children took the same test, with only two failing. The quality of children from this group was getting encouraging. In fact, it was promising to be one of the best groups that had ever been found.

The next few months would see the children stretched, fed and put through more of the weight training until they started to walk. The whole of the nursery was ecstatic with being involved in such a solid gathering of new Spears.

The Holders of the Staffs continued to read to the children. The new Spears were always quiet during the readings, listening to the voices as the readers all but sang the words out to them.

Every day, after the reading was done, the children were put through pain trials. First, the trainers of pain poked at the feet, causing the children to flinch from the surprise. After a week, the trainers actually pricked the skin, causing little points of blood to show.

The ones who carried out this training did not enjoy their work. No, they seemed to despise it, but it had to be done. It was all about the training, the training that had been handed down for years. It was the ancient custom. If they did not do this, the Spear would not have the tolerance to put up with the rest of the training as they grew older.

So they continued. And the ones who did it did not smile. All that is, but one.

The one who was a concern was Dander. He smiled when he made a child cry.

Con was the first to notice it, having observed the reaction as he walked past Dander when the trainer administered the training. It caused Con to wonder what Dander had been doing, so he held back, waiting for him to exit. Once Dander exited, Con went in and examined the child. Seeing multiple prick marks told him what had been happening.

They had seen this behaviour before in the past, but that was a long time ago. The interviewing of trainers for the young Spears usually made it safe. Every once in a while, an undesirable would slip past them and take advantage of the orphaned children, who were taken as Spears. And with that, a trial would come. Spears would stand in judgment.

"We need to do something about Dander," Con told Chail.

"Why, what have you seen?"

"Dander was pricking a child many times. His one turned into almost a dozen. The child was suffering beyond the need of the training," Con replied.

"Then we act."

"What does that mean?"

"It means nothing to you. I will call the Spears, they will judge. Be ready to be called, and to stand as witness. Do not interfere, only observe and speak when asked. Say what you are told to say, for unlike me, you are not a Spear," he said, dismissing the eunuch.

---

Dander walked into the nursery to perform the dulling, a task he enjoyed performing on the children, but took care not to show it. He always picked a child with a high tolerance, one that would not scream from the continual pricking of the needle.

This clutch had several children who would hold their screams, only moving their feet when it happened. His favourite was Thomasyn, but he would also prick Jon and Bethany from time to time.

He stopped at the entrance, looking about the room to ensure he was alone, without oversight. The still of the air told him no one was about, no one overseeing what he would do. Yes, he was a trusted tester of the Spears.

His thumb twitched as he moved into the room. Dander felt the small hairs on the nape of his neck, telling him his excitement was climaxing today the way he liked it. The shortness of his breath belied the caution he took.

Dander stopped at the foot of Thomasyn's crib and looked down at the child, anticipating the thrill. His hand fumbled in his pocket, pulling out the small needle he used to express his need. He felt the sharpness of the tip against his thumb, bringing the anticipation of his guilty pleasure to a buildup. A small tingle started to expand in his loins, making his manhood push against his pants.

Dander stopped again, looking around for a second time, thinking he was not alone. His searching showed nothing, no shadows, no clumps of clothing, nothing. He was alone except for the children. Not even a wet nurse was around him. Dander was alone, truly alone. The ache was now fully between his legs, and a small bead of sweat rolled down the side of his face.

The small needle was out now, moving slowly towards the bottom of the foot of the small child he was in front of. Thomasyn lay there, not knowing what would happen next. The child was awake, but unaware of the threat looming over him.

Dander slowly moved the needle closer and closer to the child's foot, feeling the anticipation of what he was about to do. Bit by bit, he could hardly wait to see the reaction, feeling the desire. His hand stopped less than an inch from the foot and he watched the child twitch a little. That was when he struck.

His hand moved quickly, poking the small needle into the flesh of the foot of Thomasyn. The child jerked its foot back, face frowning.

Dander giggled.

He put his hand back in the same position, ready to strike again. Thomasyn's foot returned to the same point. Moving as a child will move it. His face turned back to peace. Dander struck again, pricking at the bottom of the child's foot. Thomasyn jerked his leg back, and the frown appeared again on his face.

Dander giggled once more.

With his hand in the same place, Dander kept the needle still and Thomasyn kept putting his foot in the same place. The needle struck seven times till his excitement climax, making his body spill its seed in his pants.

A flush came over Dander's face. He reached into his underclothes and unwrap the rag from around his manhood to clean the mess he had made. The cloth was soaked from the expulsion of his body, leaving it sticky. The one part he hated was the discarding of the evidence. He would have to move fast, put the rag into the same refuse the children's bottom rags went.

The needle disappeared back into his pocket and Dander turned, bumping into Con as he did.

The eunuch stood there, staring at him. He had a look of disgust on his face that told Dander he knew what had happened.

"I do not know why you have done this to the poor child, but I know I cannot let you continue. I will call the Spears to judge you," Con said.

Dander laughed. He looked around the room, turning on the spot with his arms outstretched.

"You have nothing!" he exclaimed. "There is no one anywhere around here. No one but you has seen me and even that you cannot claim. I did nothing, nothing except clean myself. No Spear will act on just the word of a eunuch."

"You may be right," Con said, softly. "Most eunuchs are shunned. But I am a member of the Spear's council, respected and given full access to them when needed. How many of them have fed on the very breasts I approved? How many of them seek my council when faced with issues during training. It is I, a lone eunuch."

"But what good will that do you, eunuch? It is still your word against mine!"

"That is what we hoped you would say. Please attend part of the advanced training. Spears! Show yourselves," Con said.

Dander stood still, looking over his shoulder. He saw nothing for the first second, then a shadow rose and moved, turning, spinning, and forming into the shape of a man in a cloak. On the back of the man was a short spear, the spear head slender with an edge that looked like it could cut through stone if pushed hard enough. The greyness of the cloak was what concealed the shape; that combined with the wearer's knowledge of shadow and light.

The man stood there, looking from beneath the hood of the cloak, not moving or showing remorse, only sadness.

"You had an honoured position among us. You taught us how to endure," he said.

Another shape appeared to the right, standing up from between cribs where there was once nothing but shadows. The same type of shape, but this time a woman's body was somewhat concealed under the cloak. The same type of sharpened metal spear strapped to her back.

"You took an oath to protect our young brothers and sisters; to only do what was needed to make them strong," she said, without emotion.

Dander reeled. He turned again, seeking escape, but another shape appeared from the shadows.

"Dander, you have done wrong. You have been found torturing an innocent without gain. You have been found, you will be judged," said the shadow, as it changed into the form of a man.

"No! I am the instructor! This is my duty! I had to dull them to pain!" he screamed.

He was caught, and he knew it, but that did not stop him. He was shaking, sweating, trembling. Dander's mind raced as he tried to talk his way out of what was going to happen to him. He spun to confront Con only to see another Spear standing in front of him. This Spear was huge, one of the front line that was trained for war. He stood two hands above Dander and at least another two wider. Scars could be seen on his face, telling Dander this Spear had survived the Elven war from four years ago.

Urine escaped his bladder while he looked up into the face of the Spear. "I needed to train them. You saw it. He did not cry out. I needed to train him."

"We have watched you today. You have been judged by your actions. You expressed joy, desire, excitement from what you did. You did not seek help, you instead sought to only fulfil the need you had," the big Spear said.

"Thank you for letting me do that, Chail," Con said. "I had never seen the Spear's dispense judgment before. They can be very impressive, can they not?"

"Yes, they can," Chail said, still a little shaken from the ordeal. He had not dispensed justice himself for over seven years, but now he was reminded of the brutality of it, the unfeeling that one needs to feel. His mind was still swimming with memories.

Both men looked out over the main square to examine the crowd that had assembled. The faces of the people could not be seen but they could imagine them all in their mind's eye. The population of the castle was composed of lords and ladies who depended on the Spears for their protection, just as most people in the Realm did. The centre of their attention was a man in the stocks, proclaimed to be a molester of children, and an enemy of the Spears.

The people gathered and pressed closely to look at the one who would be jailed in the castle dungeons. He would be used as practice for the Spears in flight, to teach them how to take a life if the need comes. He was but one of the dozen who had been taken alive to pay for their crimes with their lives due to the heinous nature of their wrongdoing.

A child ran up to Dander, who was displayed in the stockade, and slapped him across the face. The child then ran back into the crowd. The crowd cheered as they saw the lip of the criminal was split by the action.

Dander wept in the stalls, his hair messed as if a bird had placed it there for a nest. His wrists and neck blazed raw and red from the rubbing they endured against the wood. The clothes he wore were the same he had worn when he had been discovered and they smelled of urine and feces. The dignity of cleaning denied him as he was put on display.

The people only watched as, for the third time, a Holder of the Shaft approached and read out the charges.

# FOUR

YEAR FOUR

"The first law, a life that takes a life, is forfeit," the Speaker of the Spear said as he walked among the children. The man was old with a face covered in wrinkles, giving him a wizened look. He bent over the large tome he held in hands, emaciated from age. His knuckles were huge, swollen from the affliction that ravished the joints of his body. It sent jolts of pain through his arms when he flexed them, and lightning up his legs as he walked. His sparse hair hung to his shoulders, ragged but clean, as if he had washed it but not brushed it straight. His beard was straggly, as if during his youth, it had not learned to grow properly and left to grow uncut or shaped in any way. His bony fingers stroked the ragged beard when he asked questions of his charges, as if to pull off any ill-timed words from them.

His garb was as simple as his mind was full; a long small-shirt that went to his knees and a robe over that covered the shirt. He tied the simple garb with a plain red sash around his waist. It was plain yet elegant garb, and the red sash denoted his rank. But the white sash of the apprentice was all he ever wanted, for it was his first when he joined the Order of the Spears.

"The second law, one that steals, will return what they take double." The speaker continued to walk about the children who sat on the floor, watching him and absorbing the knowledge that came forth. They followed him with their eyes and listened to his words, knowing they would soon be able to play, once the lessons had ended. They did not write the laws down on tablets or take their eyes off him as he walked about them. The Speaker of the Spear was the centre of their attention. The children had been taught to listen, to learn, and to commit every detail to memory, for it would be needed later in their lives.

"The third law, one will not hurt another. The fourth law, one will not take another's spouse. The fifth law, one who bares false witness, shall be said to have also committed the crime. The sixth law, one shall bear witness when called. These are the basic laws of the Realm. These are the laws you will strive to uphold and maintain. You may also be called upon to invoke judgment for the people. At any time, you must know the basic laws of our land." His foot tapped the floor in rhythm to his words as he spoke this last part to the children.

"There are foundations to uphold in the law. An example of one is if one summons another for judgment, he must go. If they do not go, let the one summoning him call the bystanders to witness and then take him by force.

"If he shirks or runs away, let the one that summons lay hands on him. Unless illness or age is the hindrance, let the one that summons provide helpers to bring the summoned.

"Let the protector of a landholder be a landholder; for one of the proletariat, let anyone that cares be protector.

"When the litigants settle their case by compromise, let the Spear announce it. If they do not compromise, let them state each their own side of the case in the presence of a Spear before noon. Afterwards, let them talk it out together, while both are present. After noon, in case either party has failed to appear, let the Spear pronounce judgment in favour of the one who is present. If both are present, the hearing of the sides may last until sunset, but no later." His voice droned on through the legal text of the tome that he read.

A pebble dropped to the floor, making a skittering sound. The

Speaker of the Spear turned quickly for a man of his advanced age, searching the faces of the children at his feet.

"Who is disturbing the class? Come, tell me," he demanded. His commands were always obeyed regardless of whom he was teaching.

On the other side of the room, Bethany giggled, and the Speaker turned again, searching. Bethany went deadpan when the old man's gaze fell on her. His brow furrowed, and he closed his eyes. The Speaker of the Spear took his hand and pinched the bridge of his nose to try to relieve the pressure of the ache that was developing. His other hand closed the book he was reading from and dropped to his side.

"Children, you will need to know this when you are out in the Realm among its people. At any time, you may witness evil and have to act. Therefore, you need to know the authority on which you act, or evil will win and the peace that has been in the Realm for hundreds of years will be no more," he explained. His hand dropped from his face and he looked about the room at the silent children.

"The laws must be enforced and you will be doing the enforcing. This is a grave matter, and you need to make sure you understand it to the fullest. If you lose your way, then the Realm will be lost. Those of evil will take what they want from the weak or helpless. The people will suffer, and when the people suffer, so will the land. Your King can ill afford to take the time to look at the Realm when he must look at the shores in order to keep other lands from trying to take that which is ours. The giants are there," he extended his arm out in a sweeping motion to enforce his point, "always looking at taking our fertile lands for themselves. The gnomes are jealous of us, as well; they scheme to take from us and use the people for food." He leaned forward at the children and made a snarling face. "The Elves are the only ones who will trade but they as well would conquer if they could, and the dwarfs," he stood up as straight as his body would allow, "well, they barter their metals with us but want more of our gold and jewels from the north than they agreed to when they struck the bargain. They have been the best allies we could ever have, for they pay us for mining the mountains to the north!"

A child coughed in the group and, this time, the Speaker saw him do it. He moved about the children till he came to Jon, who sniffled a little when he looked up at the Speaker.

The Speaker bent down and placed the back of his hand against the child's forehead. After a second, he nodded and straightened.

"Jon, take yourself to Tess to see if she can give you something for the cough. If not, then you will need to see Wooder Stevens. Off now."

Jon stood and moved from the room with thirty-two watchful eyes following him.

"The rest of you, off to the yard for practice. Move it now! Off! I don't want to have any one of you advanced more than their fellows."

With that, the Speaker turned and walked from the room.

---

The children made their way to the practice yard, biding their time till they reached the point where they were allowed to run and enjoy their brief respite together without the trainers shadowing them. The yard was a pool of mud from the morning rain that had pelted the area for hours. The cloud cover was just breaking up, allowing the sun to come out and try to furiously bake the earth to a hard surface again.

The ground had seen thousands of years of the feet of Spears in Flight marching on; countless children training to be full Spears had pushed the soles of their feet into the ground as if attempting to make the earth yield to their need for practice. The sloshing dirt packed down in order to support the trampling feet that ran across it as this new hoard broke from the passage to enter the yard. In no time, the children had organized a game of tag, picking who would start and making a safe zone. It was one of those fast and fun games everyone enjoyed.

The children played, running, tagging and laughing as they slid and became caked in mud from head to foot. After an hour, the trainers came out to the yard to start the afternoon, but waited until Chail emerged from the corridor to call order to the group.

"Children! Come and attend," Chail called.

The children stopped their playing and quickly gathered around

Chail. Their respect for the man was evident in their faces as they watched the one who had been looking after them all their lives.

It was a common routine for them to be called to train, and today was no different. The adults would complement them and praise their achievements, as well as assist them in being the best they could be. It was rewarding, for not one person belittled a child. It was not needed; nor was it acceptable, each child being a valuable asset to their group, and ultimately, the Realm.

Jon joined the group after visiting with Tess. Chail had noticed her love for them from the start. She would fawn over every one of the children, having been with them since they came to the Spear training ground. Tess was different from any of the other wet nurses, not just there for shelter and receiving the few copper points a week for feeding the children. She actually used some of her payment to buy small things for her charges, setting her aside from those who were hired with her.

So, instead of releasing her from employment when they weaned the children off breast milk, Chail requested dispensation to have her join the trainers as a nanny. His request was approved, and he approached her with the offer. Tess accepted, knowing she would be around the children that she loved and loved her.

"Today, we will be learning the art of striking and blocking. It is important to first stretch. Children, pair off and do your stretches," Chail said.

It was all that needed to be said for them to start. The children paired off and commenced to stretch, each assisting the other in limbering up their bodies to move in their full range of motion. For ten minutes, they pushed their bodies to the limit in order to prepare for the training to come. The trainers moved about them, looking closely at their movements, ready to correct any errors, but of course, they saw none. The children had started stretching by themselves and in groups each day after the age of three, and now at the age of four, they stretched continually, all day, making the practice second nature.

Once they finished, Chail looked about and smiled.

"Children, you are performing very well. You please me, and bring great honour to those who love you as all the trainers do. Now, let us begin. Stay in your pairs, face each other and stand two paces apart," Chail instructed, watching the children do exactly as he said.

Chail motioned for another trainer to come forward to help him demonstrate what was needed. They faced each other, nodded and took up a hand fighting stance. Chail's was a classic one, left foot forward, pointing straight at his opponent and right foot back, turned slightly sideways. He kept his legs bent with the weight on the rear one, bringing his arms up, left arm vertical, fist opened, not clenched. His right arm was parallel to the ground, palm down, and hand opened.

His opponent took an unorthodox stance, similar in form but both arms parallel to the ground, legs bent and both feet pointing towards Chail. They both appeared relaxed, like snakes ready to strike, but waiting before they expend any energy. Chail nodded and his opponent struck out at him. He blocked it easily and struck out with his right hand, stopping just shy of his opponent's windpipe.

"This is a killing blow. You may practice it but do not strike. Stop one inch before hitting your sparring partner. Decide which one will strike and which one will receive. Begin."

As if they were one person, the children moved at the same speed. Chail smiled, for it looked like a well-choreographed dance, the children moving as one. He saw very little mistakes, and those who made them were quickly found and corrected with care and kindness. While they practiced the move, Chail spoke out to them.

"This is the first basic movement in hand fighting. It is also the most effective. It is so effective that over three hundred years ago, it was adopted as the first basic move for Spears to learn.

"When the Realm was young, the Spears used this technique of striking against an Elfish invasion. The Elves did not fight hand to hand very well, they prefer bows and long shaft spears. Our forces, the Spears of old, knew this and when they engaged the invaders, they closed the distance between them and the Elves quickly. It took away the advantage the Elves had and allowed our Spears of old to overcome a superior force. It was told to us that the Elves outnumbered our brothers and sisters four to one, but using the basic fighting skills you will learn over the next year, they overcame their foe. They had charged the Elvin line, making it difficult for the Elvers to hit them with arrows. And once they were in range to strike with their hands, the invasion force could not defend."

Chail watched how the children moved. Their movements were fluid and strong, with purpose. He was pleased at what was happening; this group would be the best that had ever been trained.

He had the children continue for a few more minutes till he was satisfied of their ability to mimic the move.

"Children, attend," Chail ordered.

"You should know how to defend from this blow. It is done such." He demonstrated it. "Please perform."

He continued to explain the use of the block, giving examples of how to use it and why. The history that poured forth was rich and colourful, a history of the Spears.

He continued training them for an hour, making sure the children worked hard and long. During the practice, he explained a number of stories about the history of Spears, and the battles they had won defending the Realm against those who meant it harm. It was always defend, never attack. The Spears were defenders, not attackers. Chail kept reiterating that the Spears defended the Realm, never attacking foreign lands.

When the hour was over, the children had learned several methods of attack and defense. Chail felt this day was completed. He smiled at the children. They looked like mud puppets, all of them covered from head to toe. He let out a chuckle and shook his head; they would have to bathe extra-long to clean themselves this day. Tess would be furious with him.

***

The children walked into the bathing room, stripped down, and climbed into the water that filled the tanks and proceeded to scrub themselves clean. Both boys and girls washed in front of each other. It was something they had been doing all their lives, still being young and innocent.

After cleaning, they walked back to the nursery, wrapped in towels, to dress only to find all their clothes had been removed. The children were confused, and once they saw Tess they went towards her, questions on their lips.

"Children, please. You have outgrown the nursery; it is time to go to the barracks now. You will be there until you are no longer in flight," she told them, getting up and motioning them to follow her.

"Come, we have everything there for you," she said, leading them out of the nursery to the main barracks.

———

Their new barracks were organized, clean, and set up for them. They each located their beds, seeing their clothes all laid out for them.

"Change into your walking clothes, children. Chail wants to take you outside of the gates on a walk," Tess said to them.

"We're going outside?" Thomasyn asked.

"Are we?" Bethany echoed.

"Yes, he is taking you outside for a walk. Get dressed now, please."

Each locker contained new clothing that marked them as Spears in Flight, meaning they were in training. Thomasyn, Bethany, and Jon had bunks close to each other, and they smiled. It was like someone knew of their friendship. They all held up their clothes for each other to see.

It did not take long for them to put on their new uniforms, and Tess moved about, making sure each had dressed correctly as she had been shown. The small clothes first, with the leathers on top. Once that was done, a small sash was placed over their shoulders, marking their current station in the Spears. They all beamed with pride as they looked at each other in their new attire.

Chail came into the barracks dressed in his parade best. Across his back was a small spear with a throwing stick known as a bone. Over his right shoulder, the children could see the large sword he only carried on special occasions. The pommel of the weapon was wrapped in supple leather, tan and worn. It ended at the butt of the pommel with a tassel of red silk with a light green rope woven throughout. The tassel swayed in the air as Chail walked down the centre of the barracks. The last of his weapons was a small dirk, secured to the sash of office that was tied around his waist. It marked him as a Master Spear, one of the highest honours before being assigned as a member of the Spear Council.

"You all look very well dressed, children. I want to make sure you understand. We are about to enter the city proper, where you have never been before. There will be many people about, and children also, so please stay together. I do not want to lose any of you," Chail said to the children. He looked at each one of them in turn, all thirty-two of them.

"Okay, children, just as we practiced before. Form ranks!"

The children quickly formed three lines of ten, straight and even. They waited there, expecting the order to move out of their new sleeping area. They wanted badly to move out to the city proper, for they had never been out of the training compound.

It was Thomasyn's duty to lead the front and Jon's to bring up the rear of the formation, and they stood, beaming with pride. Chail watched the two of them, chests out and proud as could be. They could push over a mountain if they wanted to, now, he thought. He, himself, could not have felt more honour being their master trainer. His own chest stuck out as he gave the order.

"Move out!"

"They're coming," Frail said in a hushed voice. His throat hurt and masking his speech in such a low tone that it caused a thundering pain to shudder through it. He knew the first outing of the young Spears was coming, and today a little rat told him when it would happen.

"Get your ass in here before you're seen, ya git," Bosco hissed at his friend. "If ya seen, we lose out on tha grab."

Frail moved back to where Bosco was standing, in the shadows of the alley. They wore dark leggings and jerkins, all made from rough-spun wool. The two of them carried small dirks in their belts, ready to use if needed.

They were waiting for the signal from the other two members of their group. It was something they had been planning for a while, and now they had the chance to do it. Today, they would be taking two of the Spear children. They were hoping for the boys, for they would fetch a higher price in the Western Land than the girls. Their scheme was simple, but in reality, it would be a difficult task.

First, they would need a diversion, something that would make the lines break. They figured a small fight breaking out would be the best way to distract them. The children would do what they had been trained to do, work on keeping the crowd from hurting one another. But that was just the start. From there, Frail and Bosco would swoop in and take two of the children from behind and run out of the city quickly, something they decided on because they were the biggest ones out of the group. They would head for the sewers and use them to get to the shallow shore, where they had a small skiff waiting.

At four years old, the male children would be great for the perverted pleasures of the ruling class of the Western Land. They seemed to have a thing for little boys. It was said that they made eunuchs of them before they took them, enjoying the lack of sexuality it produced. But they did not like them when they were older; it spoiled the pleasure for them.

Frail sneezed, letting out flecks of food from between his teeth. Bosco slapped his back to motion him to stop making such noises, and he was about to tell him off again, but the signal was given. The children were approaching.

A man with red hair had started the fight that signalled Bosco and Frail. His fist punched another man with brown hair, causing him to stumble back. Onlookers caught him and pushed him forward, telling him to strike back. The brown hair man complied with the request; he grabbed the redheaded man, swung him around and hit him in the nose. Blood erupted, and the fight began.

The fight had caused a crowd to gather. Cheers went up, for people felt the need to cheer the fighters on. Bosco made them wait in the alley, watching for the children to show up. Without fail, it happened. The children came around to help control the crowd as their trainer took charge of the situation. All they did was form a protective circle, allowing Chail to handle the two combatants.

The ruffians moved on cue, slowly at first, till they came to the mouth of the alley, where they stopped. They stood there in the shadows, spying their prey. Bosco moved first, followed by Frail. They broke from the cover of shadows and moved out to the yard area. The two found their prey easy enough, two boys close together, and unaware of the danger they were in. Bosco and Frail swooped down on them like birds of prey, and grabbed them from behind and clamping big, rough hands over their mouths. The children struggled, striking out with arms and legs as if treading water, but the two men were strong, too strong to escape from.

As the men turned back to the alley with their prizes, they found their way blocked by two more boys. They stood there defiantly with arms crossed, as if they could block the men from taking their comrades, two small boys facing two grown men.

Bosco started to relax. He actually smiled at the two boys.

"Frail, ya think we could grab them, too? Double our take with less trouble?"

"Something tells me that would be a good idea," Frail said. His captive wiggled about till he clubbed him with his free hand.

"One who steals will return double. What is the cost of the life of a Spear?" Thomasyn asked the men.

"A child like you dares to question me?" Bosco asked, advancing on the children with a leering smile on his face. "I reckon we have doubled the take now, Frail."

His partner had a worried expression on his face. He was not looking back at Bosco, he was glancing back and forth. The other children were gathering, moving and starting to surround them. They were all saying the same thing in a low voice, repeating, increasing their volume. It was the second law.

"One that steals will return double. What is the cost of the life of a Spear?" they chanted in unison. "One that steals will return double. What is the cost of the life of a Spear?" they echoed again, and this time members of the crowd turned, and seeing the scene, they took up the chant. "One that steals will return double. What is the cost of the life of a Spear?" they chanted in unison, and the children circled the two men. "One that steals will return double. What is the cost of the life of a Spear?" was the sound that came from the crowd, calling out the mantra.

Bosco dropped the child he was carrying, looking scared, afraid for his life. "One that steals will return double. What is the cost of the life of a Spear?" came the litany from the crowd as the children completed the encircling of the men. Frail dropped his charge and whimpered.

"I... I... I released 'em. Ca... ca... can I go?" He let out a crying whimper, wanting to know if his sin could be forgiven.

"No, neither of you can. In fact, you will tell me who else besides these sorry two are involved in this foul plan." It was not a question, but a statement emitted by Chail. And as he entered the circle of children, he pushed two men forward. It was the fighters, and they stumbled from the shove, falling to their knees. Both had hands tied behind their backs, ensuring they would go nowhere.

"But I do not expect you to tell me now, not here. I will ask you once again later, and you will tell me. Or, instead of a cell, you will be used to train these very impressive Spears."

Bosco shook his head and held out his hand towards Chail.

"No, you're not getting me into that cell, let alone as practice for killing," he screamed and suddenly turned, bolting towards Jon and Thomasyn, hoping to break through them.

Chail moved quickly and fluidly. He pulled the small spear and throwing staff from his back, setting it and hurling the weapon at Bosco. It flew true towards its target; and so powerful was the force it had been thrown with. Onlookers would later swear it travelled without arc. Bosco was only yards away from Chail and the spear met its target quickly, slicing through the woolen jerkin as if it was paper. Its tip entered the man's body to the left of the spine. The spear slipped between the ribs, slicing into the muscles, and piercing the heart. But it did not stop there. The spear erupted from Bosco's chest and burst through the front of the jerkin, stopping just as it protruded.

Bosco fell forward, driving the point of the spear into the ground, supporting the body.

# FIVE



## YEAR FIVE

The five who controlled the lives of the Spears met in the small room near the barracks. Tess, trusted implicitly with the children, was now invited to these special meetings. The little ones had started calling her Nanny of Spears. Chail chuckled when he heard it; such an innocent title only children could come up with.

"Have they been properly prepared?" Con asked. He already knew the answer.

Tess looked upset, not really wanting to be involved with this phase of the testing the children were going through the poison trial. She had been told about the test, but was still shocked when she was told it had started. Chail had informed her it was always necessary, adding a little of the poison to the children's food, and it was done when they reached five years of age. A necessary part of becoming a Spear, they had said. One possibility could arise so they make sure the children could handle poison now, for when they became full Spears they would be exposed to it from enemies.

"They have been exposed to the poisons it calls for, slowly in their food," Chail said.

"Some have been sick, unable to keep the food down," Tess said a little shakily.

"It is to be expected," the Speaker of the Spear said. "Their bodies are being subjected to a small poison that would kill most children of their size and age. If not for their training, they would be dead by now.

"From centuries ago, we have been taught the ancient way of how to raise the Spears. What training they are to have, what tests they are to have done to them, even what food to feed them. It has protected the Realm. Now, with the giants marching on us, we are in need of them. If those Spears had not had this testing, they surely would die. The giants are known for using poisons like this to taint the water and food. They are large and can handle the poison, so we make our Spears immune to it in this way."

"I still don't like it. I did not know this would happen. Are there any other tests I should know about?" Tess asked.

"There are many, my child. Many tests that happen every day, every week, every month and every year. It is the ones that happen during the year you have to be concerned about. They are the major ones. The worst is yet to come," said Con as he watched her expression turn to horror at that statement.

"I feel like a monster," Tess said.

"Don't, child," Con replied. "I know of four Spears who actually lived through poisoning because of this test. If they had failed it, the poison they ingested would have killed them quickly. It is a good thing. The children will survive this, and because of it, they will be able to survive out there when they are finished taking flight."

Tess shook her head, still feeling ill for what was happening. "It does not mean I have to like what is happening."

They all agreed on that statement. But the more important question was who was dealing with the poison the best.

"Tess, I have been watching the children also, and I think some of them are handling it better than most. Have all of them been sick at one time that you know of?" Chail asked.

"Bethany has not been sick, but she has complained a little about her stomach being upset. Likewise, Jon and Thomasyn. The three of them have been fine with the trial," Tess replied.

"Yes, I have not seen them ill, either. It is as if they are not being tested. Their response is the same, fast and sure," Falon said, one of the sub trainers.

"I think we will have a problem with Kania and Drais, they have been sicker than most, and not only have they been sick to their stomachs, their stool has been runny. They cannot get enough water in them and are always thirsty." It was Natail who spoke this time, and his eyes told Chail everything.

"Pull them," Chail said. "Give them to the Wooders so their training will not be wasted."

The council agreed and dispersed.

---

"Come, we need to talk," Chail said to Kania.

She rubbed the sleep from her eyes and sat up.

"Yes, Master Chail?" she asked respectfully.

"Come, I want to talk to you in private," he said, holding up her over shirt. Kania stood, looking a little confused, but still she pulled on her over shirt and put her cloth shoes on her feet.

"I don't understand," she said.

"It will all be explained," he told her with kindness in his voice. It was the hardest thing to tell a child that they have failed what they have been trying to achieve, and it was not one of the tasks Chail liked to do.

He guided Kania into the small room near the front of the barracks where Tess was waiting. The child was still walking uneasily and holding her stomach from the last dose they had been administered, though she showed signs of getting better. She looked at Tess, who had obviously been crying. Kania had a puzzled look on her face and went immediately to the Nanny of Spears and took her hand.

"Why are you so sad, Nanny Tess?" Kania asked, a concerned look in her eyes.

"It is because I love all of you so much, Kania," she replied. "Please, sit here beside me. Master Chail and I have something to tell you."

Kania sat in the chair beside Tess as Chail seated himself across from them. Tess had not released Kania's hand. Chail could not believe the bond between the child and this woman. He made a mental note to make sure Tess had the opportunity to bond with other groups that came to train once this clutch ended their flight. He cleared his throat softly to get their attention.

"Kania, as you know, we have been training you to be a Spear for five years now, ever since you came to be with us, here in the Realm."

"Yes, Master Chail."

"And you know we have all been pleased with how smart you are and how hard you try. We all know you would be a great addition to the Spears."

"Thank you, Master Chail, I do try hard."

"And we know it. All the trainers know you try very hard, and you are able to do what they instruct also. It is not that you are unwilling or unable to do the exercises, or that you are not able to understand. No, it was one of the tests we had to do, which told us something we have to tell you."

Kania looked at him with confusion on her face, concern showing at the corner of her eyes. She did not know what he was leading to. Something was wrong, and she was trying desperately to understand, but it was somewhat out of her grasp.

"Kania, I am trying to tell you it is not you, it is your body, and it failed the test. It was not you or how you work towards training. No, far from it, my child, it was your body..." Chail broke off for a second. He looked at the child. She was confused.

"I can try harder," she said with enthusiasm. "I will work harder than anyone and make you proud."

Tess's lower lip started to tremble, and a tear appeared from her eye, sliding down the side of her nose.

"Kania, it is not that. You remember being very sick the last couple of days?"

"Yes..."

"Well, that was a test. It turns out your body is failing. If we let you continue, you may die from the other tests which have to be done, and we love you too much to allow that to happen."

Kania looked at him, trying to understand what he was telling her.

She puzzled over it like all small children do, not fully understanding but realizing something had not gone the way it was supposed to. She decided to square her shoulders and face the challenge. It was one of the characteristics that had made her last this long, the desire to always win.

"I will work harder. I will make my body pass the test. I can do it, Master Chail," she said with pride.

"I'm sorry, Kania. It is not something you can make your body do. It has to be able to do it or it will not. I'm sorry," Chail said. He really did not enjoy this part of his duties, but it was something that had to be done.

Kania started to cry softly, as the realization of the situation forced its way into her mind. She looked up at Chail first, and then Tess, pleading. It was all she knew, the life of a Spear. She could not remember anything else, for there was nothing else. Life as she knew it had just ended. Her tears flowed freely now and her lower lip quivered.

"I... I... I... I don't... know... what... to... do!" she cried, slurring her words together between sniffles.

The door of the room opened, and Con entered, leading the Master Wooder. He was dressed as all Wooders dress, grey cloak over his shoulders, with the hood pulled up, casting a shadow over his face. As he entered, he pulled down the hood. The Wooder had a caring face of a man no more than thirty-four, but it had character, shallow lines from smiling and laughing. His brow held no creases of sorrow, and his eyes lit the room with love and caring.

The Wooder approached Kania and knelt to bring himself as close to her height as he could. He looked at her, seeing the pain she was going through, feeling her heart ache. The Wooder held out his arms to her and, having been taught to trust the Wooders explicitly, she went to him. He embraced the small child softly, comforting her.

He turned his head and whispered in her ear. Chail could not tell what it was and neither could Con, but Tess was in the right position to hear the soft voice, the comforting voice. The tears stopped falling on her face at those words, knowing Kania would be taken care of and loved.

Tess smiled and wiped away the last of her tears. She nodded with the words that came from the Wooder to the child and rejoiced. The pain of sorrow was still about her, for Kania would no longer be in her care, but she felt the child would accept the new role being offered to her. She would accept the role of a Wooder, a healer and helper of the Spears.

# Six



YEAR SIX

"Up, children, it is time to start our day!"

Chail looked up and down the barracks, watching the children rub the sleep from their eyes. It was going to be a glorious day. The sun was shining, the fresh air was still in the surrounding area, the stink of the city not yet raising from the streets, and spring had just pushed the cold of winter out the door. Today was the day they started endurance training. Today, the children would get their first glimpse of the wild.

"No, not parade clothes, workout clothes. And come to the centre of the barracks for stretching," he called out to them.

The children obeyed his directions and put their workout clothes on. Jon was a little confused; they usually washed and had breakfast first.

"Master Chail, are we not washing up for breakfast?" he called out.

"Not this morning. This morning we are going for a run," Chail said.

Groans came up from the children. Going for a run meant running the circumference of the yard for an hour. Nothing to see but mud and equipment. It was something they did every day but never this early.

"Once you have dressed, put a dirk in your belt," Chail announced. That will make them think, he thought, watching some of the faster children look up in surprise. They did do what he told them, though, following his instructions to the letter.

"Three lines, front to back, no lead or trail. You will follow me and stay close. For no reason are you to break the formation, no matter what happens or what you see. Do you understand?"

"Yes, Master Chail," they responded as one.

"Okay, my young Spears. On the march!"

He led them through the main concourse and out past the exercise yard. From there, they passed the parade square and left the training grounds behind for the main city.

It was a surprise to the children, for they had only been allowed in the main city five times. Chail was protective of his charges, not wanting to put them through any unnecessary threats from others. But now they had turned six years old, and running around the exercise square was no longer sufficient. Now they must run in the wild.

After twenty minutes of marching, they reached the main gates of the city. Two figures guarded them, dressed in fine ring mail. The small loops of metal covered their upper bodies, sparkling in the sunlight. Under the protective metal, you could see the soft spun cloth that kept the protective covering from pinching the skin. Their legs were covered in hard leather, boiled instead of tanned. Short spears with throwing sticks were held in holders on their backs, very impressive weapons. But to make sure people knew they were protectors, they wore long swords at their waists.

The children turned their heads to look at the two Spears standing guard at the entrance of the city. Soon, they could have that privilege. Chail knew this would be in their thoughts, for it had been in his when he was taken for his first run in the wild all those years ago.

Thoughts of being full-fledged Spears soon left their minds when they noticed Master Chail did not turn them around, but instead quickened his pace to a slow jog. The children quickened their pace to keep up. Smiles erupted from the young hearts who followed him, their spirits soared as they moved as one into the open fields around the city. They were no longer captive hearts; they had been allowed to fly!

The children had been running for an hour. They were tired, hungry, and they needed water. Chail knew this, for he felt hungry and thirsty. Slowing to a walk, he looked back. They had kept up with him, still in formation. The last group had broken formation when he slowed to a walk, and this group did not. Discipline, they have much more of it in them than any had thought.

He stopped and waited for them to catch up to him. They really look like I just whipped them, he thought. I guess we can rest here for a few minutes before the next couple of lessons start.

They reached him, and instead of breaking ranks, they stayed formed up, looking toward him for direction. He could not help but feel proud of their actions. Carefully, he kept it hidden.

"Break ranks!" he commanded, letting the children relax. Most sat down straight away, resting their bodies on the ground. Three turned to each other and stretched, making sure their muscles did not tighten up from the long run. The same three, those who always surpass the others. Jon, Thomasyn and Bethany, they are the ones to watch. They will be leaders among Spears one day.

"Children, gather around. I know you are hungry and thirsty, but this is not just another run. This is part of your training. So far, you have done very well in keeping up with me. I am pleased.

"Now, the next trial that you must endure. Around us is the land you will one day protect. In protecting it, you must also know how to live off it. At the best of times, we only have our wits about us, and now that is what you are faced with, your wits.

"The test is to find drink and food for yourselves with just the items you have. You will be able to do this and you have all the abilities needed to survive. The exception is you also have to supply me with food and drink, and I am hungry. I will not eat raw food; it must be a proper meal.

"Now, do what you need to do and do it now!"

Chail kept the smile off his face while the children looked a little taken aback. It was not what they expected. The children had thought all of them would be travelling back to the city in order to sit down to a great breakfast. But no, they did not have that pleasure. Today they had to feed Master Chail as well as themselves.

They did not scatter like the last group had. In fact, they did not shirk the challenge at all. That confused Chail. He watched as they all looked at Thomasyn in turn, the destined leader of the group. Thomasyn smiled. He had a plan.

"Okay, what do we have? Bethany, see what's in the pouches. Turn everything out, we need food and Master Chail is hungry. We cannot let him down," Thomasyn said to the group.

Thomasyn organized everything. The children took pouches and sent three of their group to a stream for water. He sent another ten to gather firewood and another ten to hunt for grubs. The remaining five he made into hunting groups for fowl. Bethany and Jon joined him and they dashed into the nearby forest with the wood gatherers.

Before he knew it, the children had filled each pouch with water. They had washed each one out before filling it, ensuring the water wasn't contaminated. He thanked the child, who handed him a full pouch, and took a swallow of the cold water. Two more swallows and the pouch was empty. He put it aside and the child came and picked it up, hurrying to the stream nearby to fill it and a few others again.

The wood gatherers had piled up a nice amount of wood and started to build the makings of a fire. They had already been trained in basic survival, so Chail knew they would have no problems with this task.

His main concern would be what they would be feeding him. Snails, grubs and such he would eat but did not care for. He preferred eggs with bacon burned almost black. That, unfortunately, was a little too far off the achievable now that they were not in the city. But none the less, a person could be creative in the woods if they wanted to be.

He looked up as Thomasyn, Jon and Bethany walked out of the forest with their arms fill. He sat up a little and tried to discern the prizes they had. Once they came within spying distance, he made out four quail carried by Bethany, while Jon carried five. Thomasyn had a big smile, holding what appeared to be more than two dozen eggs in his shirt. Chail smiled. He would have a great breakfast, even if his eggs did not have bacon.

---

They finished breakfast and Chail ordered they clean up the grounds, making it appear as if no one had been there. The children did an efficient job and cleaned up the spot extremely well. It was another point of pride for Chail, knowing his group was the best Spears he ever trained.

Once the site was cleaned, the children stretched for a while and then started to make the long trek back to the barracks. They would have a good sleep after getting home. He also wanted to talk with Tess about keeping an eye on the three leaders this group had developed.

But till then, he needed to get the children back to the barracks. He kept a good pace in order to get the Spears back to the barracks.

---

"Honestly, Con, the three of them know exactly where to go and what to do," Chail said, shaking his head. Four of them sat around a small table in the room near the barracks. It was another council meeting to compare their findings. All the major trainers and overseers of the children were present, making sure their voices were heard.

"It seems the three of them are always together, like they share a bond or something," Tess said.

"Well, it's downright confusing," Brandon said, the spear trainer. "It's like I'm telling them something they already know. They take to the training like a bee to a flower, no need to tell them, just point and they go."

"Then it is settled. We have three naturals in this group. It is a glorious finding it is. We have not had one in over seven hundred years and now we have three!" Chail could not believe his luck at being the one to train the naturals.

"We must be diligent and not let our desire get ahead of us. Time will tell what we are seeing and if they are truly the ones," Con stated.

---

They moved about the practice square, engaging each other with wooden swords with lead poured centres. The weight made their wrists ache, and they sweated through their clothing.

After the third hour, the children started to become sloppy from the strain, arms growing heavy. But Brandon wanted perfection, even if it meant driving them to exhaustion. And exhaustion they had been driven to. Every child was near to dropping when it happened. A scream echoed in the air as the wood of Bishop's sword splintered, a shard flying into the eye of Elana. Bishop dropped the weapon and grabbed her before she fell to the ground. Brandon was there immediately, taking Elana from Bishop's arms and running as fast as he could to the Wooder's area of the training ground.

He was met by the trainers and a Master, who took Elana from him.

"The eye has been punctured. She will not be able to see from it after we remove the wooden shard. It is lost," the Master Wooder said. His hands moved deftly, holding the child by the jaw in such a way as to induce sleep in a way only the Wooders knew how to do.

"Is there no way to save her full vision?" Brandon asked, flushed with concern for his charge.

"There is no way. See, it penetrated the centre, through the part that admits light. The eye has lost its fluid. We have no art to heal it."

"Just save her. She is more precious alive than dead. I will find something for her here," Brandon said, a tear running down his face.

He knelt, taking Elana's hand in his, stroking it and talking sweetly to her. The Master Wooder moved swiftly, pulling the wood from the eye. He then took a small knife from a kit he kept inside his robe and sliced quickly at the damaged organ. It came out of the socket easily and fell to the ground, the Wooder already pulling another instrument from his pouch.

"Ned, heat this till it glows in the fire, there. It needs to be red hot to seal the wound. I will stitch after it is sealed." When Brandon looked, the Wooder already held a needle and thread, poised to complete the repair.

Around them, the children gathered to watch their fallen comrade receive treatment to save her life. Questions were asked about how the eye could be repaired, why the eye was cut out, what the hot instrument was for.

When the instrument was hot enough, it was given back to the Master Wooder who pried opened the lids with forefinger and thumb and forced the tool into the empty eye socket, cauterizing the wound. He packed it with ointment and stitched the lids shut in order to allow it to heal.

"Take her to her cot and lay her down gently. I will be there soon to make sure she will heal. I first have to talk to Master Chail and let him know he has lost another Spear in Flight." The Master Wooder stood, turned and left.

---

Chail was sitting beside Elana's bed, holding the child's hand in his and looking upon her face with a worried expression. He could see the damage that had been repaired to the best of their abilities, and still frowned at it. He remembered years ago they cured such issues. It was through the use of the black arts that major injuries like this could be cured. The eye could regenerate, but the cost was high. He learned this from Con, for once he had been a man, but because of the black arts... Chail could not imagine it, the pain he must have endured. Con told him in the Western Land they had maji who took the manhood of male children in order to cast their dark magic. Such would grow a finger, a toe and maybe even an eye.

Alas, the dark arts were forbidden in the Realm. The sanctity of life was more precious to them than anything; that is why they used the Spears to protect the people. Chail didn't want anything to do with the mutilation of children.

So he waited by Elana's bed, holding her hand, hoping the sight of a familiar and loving face would help soften the blow from what he would have to tell her, that she could not be a Spear. No, she could not even be a Wooder. She would be destined to be part of the staff that the Spears hire to make the training centre run.

He was glad he could keep her under the protection of the centre, the God's knew she would be far worse off if she was released to the city, despite her training.

Her hand flexed a little. Her head turned, and she tried to raise her hand to her missing eye, but he held her back, speaking softly to her.

"Elana, don't try to touch your eye. It is injured and there is a bandage there," he said.

"What happened..." she started to ask. "My eye hurts."

"Elana, you remember the sparring?"

"Yes... I remember I had Bishop beaten. He was backing away. I kept moving, and he swung a wild blow that I blocked and then all was black. Master Chail, can..."

"Hush, child, you have been injured. The Master Wooder has tended you and you must let yourself heal. All will be well. You are home," he said, squeezing her hand.

Tess entered the barracks at a run, coming over to Elana's bed. Tears ran down her face. She had been helping to prepare the afternoon meal when she was informed. Not far behind her, and moving at a slower pace, was Con, full of concern for the child as well.

Chail could understand how much these young children had garnered the love of so many of the staff. It must have been their willingness to strive for perfection without question or complaints. He looked down at Elana. Her one good eye was open, staring at him. He wondered what the child saw in his face. Concern, fright, sympathy? He did not realize he was crying until a tear fell from his face on to the bed she was lying. She reached up and tenderly brushed them from his face.

"Don't cry, Master Chail, I will be alright. I know something bad has happened. I lost my eye, did I not?" she said gently.

Chail could not stop the tears from running down his face. To lose a child to illness is one thing, but to have a one maimed so badly she could not fulfill her potential was a tragedy unto itself. At forty-seven, he had never cried, not even during the testing. Now. This young child had turned him into a weeping little babe. This strong, brave child who had lost what she trained for all these years would not be able to meet her destiny. He looked over at Tess, hoping she would be able to help him, but she had averted her gaze, shoulders struggling to stay still while she muffled her sobs.

"You are strong, child, stronger than I am, I must say," Chail told Elana. "Yes, you lost your eye. There is nothing that can be done about it. There will always be a home for you, though. You will always belong."

Con approached, his concern for the child obvious on his face. He bent and unwrapped the bandage that covered her empty eye socket. He nodded his approval at the job done by the Master Wooder and wrapped it back up.

He looked at Chail and spoke softly. "We will have to arrange living quarters for her. The kitchen staff would be happy to have her there. Serving, helping and such. We could even arrange for her to serve the King if need be."

"Yes, we can arrange that. I want her to have anything she needs. Make sure she is comfortable and allowed to heal fully before she is put to work." He looked back at Elana and smiled as best he could. "I will be watching you, little one. Make sure you do your best, as if it was I who was training you for your new lot in life. You have and always will fill me with pride." He bent forward and kissed her on the forehead.

"This way, King Savoy," the squire said, bowing deeply and sweeping his arm towards the direction of the training ground.

"I know the way. Gods be damned, fool. Just walk in front like you're supposed to or I'll have you put into chains," Savoy said. He was ill of spirit today. His head felt as if a hammer was beating on it, and the sun was too warm for his liking, even though it was only late spring. "How am I going to survive the heat of this summer? The mystics say it will be warmer than last year."

"You fret too much, dear," Milon said. She was his wife and queen. He had loved her dearly in her youth, but could hardly stomach to look at her now. Her slim figure had grown rounder after each child, and he desperately wanted to send her away. The scratching of her voice annoyed him and was not helping his headache one bit.

"I will have to talk to Master Wooder about my head. Maybe he can figure what can be used to quiet the drummer, or give me a hammer to strike his head in return."

"My King has a way with jests," the squire said, bowing and sweeping his arm in the appropriate direction.

"I did not talk to you, fool. I swear, you test my patience every day," the King said. But he would not do anything to harm the man; he was the son of his brother's sister-in-law. He would cause such turmoil if he did anything anyway, and who would want their child to be squire to a king who would kill him out of hand?

"Anyway, you know the Wooders will do nothing for the day after wine, Savoy," his wife continued. She kept berating him as they moved through the grounds to the balcony overlooking the practice square. The sound of fighting could be heard from afar back, so he knew they were down there now, swatting at each other.

Master Chail was standing in the archway leading to the balcony, along with Con, the eunuch. Savoy tried to get Con replaced when he came to power, but Master Chail told him they could not do without his service. He mentioned no woman would bare her breasts for inspection to a normal man, being afraid she would be picked because she was comely. No woman would judge well, for they would see the need in the other's eyes, thus picking poorly, he had argued. No, a eunuch was the best for such a job, less emotion and no ire to rise when feeling or touching. Yes, the eunuch was the best for the position of picking wet nurses and watching over them.

So it was agreement; even though he did not like the sexless man, he had to agree. He was the best for the job.

When Savoy saw him there, he remembered just how much he felt ill at ease around the eunuch. It made his skin crawl that the man had nothing between his legs. The strangeness of it all confused him. What was the motive for him to serve the crown? Men would serve in order to ensure their children had a future, but what about Chail? He was not married, nor did he have any children. The questions caused his head to ache even more.

The two men greeted him as he approached, bowing deep to show their respect. Savoy walked past, looking out on the yard at the children fighting with wooden swords.

"So, they are six now. What are they using, wooden swords?" he asked.

"Yes, wooden swords with the centres bored out and filled with lead. Each sword weighs more than a real sword of the same size. It is used to strengthen their wrists so they can fight for hours. Right now they have been practicing for approximately an hour," Chail said with pride. He came up beside the King on his right-hand side, knowing only a few people were allowed to do so.

"What weapons have they been trained on?" Savoy asked.

"The basic ones. First, we trained them on daggers, of course. Short and long. The sword now, we are almost finished with that training. Next, will be the mace and morning star, and ending with the fauchard, to make sure they have a fully rounded education."

"When do they move onto tactics? What is the timeline we are looking at?"

"My liege, these children are still seven, eight years away from being duty ready. We have to finish their basic training in fighting and then prepare them for endurance. That alone will take another year. Once that is done, we will be pushing the law into them with determination, challenges and such. Once that is done, they have at least a year with the Wooders to learn basic medicine. We have a number of years of training after that, honing their skills and making them the defenders we will need," Chail said, looking distraught at the King. He was not sure what the meaning of the question was, but he was sure he would not let any of his children be moved too quickly through training.

He stopped for a second. He realized he was thinking of these children as his own, as if he was their father. But he was not. He had never married, even though Spears were allowed to wed. He had forsaken it. When he was moved to a master trainer he vowed never to let anything get in his way of serving the Realm, so he never sought out a woman to share his life. He never complained about it. The children made his life rich with love, especially this group. They loved him and he loved each one of them in return.

"Chail!" Savoy spoke to him loudly. "Are you sleeping with your eyes open? I want to know if there is any way of speeding up the process of their training. I want to have them ready for an assignment sooner. Move up your timetable for this group. They are more advanced than the group recruited before them and should be able to handle it."

"But my liege, that group had setbacks. This group has not. They are progressing wonderfully, but not fast enough to outpace their predecessors."

"They never understand," Savoy said to his squire. "None of them do. It is enough to have to feed them for fourteen years, yes it is. I should be the one to set the rules. I am the King of the Realm. I wear the crown, do I not?"

"Yes, my liege," the squire said, acting more like a fool than anything.

"Then why do they not obey me without question?"

"My King," Chail said. "It is not that I do not obey you without question, it is just their training will not be completed in the time you request. They would not have the necessary knowledge or abilities. It would be like going into battle without sharpening your sword. We have to let them train. That way, they are Spears, not slingshots!"

"But I want them ready before," Savoy said. He did not tell Chail why. No one knew of his plans to invade the Western Land. They had all the jewels there, and he wanted them. He wanted to strike fear in them. If he had the Spears march in, the ruler of the Western Land would soil his garments and give up, trembling. The land would be his. He could plunder it for all its worth and leave their cities in ruin. Yes, that was the plan he had for that land, and the Spears. But he would need many of them. More than he had now. Lots more. He had been trying to increase the amount of Spears for years, but children were hard to find when they were young. Slavers usually took the innocent at birth when the parents passed away. Yes, even the brothels supplied less and less children each year. He was not sure why, but they did.

Savoy found everyone on the balcony looking at him in wonder. He was curious if they had actually heard the conversation in his head or not. Nonetheless, they were his servants and they would do as he said.

"Master Chail, these children will be ready sooner than you say. See to it that their training is advanced to the next stage sooner rather than later." He turned and strode off the balcony with a purpose no one knew.

---

THE EVENING WAS FOUL, RAIN COMING DOWN IN SHEETS ALL about them. It had been two weeks since Chail met with the King, and he had done exactly what he was told to do, advance the training.

Unfortunately, that advancement had cost a life today.

Chandra had been working on the training dummies with the fauchard when her slice had taken too much off the dummy's arm, causing the blunt mace to fall on her, striking her temple just at the right angle. She passed away in Chail's arms. He had wept. The other children watched, expecting the Wooders to work some type of magic and bring her back to life, but alas, that was not to be.

Chandra's body was taken into the barracks, washed tenderly by Tess and dressed in her good dress. Now, in the evening, they brought forth a pyre to lay Chandra's body on, ready to send her remains back to the Gods.

Every Spear in the city, save those who stood watch, came to the funeral. Every In Flight came to attend the fallen one. They needed to say their goodbyes, even if they did not know her. They paid her respect in order to ensure they themselves would not be forgotten, that respect would be given to them as well. They needed to make sure they would be offered the same, the ability to see the Gods after their death.

"And the five brother gods roamed the sky, which was black. One God took the sparkles from his eyes and placed them in the heavens, saying that 'The light from my eyes will light the sky'.

"The second God took the light from his mind and placed it among the stars, making a large glowing ball, saying 'The light from my mind will brighten our lives'.

"The third God loved the two brothers, he placed a part of his body balanced between the two, saying 'Your lights in the sky need to have something to shine on, so I give you both something from me to shine on, to show you are both powerful and beautiful, and we will call this earth'.

"The fourth God looked at his brothers and spread his body on the earth, filled it with trees and animals, filling the big depths with water and the high peaks with snow, 'My body will supply life to the earth so life will abound, I do this for the love of you all'.

"The fifth God looked at his brothers with pride. He came to the earth and saw the day with the light and the night with the sparkles. He moved upon the land and saw the trees and plants that grew. He cried, and the tears created fish in the sea, beasts in the fields, and man. He cried till man came forth and his tears carried his soul into them. He faded away, saying to his brothers, 'The men will walk your earth under your stars and sun and among your trees and flowers to appreciate what you have done. They will love us and remember us and cherish us. I give them a soul so they can be forever with us,' and he faded away into the children he created.

"The bothers wept for their loss and created the lesser races of the elves, and the dwarfs, and the gnomes, and the giants, and they all disappeared into their creations. Thus we are all gods. And to return to the sky we burn the bodies, spreading the ashes on the ground to bring us closer to the one God who created us, and the smoke from the fire will bring us to the brothers who he loved."

The Chanter of the Word rolled the scroll closed and handed it to the Singer of the Word, his assistant, during these important funerals. He looked upon the children who stood closest to him, understanding of their pain in his eyes. He spread his arms as if to embrace them all and brought his palms to his eyes, covering them. The two speakers of the Word who attended him held bowls under his elbows and all watched as tears streamed from between the Chanter of the Word's fingers down his arms and into the bowls. Once he was done crying, he held out his hands and the Chanters placed the bowls in his hands. He turned and emptied the contents on Chandra's body.

Once all the tears had been poured on the pyre, a spark magically ignited in the centre, lighting the tinder and wood into flames. It was impressive, the blue and orange that lit up the sky from the climbing flames. The Chanter stepped back from the fire.

All the children whom had never been that close to see what happened took a deep breath at the ignition of the pyre. They were taken aback by the simple but elegant delivery. The memory of this night would last a lifetime, and they moved forward as Spears, knowing their lives would always be remembered.

The fire blazed for over an hour, and during that hour the Spears who had gathered started to sign. The song had been heard before by the children but not fully understood till now. The lyrics had been passed down from generation to generation of Spear for thousands of years, since the Spears were first formed.

*The life of a Spear is to fly from the arm*
*Protecting those they see*
*The need for protection is one they give*
*For they save the lives with charm*

*A Spear starts their life learning the law*
*A Spear starts their life protecting*
*A Spear starts their life learning to fight*
*A Spear gives their life to the Realm*

*The life of a Spear is to fly through the air*
*Spreading the word of the law*
*The protection they give is for the land*
*Dispensing justice making it fair*

*A Spear starts their life learning the law*
*A Spear starts their life protecting*
*A Spear starts their life learning to fight*
*A Spear gives their life to the Realm*

*From the start of the flight a Spear gives their life*
*Not asking not taking only giving*
*They ask not for anything other than love*
*For the time they give without dread*

> *A Spear starts their life learning the law*
> *A Spear starts their life protecting*
> *A Spear starts their life learning to fight*
> *A Spear gives their life to the Realm*

The song drilled deeply into the minds of the children, making them realize they were not alone, whether they were alive, dead or wounded. It was something they had wondered about, what would happen. They had seen a number of their friends and fellows injured and drop from the training, but they had not really left. The two who had not passed the test last year, Kania and Drais, had been assigned to the Wooders.

They also realized Elana, who had been injured and not able to continue or join the Wooders, was still there with them in another role. Yes, they would not be forgotten or left aside.

Yes, they only had to remember that day in the city when the whole of their group raised against two large men to help protect two of their own, and Master Chail dispensed Spear justice on the one who tried to make off without justice.

No, they were not alone.

# SEVEN

YEAR SEVEN

Thomasyn stepped back a little, and squinted his eyes against the glare of the sun as he had been taught. He brought his arm back, the knife blade held between thumb and forefinger, and then flipped it forward, letting the blade go just at the right moment. The weapon flew forward, end over end. His aim was true, and the knife dug its tip into the target, dead centre.

He frowned; the balance of the blade had thrown the tumble off, leaving the hilt pointing toward the ground. Thomasyn shook his head and stepped back.

"You spin like you sleep all over the place," Bethany said, laughing. She stepped up to her target and let fly her knife. It hit dead centre on her target, handle pointing directly back at her perfectly. She looked at Thomasyn and winked.

"Gee, you two, I think Master Chail would want you to work harder than that," Jon said. "Anyway, we have a run coming up."

And what a run Master Chail had planned. He took the children out of the city at a fast pace, not the usual light jog. Through the gates and out to the road. He tested them. Running over to the fields, and pushed them harder than he had ever pushed them in the past. They passed the area where they had broken their fast for the first run out of the city and kept going. They moved quickly and with sure feet. It was a brisk and fast run.

After an hour, the clutch of Spears had run double the distance they jogged the first run but they kept going. Master Chail ran them for an hour and a half, till his lungs started to ache. When he knew he could go no further, he slowed to a brisk walk, looking back at the children. The perfect formation they had started with had been maintained. Yes, they were perspiring but not breathing heavy, nor did any of them look tired.

They have finally surpassed me, he thought, with a smile. I have trained a wonderful group of children with the help of some of the best people. Now it is time to show them how to kill.

In order to train the children how to kill, they needed a criminal. But not just any criminal, only the ones who had taken a life would forfeit theirs for training the Spears. They now entered the town which contained such criminals.

It was a town of just over eight hundred souls, and most of them bad. The small jail was stuffed with twelve criminals, each of whom had recently murdered someone. The two Spears assigned to the town kept them in jail, instead of dispensing justice. They knew the need of the Spears in Flight, and the group they caught would best have justice served by the young Spears, teaching them how to kill.

Chail marched the children into the town and up to the garrison hold. One Spear waited for them, dressed in his ring mail shirt and leather leggings. He smiled. Master Chail and the Spear grasped arms.

"Master Chail, it is great to see you again. I see you have another group of Flights you're training. How are they?"

"Tal! It has been many years since your training completed, and I see you are doing well here," Chail said.

"Yes, but I am more interested in this assembly of amazing Spears behind you. Did you run all this way from the city?" he asked, looking impressed.

"Yes, they handled it well, better than I did."

"Well, you are old and they are young," Tal said, winking at the children.

The two men laughed and embraced as if they had been friends for a long time. Tal looked at the young Spears and addressed them.

"Master Chail trained me. He was the best trainer then and I know he is the best trainer still. Listen to him and learn," he said.

"I bet the whole group thinks we are both old and over the hill," Chail said, laughing. "I need to feed this bunch and get them on their way again. It will be a long march back to the city with those law breakers you have captured."

"Agreed. The tavern can put food in their bellies and make them happy. The food they prepare is tasty, and has a good bite to it from the local peppers that grow in the woods," Tal said, and pointed the way.

He joined the group on their trip to the tavern. It was a small building, adjoined to a stable. Two small boys, roughly the same age as the young Spears, were raking out the hay from the stalls. They stopped and watched as the troop came into the building, totally amazed by the children. They put down their pitch forks and went to the tavern door to watch.

The children had never been in a tavern. The door stood tall in front of them and a sign hung from the wall: a crude drawing of a foaming cup.

Tal opened the door for Master Chail, and walked in behind his friend, letting the children follow them. The prevailing odor was of stale ale. The floor was made of wooden planks, dirt from the muddy boots of the patrons from over the years. Tables littered the area, and a bench ran around three walls, a serving bar stood against the fourth. A plump woman with graying hair stood behind it, her complexion ashen. She looked up and gave a toothless smile.

"Oh, ya all want some ale? You and the small ones?" she called out.

"No ale for us. Water please, for the whole group. What does your husband have cooking?" Tal asked.

"He has mutton stew with carrots and potatoes. Loads of good food for the children 'ere. Bread just baked has cooled enough for them to soak it up if they can handle the peppers," she replied.

"Then yes, water for all and the mutton stew with bread. And tell your husband not to skimp on the meat in the stew for the children, I'll be watching," he said.

She scowled at him for a second, then walked to the back of the tavern, opening a door and yelled something incoherent at the person in there. A reply came back, and satisfied with it, she closed the door and started putting cups on the bar.

"Just pick any seat will ya. I'll have ya water in a second."

They sat together, the children circled around the two men, listening to tales of how the land had changed. Tal had many stories of the justice dispensed in the area, and Chail went over the children's progress. He spoke with pride and Tal did not fail to point that out.

Several minutes had passed when the woman discovered the two stable boys had snuck into the tavern, and were listening to the tales. She came around and grabbed each of them by their ear, and yanked them to their feet.

"I don't pay ya to listen to long tales from Spears. I pay ya for keeping the stalls clean!" she yelled. Both boys cringed as if they knew what was coming. "Now get out there and clean before I tan your hides with the spoon." She pushed them to the door, and stood there for a moment with her hands on her hips. "I'll skin ya alive if the stalls aren't cleaned before sup' time. If they aren't, ya will be without food for the night!"

"Woman!" a yell came from the back of the tavern. She hurried back and opened the door, disappearing behind it. She returned a few moments later with bowls in one basket and bread balls in the other.

She placed a bowl in front of the men and each child, ruffling the hair of a couple of them as she passed. The basket of bread balls she emptied between the three tables they occupied and hurried to the back of the tavern. A few minutes later she returned, carrying a large pot and ladle, and proceeded to serve the stew to the hungry guests.

The stew was rich and heavy, it contained big chunks of carrots and potatoes with a bite from the peppers Tal had warned them about. Throughout the stew, small pieces of meat made their appearance. It was enough to make it well stocked, but not too much to say it was overdone. Chail found it delightful and the children devoured it in earnest.

During the meal, Tal explained about the men who would be going back with them. He also took the time to warn them about the twelve, and the deeds they had done.

"They are a sorry lot. It was interesting at first, trying to figure out who had killed the twenty people in the Dooly family. After investigating, I found they had quarreled over livestock for years. One family would claim the goats and cows, and then the other would. They mixed their herds and bred between the two and each family claimed the calves for their own. Well, as everyone knows, the calves always belong to the one who owns the cow, not the bull.

"So, I watched and waited. Sure enough, one family had no cows, only bulls. When the deaths stopped and I inspected the herd, the bulls now had cows to mate with. I confronted them with the findings and instead of disagreeing or saying they purchased the cows, they attacked me and Jenkins! A family of farmers trying to overcome two Spears! Have you ever heard of that?

"Well, the family also seemed to be breeding their children between themselves. After many years they had the strange appearance come out. You know, white hair and a pink complexion with pale blue eyes. I charged them with incest, explaining it is not only a sin but against the King's law. We need healthy people, not inbred ones. That was when we rounded them up.

"I searched and found human bones, of all things, buried in their dug storage. I figured about twenty or so bodies. Enough to close the investigations on more than half our missing reports. When confronted with this, they confessed to eating humans instead of their cattle. They had no cows you see, so they ate people. It figured with them that people of lesser sorts were cattle anyways, so they took them at night, and boiled them after gutting them alive. They ate just about everything, and what they could not eat they buried."

The children were aghast that people had been eating one another. It was Thomasyn who spoke. He always seemed to be the one to speak for the group.

"Could they not have hunted in the forest for food?" he asked.

"That's a good question. I think yes, but when I asked them, they said it took too long and they could not get anything big enough to feed all the mouths they had. It was easier to take one of the people who would not really be missed by anyone," Tal said.

By then they had all eaten their fill of soup and bread, feeling the warming effect of the peppers. The water was all but drunk and they needed to get going soon.

Chail stood and approached the woman, to pay for their meal.

"What? Me take coin off a Spear, for a slop of soup? No, I won't take ya money from ya. That Tal saved a lot o' folk here, and without that, me tavern would be empty, same with me purse. If not that, I woulda say he saved me two boys out there from being eaten by that family. I won't have any of it. Nope, keep ya money. But do me a kindness?" she asked.

"Yes, I will. What is it you need?" Chail asked.

"Make sure ya do a good job punishing those folks. They killed some good people around here, and revenge is something that is needed."

"Revenge and justice are two different things. I would suggest seeking justice for the dead only," Chail said. "But yes, they will be dealt with. We will be using them to instruct this group of Spears in the art of killing."

With that, he motioned for the children to thank the woman for her kindness. They lined up, each bowing with gratitude, exiting right after. By the time the last one had voiced their appreciation towards her for the meal, she had a tear or happiness in her eye, and a smile lighting her face.

They walked back to the garrison in silence, the children trying to comprehend the story about the prisoners. It was a wonder they had stayed and waited to be caught. Why not simply flee the area? Take their livestock and run?

It made no sense to them but they figured it was an adult thing, or something to do with the wild people beyond the city walls and outside the small towns. They all wanted to make sure they did not have to deal with such animals.

When they made it back to the garrison, Chail told the children to wait outside while he entered with Tal. After what felt like forever, they came out with the twelve prisoners, five women and seven men, all chained together at the ankles. Their hands were shackled in front of them, and those shackles chained around their waists. They looked defeated in their home spun clothing of wool and cloth.

They had no shoes, and their bare feed were covered in grime. The young boys and girls had white hair and pink complexions with pale blue eyes. It was obvious they had been born of closely related, maybe even siblings. It was an incredible sin against the five Gods.

The whole family was chained in single file, tallest to shortest. Each one looked like they believed it was them that had been wronged, not that their actions had wronged others. It caused them to snarl and grunt when one of the children came close to them.

Chail ordered the children to form two groups, on for the front, and one for the rear. He checked the chains of each captive, making sure they would not be able to escape.

It took a long time for them to get back to the city. The captives moved slowly, a lot slower than the children would have walked by themselves. It was not a hard walk to the city, but the family complained all the way, demanding to stop every hour to either drink or relieve themselves. They complained about the chains when they needed to make water, when one moved too fast or too slow, but finding it did nothing to get them released regardless of how loud they were.

When they made it to the gates of the city, the captives realized they had reached the end and started to cause problems. The biggest one stopped and sat down, causing the rest to fall to their knees. The younger ones shuffled their feet in place, and did not want to move forward as well. After being prodded by Chail's spear they eventually resumed their forced march.

As they paraded through the city, refuse was thrown at the family as the people showed their disgust. It was like that all the way to the training grounds. And once there, older Spears took charge of the captives, and moved them into a secure area, keeping the shackles on both wrists and ankles.

"Tess, I just wanted to tell you it has been great having you here for the children. And I find your company nice," Chail said to Tess in a whisper during the evening meal. They were sitting in the great hall, the children at one end of the table and them at the other. They could not have been heard by the children even if they talked in their normal voices due to the noise from all who sat around them.

"Master Chail, I have always enjoyed the time I spend here at the training hall. You and the others have been very kind to me," she said.

"You never talk about why you came to us."

"It was sad. My husband was sick after I came with child. But it was not the coughing that caused him to pass. He was killed by a robber for the three copper buts he carried, which we needed for a midwife. I could not afford to pay a midwife to birth my child, but he did come out easy. He was small and weak, but I loved him still. After two days he got the cough, and soon afterwards. I had just enough to bury him next to my husband. I cried till my eyes would no longer open. If it was not for the Spears..."

"I'm sorry if I am upsetting you. We don't have to continue..." he started.

"No," Tess said, reaching over and touching his hand. "We have never really talked about it." She took a deep breath and looked into his eyes. She noticed the way he was looking at her, and realized he was actually attracted to her. That realization told her to look a little closer at him. He was a handsome man, strong of features and clear eyes. "I traveled here to the city in order to find a place to belong, and the Spear's crier announced the need. I realized I would be of use, so I came and Master Con accepted me. The rest is just what happened."

He looked at her, the long, brunette hair tied neatly behind her head. She was a fine woman, a small nose and soft, brown eyes. He liked the way of her, and placed his hand on top of hers, squeezing it a little.

"I'm sorry you lost your child," he said.

"Don't be. I would not have been able to survive with no husband and a new born child. This way, I not only found a place to belong, but I also gained many children, all of whom I love."

"Then you are happy here?" he asked.

"Very happy," she said.

He noticed Tess had not removed her hand from his, instead, she turned her right one over to hold his properly.

"So what does this mean, Chail?"

"I guess," he said, "that we have something to build on, besides our love for the children."

---

The children were told to gather in the training square with the knowledge today would be the day. They had only been back from securing the twelve for three days, and they had not been out since.

The square had been cleared of all the usual objects, targets and practice. Instead, two of the captive men stood there, unchained and stripped to the waist.

Chail stood on a raised dais looking over the square, wondering which child would be the first to kill one of the captives, and learn how to spill blood. This part of the training was not something he looked forward to. It was barbaric, old learning that was passed down over years and years of ancient custom. It was also a necessary part of the training. It ensured they would not freeze in the future if they had to take a life in self-defense or in defense of others.

"Who will be first?" Chail asked.

They contemplated one another, and returned their trainer's gaze with a question in their eyes, all but Thomasyn and Bethany. The pair stepped forward.

"Thomasyn, Bethany, down to your small clothes," he called out.

They looked at each other and stripped off their clothes, except the wrappings around their lowers. Those they kept on, for it would keep some form of modesty for them. They removed their shoes and placed them with the rest of their uniforms.

"As a Spear you will always need to be mindful of your surroundings. You will also need to protect yourself at all times.

"In the middle of the square are two criminals who have taken lives. These two are afforded the privilege to either kill or be killed. If they are killed then their lives are gone from them forever. If they kill, then freedom is their reward. For them, it is a fight for the right to live.

"You on the other hand, will be fighting to hold them or kill them, the choice is yours. You do not need to kill them, but remember, they will be trying to kill you in any way they can.

"So, be mindful of what is happening around you. Fight with honor, fight with bravery, fight to survive."

Chail picked up four short swords and walked out on the practice square, walking with determination and purpose. When he reached Thomasyn and Bethany he handed each of them a sword, and then walked past them. When he reached the two men he looked at them squarely, measuring them.

"So we kill da kids and we go free, aye?" the bigger one asked.

Chail looked him up and down. Yes, he was a large man, strong and fed after his journey to the city. He looked like he could fight, but how well? His face was scruffy with a week's growth of beard, it partially hid the ugly gash on his cheek. Eyes under bushy eyebrows had a crafty look, unlike his companion who appeared to use them only to glance around with nervousness.

"If you live, you go free," Chail said to him. "I suggest you don't underestimate the children, they have been training since birth."

With that he dropped the two swords at their feet, and turned away.

"Children, leave the parade square and go to the dais," he said, climbing the steps and then sitting on the bench. The children followed, picking seats and looking out at the parade square, wondering what would happen.

The captives looked at one another, stepped forward and picked up a sword each. The big one tested the blade to make sure it was keen. He nodded, satisfied, and took a few practice swings at the air. His comrade kept the sword in his hand, letting it swing softly as if it was affected by a breeze. He is the one to worry about, thought Chail. He does not waste his energy fighting the air or worrying about the sharpness of the blade, he is just waiting to kill and be released.

Thomasyn and Bethany approached the center of the training square as they had been trained. They looked at the two they had to fight and bowed slightly. The big one raised his sword; his companion turned sideways, keeping the sword low and non-threatening.

The big one was the first to move. He jumped towards Bethany with a clumsy, lumbering movement. He held his sword high, swinging it down with all his weight towards her. He had a mad, teeth gritted smile, spittle flying out with a large exhalation of breath. His eyes were wide with madness, a desire to spill blood. He could see it, the blade swinging down. He envisioned the killing blow cleaving her head in two.

But she moved, sideways and forward. She moved quickly and sure footed, knowing his clumsy swing would take time to deliver with the short sword, and that to reach her he would have to over extend his reach. She also realized she was faster than he was. Not because he was slow, no he was anything but slow. It was because of her training, she had been taught to be as fluid as water over rocks.

She side-stepped his swing and rolled forward to her feet and turned, driving the tip of the sword into his calf muscle. Not deeply, just enough to cause a great deal of pain.

Thomasyn heard this happen, but his full gaze was on his opponent who stood in front of him. He realized by the man's stance and the way he did not lunge forward that he had trained in fighting. But to what degree, he did not know.

They stood there, looking at one another while Bethany and her opponent danced around the parade square. He would advance in a lumbering swing and she would dance to the side, delivering a stinging pinch to him from the tip of her sword.

Chail watched from the dais, realizing what Bethany was doing. She was trying to wear the big man out, to cause him to make mistakes and flounder. She needed him to fail so she could move in for a killing blow without any harm to herself. And her strategy was working very quickly.

Thomasyn's opponent feinted, but he saw through it and did not react. A smile crossed the man's lips and Thomasyn wondered why he would smile. Nothing had happened and his feint did not tell him anything. But Thomasyn was wrong. The feint told his opponent he would probably die today, the young Spear being trained to ignore feints and concentrate on the blows.

He lunged, moving his arm up and forward swiftly, trying to catch Thomasyn unaware. He did not.

Thomasyn saw the blade come up and, like an expert, he moved forward, bringing his body to the outside of the attack. When the arm carrying the sword was parallel to the ground, Thomasyn was beside the man, pulling his sword across his opponent's belly.

The smile on the man's face went from a wide grin to an expression of shock and surprise. His stomach opened and guts fell out. The blue snake of his insides hit the ground a scant moment before the rest of his body did. His eyes remained opened, staring at nothing, his mouth open, and tongue extended as if reaching for the sand, just moments before his head struck the ground.

Thomasyn looked at the man, his blood was soaking into the dried mud. He took his sword and wiped it on the leggings of his opponent. He looked up at Master Chail and bowed.

Bethany was moving around her opponent with ease. The man was tiring, and suffering from over two dozen pricks of her short sword. Blood was flowing out of his biceps and calf's. She danced around him as he moved, slashing with desperation and trying to find her before his life ended, but all he hit was air. And then she would prick him again with the point of her sword. The pain she inflicted was driving him mad, and the frustration was pushing him over the breaking point as she watched beads of sweat form on his brow.

She moved behind him again, and he turned with frustration. Bethany saw that his body was slow now, having lost a lot of blood from her little stings. His sword went up again and this time she moved in. Bethany had seen his shifting weight. She knew he did not mean to bring his sword down in front of him, but to turn and slice to the side, where he knew she would have to go, for the side wall of the practice yard was at his left, and she could only evade to the right.

He smiled and let out a great howl of victory as he brought his sword down and to the side. But she was not there. Bethany had stepped forward, driving her sword tip upward and through the underside of his jaw, up through his brain. He was stunned by the move as life left him, and his body started to fall forward, threatening to collapse on her.

Bethany yanked the sword out of his head, and tucked and rolled between his legs, coming to her feet behind him.

"Yours looks like a big worm is eating him," she said to Thomasyn.

"Ya, but you had to show off again, hitting such a small target as his brain," he smiled back.

Bethany turned and cleaned her sword the same way Thomasyn had cleaned his, wiping it on the pants of her victim. When it was clean she turned and faced Master Chail, bowed and smiled.

"Very good," he said, truly impressed. Not only did they live, but they had judged correctly according to the law. "But remember, all life is sacred. Prepare the bodies for burial. I will fetch a Wooder to lay them to rest."

———

Chail was dressed in the clothes of a commoner, light cloth pants with a tunic over his cotton shirt. He left the throwing spear in his quarters. Chail was on his way to meet Tess and go to the main city. They had arranged to meet just outside the children's barracks, making it seem a chance encounter to any who noticed, especially the children.

The afternoon was turning into evening, the sun starting to dip below the walls of the castle proper. He planned to take her to the Howling Tavern for a supper that did not involve making sure the children ate. The Howling Tavern was known for its visiting minstrels and their excellent songs, so it would be a nice change for them.

He turned a corner in the barracks proper and saw her. She had taken the time to dress in a gown of forest green, and had let her hair down and brushed it over her left shoulder. Tess's face had been cleaned of all dust and constant worry for wellbeing of the children. A hint of rouge on her cheeks highlighted her gentle features. Her lips were painted with a light red dye, telling him she had planned to be attractive for him. He appreciated it, knowing he had taken time to groom himself and cut back his usually ruffled hair.

Their meeting did not go unnoticed by the children who were on their way to supper. They noticed when he held out his hands and she put hers in his, as a sign of affection. The children who had not observed the two were nudged and made to look. A cooing sound raised in volume as the children showed their approval of the two of them being together.

"Okay now, hush and get ready for supper. We will see you when we return," Tess said to them with a wink.

The children quickly got ready and shuffled out of the barracks, past the two adults. Chail did not see the approving nods of the boys and swooning looks from the girls as they passed.

He turned his attention to the woman who had captured his heart. They stood, admiring one another. Tess blushed and lowered her eyes, only to gaze up at him with her head inclined.

"I think we better get going before they come back from supper, or we will have a lot of questions to answer," he said.

"I think we will have a lot of questions to answer when we get back," she said, giggling. She dropped one of his hands and pulled him towards the door that led to the courtyard, and in turn, to the city. "Besides, did you see the glare Bethany gave you when she saw us together just now?"

"No, but she has always had a soft heart for me."

"Soft? Ha! She has been in love with you for several years now. It is fortunate she is fond of me as well or I would be fearful for my life."

They laughed easily at that little jest, a light and enjoying laugh between people who cared for one another. Tess is easy to be with, he thought, squeezing her hand a little. She glanced at him and squeezed back, smiling.

---

"Where are they?" Bethany asked. The children had returned from supper, stretched and exercised as always but neither Chail nor Tess had met them. Now, as bed time approached, neither had not come to bid them goodnight as was their wanted custom.

"How should I know? I have been here with you all this time," Jon replied. He changed his clothes, replacing his day wear with his sleep shirt. "Besides, they went out together. Master Chail can take care for both of them. Remember how he took out that giant man two years ago?"

Bethany did not care. She was upset Chail had taken Tess out on the town instead of her. Bethany loved him and knew he cared deeply for her. Of course she knew that he cared for all the children, you could see it in his eyes, but he cared more deeply for her and she could tell. Bethany had seen it one day; it was in his eyes, a little twinkle when he spoke to her. It was a young girl's crush on a powerful man Bethany felt.

"Well, I'm not sleeping till they come back," she said.

"Then let me sleep at least," said Jon as he climbed into his cot and pulled the sheets over himself.

She sat on her cot, dressed in her bed clothes but not lying down. The servants came in and snuffed out most of the candles and still she waited.

Soon, the whole of the barracks was filled with children dreaming strange dreams, all except one. Bethany struggled to stay awake, her head nodding a little more every few minutes. But she was able to push past it, keeping her eyes opened as she waited.

Her patience paid off when the two adults came through from the outer door. They moved quietly but not steadily. It is as if they forgot how to stand straight, she thought.

Both Tess and Chail stumbled into the barracks with a hushed laughter, having drunk their fair share of wine at the tavern. Tess was walking past the children, naming them by their shapes. Chail told her his aspirations for each one of them. This one was great with a knife, this one will be the best at stalking, this one was unbeatable with a bow, and on it went. They kept this going till they came to Bethany, who was waiting for them.

"Child, why are you still awake?" Tess asked, giving her a hug.

"I waited for you. I wanted to say goodnight," she yawned, covering her mouth at the last moment and remembering her manners. "Excuse me."

"Bethany, you don't have to say goodnight to us every night. We know what is in your heart," Chail said, squatting down in front of her. "But I am glad you did, child." And he leaned forward, kissing her cheek. "Go to sleep now, my child. We will see you tomorrow."

"But I wanted you to take me to supper," she said, struggling to keep her eyes open.

"Maybe later, in a few years. Now, you need your sleep."

He laid Bethany down in her cot and pulled the covers over the child as she fell asleep.

———

"I saw Master Dress, he was giving special instructions to Michael, again," Thomasyn said to Bethany and Jon. "He was there." He pointed to the back of the barracks. "And Michael's pants were down. Master Dress was showing him how to balance on his toes."

"I don't think that is right," Bethany said. She wrinkled her nose at the thought. "I have never seen Master Dress give special instructions to anyone in the barracks. What do you think it means?"

Thomasyn puzzled over that for a few moments, not wanting to appear lacking in knowledge.

"Maybe it means Michael is not doing well?" Jon said.

"No, he's really good at everything, almost as good as Thomasyn is," Bethany said, hitting him in the arm softly. "Are you sure Master Dress was teaching Michael something? Was he maybe touching him as well? Michael has been sick more this year than he was last year. Could it be Master Dress was trying to help him?"

"With both of them with their pants down?" Thomasyn asked. He shuddered at the memory. "I don't think they were practicing anything."

They stopped talking as Sandra entered the barracks at the other end. Sandra looked at both Bethany and Jon but smiled at Thomasyn; he smiled back with a wave. Her look told him she liked him and he liked her. Bethany hit Thomasyn on the shoulder again, this time harder.

"Ow! Why did you do that?" he asked.

"Why are you waving and all giddy with Sandra?" she asked.

"Why would you want to know?" he asked. "You want to be holding hands with Master Chail."

She hit him again, harder. He rolled his shoulder to lighten the blow. Bethany might be a girl but she had one heck of a slug when she wanted to. He stuck his tongue out at her.

"If I grab that thing I will pull it from your mouth," she said, making a quick grab at it.

Thomasyn sucked his tongue back into his mouth and screwed up his eyes while pursing his lips at her. He then turned and ran out the door while she screamed at him.

"And you're my friend!" she bellowed.

He laughed as he ran, and once he reached Sandra he slowed to walk beside her. She smiled at him and he smiled back. Sandra was a little taller than him but that did not matter, he would catch up soon. Her large, blue eyes lit her face which was framed by long, blonde hair. Sandra was a pretty girl, one of the prettiest.

"So, have you been out in the yard today?" she asked shyly.

"Oh, yes. It is a good fall day today. The sun stayed out from behind the clouds all morning. Bethany, Jon and I played hold the clouds for hours," he said.

She winced a little at the mention of Bethany's name, but recovered fast. Everyone knew Bethany was a close friend of Thomasyn's as well as Jon. But for some reason everyone thought the two of them would always be together. It was not true, of course. They stayed friends because Bethany was the only one who could keep up with Thomasyn during sparing. Jon was the third best fighter.

Thomasyn reached out and took Sandra's hand, a move which surprised her. He heard Bethany give a loud growl of frustration from the other side of the barracks as she hit Jon, the only target close to her.

"What did I do?" Jon asked, wincing from the strike.

"Boys!" she cried, and walked out the barracks door to the practice yard.

———

"Yes, I saw Master Dress and Michael practicing a couple of times. It is strange he makes him do that with their pants down, but I guess that is the only way he can touch him," Sandra said as they entered the small room off the hallway.

"But how was he touching Master Dress?" Thomasyn asked.

"Here, let me show you," she said, getting down on her knees.

Thomasyn thought it was strange she would be so quick at wanting to demonstrate the special training, but he did not argue. He always wanted to be his best, and if Michael was getting special instructions, then he wanted to get those instructions also, even if it was from someone who had only seen it happen.

Sandra lowered his pants to his ankles, exposing him to her. She smiled and pulled her pants down also. They all knew the difference between boys and girls, having lived together for years, but they never made much of a big deal about it.

Thomasyn did not think much of the training so far, as he stood there with himself exposed. It was not till she started that he was surprised. She leaned forward and took him in her mouth. It felt good, but something told him it was wrong. She held him in her mouth and brushed her tongue around him and he felt himself growing hard. She kept at it and he started to feel a little pain. It was like something trying to happen that could not at this time. It was confusing.

Tess opened the door and walked in the small room. She dropped the clothes she was carrying and pulled Sandra off Thomasyn. She looked at them with a shocked expression on her face.

"What are you two doing?" Tess asked, not believing what she walked in on.

"Its okay, Nanny Tess, Sandra was just helping me train," Thomasyn said.

"Yes. We saw Master Dress giving Michael the lessons and wanted to make sure we could do it also," Sandra said.

Tess stared at them, Thomasyn standing there with his small manhood all but pressing against his stomach, pointing to the sky, and Sandra so innocent. Her mind raced and finally focused on what they had said, Master Dress had been having Michael do this to him? He had been molesting the child? What could that mean? He would never break the sacred trust the Spears had given him.

And then she realized, Dress was not really a Spear. He had not been trained like the children or Chail had. He came from the sandy sea, almost fully grown from what she had been told. Who knows what went through his mind.

"Children, clothe yourselves right now. We need to talk to Master Chail." She waited for them to pull up their pants before grabbing their hands and marching them out of the little room. She headed down the corridor towards the practice area, hoping to find Chail.

The first person she stumbled upon was Dress, leaning against the wall, talking to one of the wet nurses for the newest bunch of Spears. She was blushing as he spoke, the back of his hand brushing against her cheek.

He is flirting with her! Making himself out to be the innocent! Her anger rose and she walked quickly, moving past him.

Dress called out to her as she passed but she only gave him an evil look. He did not understand it, so he turned back to the wet nurse, talking sweetly to her.

Tess pulled the children out of the corridor and through the doors to the training square. She spied Chail instructing two children on the proper technique of opening the belly of a clumsy attacker. She marched up to him, all the fire in the world in her manner.

"Master Chail! I need to have a word with you, right now."

Chail did not turn right away. Instead, he smiled at the children he was instructing as he completed his instructions.

"Please, continue with your practice. I have to attend Nanny Tess for a few moments."

He stood and turned to her and realized something was wrong. She was pulling Sandra and Thomasyn by their arms and he knew she was very upset with the children. He could only believe they had let her pull them to him, for she had not been trained in fighting. These two children could have easily gotten loose from her sloppy grip if they wanted to. He shook his head and began to count to ten. He did not get as far as three.

"Do you know what your children are practicing?" she asked him in a confrontational tone.

"How to split open the belly of an attacker. Thomasyn had showed them the art a few days ago," he said with sarcasm.

Tess swore under her breath to keep from screaming at him. She tapped her foot and kept a firm grasp on Thomasyn and Sandra. They stayed in her hold not because they had to, but because they dared not break it. They knew when an adult was angry and they knew when they could get away with something. This was not a day to test if they could get away with anything.

Chail, on the other hand, seemed to have forgotten that lesson. He held Tess in his gaze, hoping that she would smile at his little joke. It did not take long for him to notice she was not laughing, but indeed turning red-faced as she stood there, telling Chail he needed to get her off the practice square.

"Okay, come with me," he said, making his way in the direction she had come from. She followed him, bringing the two children with her.

They passed through the doors and into the corridor. As Chail passed Dress, he paused for a second.

"Dress, should you not be instructing a class of children?" he asked.

"Oh, ah, yes, Master Chail. Right away," he said and moved away from the wet nurse and out to the practice square.

Chail turned his attention to the wet nurse who blushed and excused herself, moving into the building towards the nursery.

"He... She... Errrr... I am so angry I could--" Tess started, but Chail cut her off.

"Not here. I see you're frustrated about something but I want to hear it in private first," he said, and guided her to the small meeting room. He made the children sit outside while they talked.

"So, tell me what has you so upset you would come out and disturb instructions in mid-lesson?" he asked, as he sat down.

Tess started to pace, stopped, put her palm to her forehead and paced with it there. She stopped abruptly and faced him.

"He's doing things to the children, and now they are copying him," she spoke her words at him and pointed to the children on the other side of the door.

"First off, I am not aware of anyone doing anything to the children they would mimic that would get you so upset." He stood up and walked to her. "Tess, something has you enraged. I know that, I see that.

I do not believe the resentment is directed at me. So, tell me what you saw and we will see what we can do about it."

She took a deep breath and examined his face for a second. He was a wonderful man, she knew that. He loved the children and he would do anything for them. She also knew that. Her thoughts rolled around her head as she tried to make sense of them all. Tears started to form, blurring her vision. She moved toward him, put her arms around his middle and pulled him to her as she cried.

Chail did not know what to do, so he did what she did, put his arms around her and held her. He kept her like this till her crying subsided to a sniffle. When he was sure she was settled enough, he whispered to her.

"What has you so upset, Tess?"

"I... I walked in on Sandra and Thomasyn. They... They were... Their pants were down and she had him in her mouth," she blurted out.

Chail mouth dropped and a look or utter disbelieve washed over his face. He did not know what to say. He did what he thought was the best thing to do.

"Children! Thomasyn, Sandra, in here now!"

# EIGHT

C hail could hardly believe what these young Spears were saying. To hear it from their mouths was shocking.

He sat, his head on one hand. His mind was reeling with the information they had started to tell him. When the children explained about mimicking what Master Dress had been doing with Michael, his head snapped up, a look of horror on his face.

"I don't believe it," he said. It made sense to him though. Dress was from the wasteland, and they had been known to tolerate children molesters. It did not excuse the violation of the ancient trust. Nothing like this could be forgiven.

"Where is Michael, now?" he asked.

"I don't know. I can get him..." Tess said.

"Yes, right away."

Tess ran from the room towards the barracks. On her way, she was met by Lyla, one of the maids from the Spear's training center. Tears ran from her eyes, and her shoulders heaved as she wept. Lyla grabbed Tess by the arm, pulling her towards the barracks with earnest.

"Tess! You need to come, quickly! It's Michael... he... he... he's dead!"

"Dead!" Tess put a hand to her mouth, she looked into Lyla's eyes, searching for anything to tell her it was a rouse, a jest, but found no hint of deception. Tess started to run with Lyla, following her to where Michael was.

He was in the barracks alone. The rest of the children were out training. Michael must have snuck back inside when no one was looking. The rope he had used could have been brought from the training area, where a number of such items always lay unguarded. His climb up to the ceiling support would not have been difficult, knowing the training. He had tied it off, slipped the noose over his head and stepped off the truss.

Tess fell to her knees, sobbing at the sight of the small body swaying lifeless. Two Wooders were called over from their training center. They took Michael's body down, and laid him on his bed. One Wooder examined the body, and told her there was nothing that could be done, his neck had snapped when he jumped from the rafters.

She just knelt there, tears flowing. The realization she could not save the child hit her hard, and grief welled up in her soul. As her tears slowed, her thoughts went to the one who had caused this. Dress.

---

Chail sat with the children for ten minutes, and wondered what was taking Tess so long. Thomasyn and Sandra had been informed their behavior was inappropriate for their age, and they were to cease doing it immediately. He did not care how long they had been doing it, or how many times. He told them they would understand later on, when they were older.

Falon pushed open the door as he rapped on it, entering the room without permission. He was ragged looking, as if a great weight was on his mind. Chail bade him to let loose his sorrows.

"It is Michael, Master Chail. He killed himself not an hour ago."

It was more than his mind could comprehend; a Spear, let alone a child, taking their own life.

"But how? Why?" but he knew why, it was obvious. Dress.

"He fashioned a noose, and hung himself in the barracks, sir," Falon said.

"No, that could not be," Thomasyn said. "Michael is afraid of heights."

Chail looked at Thomasyn, The child cannot even comprehend Michael is dead, he though. But he understood the reference, for he also knew Michael was afraid of heights. You do not kill yourself by doing something that you are deathly afraid of.

Suddenly, his mind focused on one thought, If the children... and he stood.

"Call the Spears; we must seek out justice now! Before it is too late." And he moved out of the office and ran down the hall to the barracks to ensure the children did not overstep their bounds by seeking vengeance, rather than justice.

Thomasy and Sandra sat uncertain what they should do next. They waited in awkward silence. Sandra continued to stare at her feet.

"It is not our fault," Thomasyn said. "It was Master Dress, he was the one who did something wrong."

"But Master Chail is mad at us," she mumbled.

"No, he is not. He is mad at Master Dress." His voice grew angry as he realized what had happened. "Master Dress killed Michael."

He stood, and held out his hand to her. She regarded his outstretched hand from beneath her eyelashes, trying to decide what she would do. The thoughts that drove through her mind stopped, and she remembered the law.

"A life that takes a life is forfeit," she said.

"Yes, forfeit. We are Spears. Young, but still Spears. We dispense justice."

She took his hand and stood.

"We dispense justice," she said, and they walked out of the room together.

Dress stood beside Angela, a wet nurse in the nursery of the new clutch of Spears. He talked about his travels as she fed one of the newest members of this year's children. Angela smiled and laughed as she talked with Dress, he was very funny at times.

He is an attractive man, she thought, as Dress leaned towards her, whispering a lewd suggestion. She had not been with a man for six months, around when her pregnancy started to show, and then when the child had come too soon and died she had to wait, and heal. Now, after two months, she wanted to feel a man between her legs again, and Dress was trying very hard to be that man.

Dress reached out and brushed a strand of hair out of her eyes, brushing the back of his hand against her cheek. Angela looked up into his eyes, wondering how hard she should make him try. Maybe a little longer, let him wait just a little longer.

Thomasyn walked into the nursery, followed by twenty seven children, all dressed in their practice leathers with dirks in their belts. They entered slowly, looking at the children in the cribs, and hushing their cries. Gradually, they made their way around the room, circling, and being coy with their intentions.

Once their circle was completed, the children turned and started to tighten their noose.

---

"Where is Dress?" Chail asked. He had found Natail in the barracks of the Spears packing Michael's kit.

"I have not seen him since this morning," Natail said, shrugging his shoulders. "He was chatting with a wet nurse last I saw."

"Master Chail! Come quickly," Falon called as he rushed into the barracks.

Chail turned to see the back of Falon through the barrack doors, so he ran after him. He followed him through the hall and into the practice square.

What he saw made him draw up short. In the practice square, Dress was facing Thomasyn, with Sandra between the two. Both held a curved short sword, and were naked to the waist, exactly as the judgment ceremony calls for. Both had boiled leather strappings on their legs, soft leather shoes, and silken judgment belts with the cloth trailing down from the knots.

The other children stood around them in a loose circle, each carrying their dirks, still tucked in their belts. Sandra was speaking, saying the law and offering Dress a choice.

"You have been judged. You have confessed your crime, or other crimes against children, and the Spears. Particularly Michael. You have trained many of us, but now we must train you.

"The choice is to fight or be killed. If you fight with honor and win you will be free to leave, no one will stand in your way; that is the way of the Spears; that is what we choose. If you do not fight, then you will be killed outright by the Spears. We dispense justice."

"I will fight, but are you ready to die, Thomasyn?" Dress said.

Sandra spoke directly to him. "You may find that hard to do, coward. For only a coward would force themselves on one so young." She smiled at Thomasyn, then turned and faced Dress. "Each Spear here wanted to have the honor of killing you, but we know how you fight. Thomasyn has not had that pleasure. You have always avoided training him. We do not know why, but we do know that is a good thing. Make your peace, Master Dress, you are about to have sentence pronounced."

She stepped back, entering the space in the circle they had left for her. Dress smiled at Thomaysn, and tested the edge of the sword they had given him. It was sharp, clean, and balanced.

Chail waited, knowing if he interfered he would undermine the justice, and it would be an emotional blow to the children.

Dress stood there, measuring Thomasyn and remembering the first time the child spilled blood. Speed, sure of foot, and clean efficiency, he vowed not let this outcome be the same. No, he would not let the child take his life.

Thomasyn studied the older man, taking in all movements. The way Dress's left eye twitched when he adjusted his grip on the pommel of the sword, of how the trainer used a breathing technic to match breathe with the movements of his feet. He sweats, thought Thomasyn, as he saw a bead form on the brow of the man. Dress tighten his neck, telling Thomasyn the attack was coming.

Dress went into a fighting stance, one foot forward and one back. His gesture showed contempt for the child; as if he thought he had already won.

He has already lost, and he does not know it, Chail thought.

Dress advanced, not lifting the sword high, but keeping it in front of him. Thomasyn held his ground; the tip of his sword extended to meet his attacker, but the blow never came. Dress touched the tip of his sword to Thomasyn's, and stayed back. Thomasyn tapped the tip of Dress' sword in return, not taking the bait.

Dress circled to his left, making Thomasyn turn right, hoping the child would turn, exposing the arm not holding the sword, but the child did something that shocked Dress, he switched hands. He tossed the sword to his left hand, switching the position of his feet. Dress found himself circling to the striking area, just as Thomasyn wanted.

Dress stopped, reversed direction, and Thomasyn switched hands again. Dress changed his tactic, advanced two quick, short steps, and swung the sword strong at Thomasyn. The swing cut through air and he expected the child to move into his blind side. Expecting it, he did a rounding swing, arcing the blade completely, bringing it sideways to block a cutting slice to his midsection. None was there.

Thomasyn stood in the same spot, his sword in the same position. Dress shuffled his feet back so he could look at him. He was surprised and tried not to show it. He was expecting the child to try and end the fight quickly, but Thomasyn did not. Another surprise for Dress, but not the last. He took his fighting stance again, tapping Thomasyn's sword tips once more.

Thomasyn reacted on the third tapping of the points. He extended his reach and nipped Dress's forearm. Not hard, but with enough force to cut the skin open. Dress leapt back in response, he had not expected the slight movement that opened the little cut on his arm.

Dress glared at Thomasyn in surprise. The child looked back with no emotion in his eyes. Dress knew he would have to finish the fight fast now; the cut was not mortal, but would cause problems with his grip when the blood reached his hand, making the handle of the sword slippery. He also knew it would cause difficulties with his arm, for it would tire faster now.

He lunged, thrusting his sword forward. Thomasyn parried, turning it to his right. He was facing Dress's right side but knew what was about to happen. He saw the telltale sign from the shifting of Dress's feet. Thomasyn ducked, just as his opponent's sword slashed over his head, taking a little bit of hair from his head, and leaving Dress vulnerable to attack.

Thomasyn pushed his body forward, thrust out his sword and sliced into Dress's calf. He did not stop though, he carried his body forward, and as he rolled between the man's legs, he pulled his sword in a backhanded motion, cutting another swath from Dress's inner thigh. He continued his roll, coming to his feet behind the man. Thomasyn did not attack again.

Dress screamed in frustration and turned towards Thomasyn with pure furry in his eyes. He reached down and felt the cut through the leather, and the moisture of the blood leaking out of his body. He knew from the amount spurting out of his leg he had been killed. Dress glared at Thomasyn, who just stood there, without emotion.

Dress stepped forward and stopped. He looked down again and saw his life blood pooling on the ground. He wavered and saw Thomasyn, the child nodded, slowly closed and opened his eyes again. Dress dropped to his knees, face paling, the blood now pooling around him. His sword fell from his hand, and his body slumped forward. He stuck out his other arm to keep from falling on his face, supporting himself in an effort to hold on to his life a little longer.

Thomasyn moved within a few feet of him and knelt. His voice was soft and without malice.

"You have paid for breaking the first law." He stood, turned, and walked away, dropping his sword.

---

THE CHILDREN STOOD IN FRONT OF THEIR COTS. THE barracks were quiet; the only sound that could be heard was the children breathing. Chail sighed and glanced at them from the main door. He had never been disappointed with the children, not even when they did something wrong. But today they had overstepped their authority; they had dispensed justice without the mandate to do so. He looked upon it as a chance to teach them right from wrong, good from evil, proper from inappropriate.

Tess fidgeted beside him, waiting for his lead. She had dressed as she always did, but now a black wrap covered her shoulders.

For five minutes they waited for their minds to stop reeling with emotion. Chail did not know what he was going to do this time; two of his trainers had turned out to be something he had not wanted. Now, it was time for the talk.

"Children, if anyone touches you strangely when you are alone with them, please tell either Tess or me. It is something that should not happen, so make sure we are told.

"Other than that, we are happy, proud. You have been able to understand a law was broken. It is a lesson we really did not want you to learn this way, but we are glad you learned it well. We are proud you did it the way you did, offering honor to the person, and a chance to redeem themself. You have truly shown you are Spears."

Tess turned paled, understanding what Chail was saying. The have truly learned to kill. They are no longer innocents, she thought.


## Year Nine

"You have all been trained on every weapon here." Chail motioned to the rack of weapons at the side of the training grounds. "You are proficient on each of them. The spears here," he motioned to the other side of the training ground, "must be added to your weapon list. Especially the short spear, the weapon you are named for.

"The short spear is used for thrusting." Chail took the spear off his back, and thrust if forward. "Or blocking." He used the spear to block an imaginary attacker. "You can use it to stab." He shortened his grip on the weapon, and used it as a dagger. "Or you can throw it short." Chail threw the spear short, into the ground a few feet in front of him. "But more importantly, it is a weapon of two parts. The throwing arm, or bone, as it is called, allows you to put your full weight into a toss, making this a very dangerous weapon indeed." He pulled the spear from the ground, and took out another stick with a small hook on the end. It was the same length as the spear. Chail placed the hook in the small indent at the end of the spear's shaft.

"Now, children, watch," he said, as he drew back his arm, Chail stepped back with his right leg, shifting his weight to it. With a quick and fluid motion he shifted his weight forward, turning his shoulders, and propelling the spear with his throwing arm. His wrist turned at the last moment, moving the bone in an arc and propelling the spear with force.

The spear traveled forward in a slight arc. It went towards the target at the far end of the practice square, fifty yards away. It entered the wooden planks with a splintering sound, and burying itself into the packed straw behind it till it all but disappeared.

"That, my children, is how a spear is thrown, and how a Spear throws," he said. Chail jumped off the demonstration disc and walked towards the target. He wanted to show the children they had nothing to fear from the weapon, it was their friend and closest ally.

An older man stepped to the disc and looked at the Spears. His name was Master Gation, and he was one of the oldest Spears the children had ever seen. He was even older than Master Chail. Master Gation had one job to do at the training grounds, to teach the new Spears how to throw like he did.

"Master Chail is one of my best students. If you can throw a spear like him, I will be proud of you, and so will he." Master Gation looked over at his favorite student with pride, motioning him to come up to the dais. "Master Chail, please demonstrate the technique for the children again."

Chail climbed to the dais and pulled another short spear from the holder on his back. He placed it in the bone, reached back and propelled the spear forward, twisting his wrist as he did. Master Gation raised his eyebrow at that move, but did not say anything. The spear traveled level and much faster than the last. It splintered the target and buried itself deep in it, with no part protruding.

Master Gation looked at Chail with a sideways glance, his eyebrow still raised. He stepped down and walked to the target. He reached into the hole and pulled out his arm, empty-handed. He went around to the back of the target, and found the spear imbedded in the fence behind it.

Master Gation pulled the spear out of the fence and returned to the dais. He climbed up and handed the spear back to Chail.

"It seems some masters can be surpassed by their students," he said. Chail blushed. "It is something every master wants to see, even if it is something they never want to hear." Master Gation noticed the smiling faces of the children. He shook his head, and looked at Chail. "Have they seen you throw before?" Master Gation asked. "You know they are not supposed to have spear training before now. Have you shown them how to throw a spear yet?"

Chail nodded towards the children. "I did not show them on purpose. They saw me throw a spear a few years ago. It was in their protection, so they have seen the technique, but only once. I would tell you they are observant, and can probably throw just as well as any Spear out there now. Let me demonstrate. Bethany, Thomasyn, Jon, please come up here."

"Have they practiced throwing a spear since that time they saw you?"

"No, I am sure of it."

The three children climbed up on the dais and awaited instruction. Chail took three spears and bones from the weapons rack and handed one of each of his waiting charges. He pointed at the target and said, "Throw," and they threw.

Their spears flew through the air at a good rate of speed, arcing a little more than Master Gation's, and traveling with a little less speed. The spears splintered their way into the target. Master Gration let out a "humph" and turned to the children with a little more respect showing in his eyes.

"That was better than most students achieve within a year. Yes, you children are impressive." He turned to Chail. "And you must show me the technique you used to throw your spear."

---

Chail and Gation walked among the children, correcting the stances when they saw problems with technique. The changes to the throwing style came slowly, as a master sculptor removes small amounts of material to bring out a well formed piece of art.

By the end of the day, all the children had the ability to throw spears using the bones.

"Children, you are dismissed for dinner," Chail told them.

"You and I need to talk," Gation said, as he pulled Chail aside. He motioned for them to walk.

They moved through the practice area, and out to the city. It was not the usual walk; Gation took them into the old part of the city. Small shops started to appear on the side, trying to sell small baubles and trinkets. A few of the stalls had food over small cooking fires. Gation maneuvered them into this area, and Chail followed, wondering when his old instructor would open up with what was on his mind.

Gation stopped at a stall where a merchant had a large pot of stew boiling over a fire. Small bread balls filled a sack he had, and in each hand he held one, holding it out to the people walking by, to entice them.

"Stew! Chicken Stew. Vegetables and chicken. A meal for all to love. Two coppers only!" he was crying out to the crowd. "Spears. Come, the best food here for you. Three coppers for two bowls. Special for Spears, our protectors."

The man looked as if he had washed that day, and kept himself clean. "Look, fresh bread! I cut out the center and fill with broth, you eat well, yes?" He held out the bread balls, and Gation took one, examined it, and nodded as he handed it back.

"Here, three coppers," he said handing the coins to the man who smiled broadly. The man prepared the meal for the two men and handed one to Gation, and then one to Chail, who smiled and smelled the stew. He glanced at the merchant, dipped the bread piece in the stew and tasted it.

"Oh, that is good," he said, reaching into his belt and pulling three coppers out. He handed them to the merchant who accepted them with a puzzled look on his face. Chail smiled at him. "Food this good should cost double what you charge," he said in a loud voice. The merchant bowed, accepting the coins and the endorsement from him.

"You honor me, Master of Spears. Thank you."

They ate the stew and bread, still with silence between them. The movement of the city played out in front of them. Chail noticed a child reaching for a purse and he cleared his throat, shaking his head when the urchin looked at him, and that was the last he saw of the boy.

Gation licked his fingers, and patted his stomach. "Now that was a good meal," he said, and wiped his mouth with his sleeve. "I must say, it reminds me of my Gillian's cooking, she can make a stew as well."

"So, why did you bring me here, Gation?" Chail asked.

"I wanted to know how you were doing," he said. "It has been seven years since we talked last, and that was for a few moments. Now, we have Spears we need to train together, and we can spend a little time to get to know each other again."

"Well, it has been a long time since we talked," Chail responded.

"Yes. How have you been?"

Chail only had a bit left of the bowl and it was good. He popped it into his mouth and chewed a little, swallowed, and wiped his mouth with his arm.

"I started with forty three children and now I am down to twenty seven. I am doing well, but the children are not. I lost a lot of them."

"I heard. That was not your fault, though," Gation said.

"I know, but it still hurts. These children, they are different than the last ones I trained."

"Of course they are, you are older, that's why."

"It's not just that. The King sees it as well. He wants them fast tracked through training."

"Yes, he would want that. It would cost him less, for they would be out there working instead of training. Just tell him you cannot do it, and the training must continue as laid out by our ancient customs," Gation explained. "He will not break our customs."

"Yes, I could do that. But would it stop him from pushing?"

"The question is how are you doing? Have you decided to marry?" he asked.

"Marry. Why? To have children. I already have twenty seven of them to take care of." Chail laughed.

"No, not just to have children. To have someone to share your life with. A woman to warm your bed. And yes, to have children. What else?

You are a good man, and it would be good to have children, not just the ones who are brought for you to train.

"I married," Gation said, watching Chail's face for reaction. The eyes went up. "She was introduced to me by one of my student's years ago. She is beautiful, lovely in fact. We have three children with a fourth on its way. I will be traveling home to be there with her for the birth in a few days."

"I didn't know," Chail said.

"No, it was personal, and you had a lot of problems at that time. You remember?" Gation said.

"Yes, I had the fever," Chail said.

"Yes, and you almost died. The Wooders did pull you through, so now I am telling you. I want you to meet her soon, after the training. I think you would like my first son, his name is Chail as well."

Chail looked at his friend, smiling. He shook his head and looked back at the table.

"I am honored you did that."

"Well, it is something I would have told you sooner, but you have been here, and I have been in Fishery. It was difficult to get to you. I needed a reason, and this was the best one I could think of. Training!"

"Well, rest assured, I am seeing someone, Tess. She and I have spent time together, and I plan to ask her to marry soon. She is lovely. You met her," Chail said.

"Yes, I remember her. Mid aged and very comely. I am happy for you."

"Yes, and the children love her, also. We both love them all, and they love her. I am willing to wait till they are from flight."

Gation fell quiet, thinking about the information he had just been given. He let his friend absorb it.

The clouds thickened overhead, small droplets of rain fell lightly on the ground and people. The stew merchant scowled and started to pack up his shop.

"How many bread balls do you have there?" Chail asked the merchant.

"Oh, thirty, I believe. I should get them under cover so they do not spoil." He cursed under his breath and then looked up. "Sorry, my lord Spear, I didn't mean…"

"No, don't worry about it. I think you have enough stew. Can you bring it to the training center for the Spears?" he asked.

"Why yes. Yes, I can get it there. Are you sure? That would be a lot," the merchant said.

"Then here." He tossed a silver at the merchant. "Stew and bread over to the training area fast. Ask for Tess, and tell her Chail sent you with this for his children," he told the merchant.

"I will get it there right away. I will call my son," he said, and went to the door at the back of his stall, opened it and yelled, "Tyson! Get out here, you lazy boy, and help me."

# NINE

It had been three months since the children started training with the short spear. They mastered throwing, stabbing and blocking. Now, a new training structure was starting, the art of concealment.

Master Shail stood in the practice square, looking at the whole area around him while the children studied his actions. The air was electrified as they waited with anticipation. This was the training session they had been waiting for the whole year.

Master Shail pointed to a spot a few feet from where he stood, gesturing with exaggeration. The children all watched his hand move, and then they focused on the spot for a second. When they looked back at Master Shail, he was no longer there.

They looked around, wondering where he had gone, and slowly a shadow changed into the form of Master Shail. The children stared, their mouths agape. He smiled as he pulled his hood off his head.

"Part of being a Spear is being able to see and hear, without being seen or heard," he said. "Concealment is the key. You must know how to blend in with the shadows, the overhangs, and the small places in order to hide. Also, the shroud is your friend. It is a cloak and hood that will help you blend in with your surroundings, if you use it correctly." He motioned with his hand and a group of adult Spears walked into the practice square, each carrying a cloak. They approached the young Spears and stood behind them. With a signal from Master Shail, they placed the new cloaks on the shoulders of the children, making sure they were secured properly, and left.

They felt honored, now clothed like true Spears. The fine cloth rippled in the slight breeze as if it had a life of its own.

"It is more than cloth, more than a covering. The material is spun from the web of caterpillars found only in the forests of the Woodland home. The power of the silk holds may only be collected during the full moon of the summer season, before the moon sets, but not before the full moon rises. It is the essence of the power allows us to blend, to mold, and to disappear when we need.

"The honor we are bestowing on you today will be with you till you pass from this world, to be at the seats of the five Gods. It will keep you pure, unspotted by evil, untarnished by vice. Your cloak is a symbol of purity of heart, for the law is to be given in that way alone. You may not don this cloak if for any reason your heart be not true. It is to be cared for and honored, as those before you have always done.

"The cloak, when displayed high, shall be a sign of warning to others that a Spear needs assistance. If you see a cloak displayed in such a manner, you are to take heed and join with your fellow, forming a point of defense that will be the basis of mutual trust and honor. Seek to help any Spear in need, and keep your heart pure.

"Remember, if you do not dishonor the cloak, it will not dishonor you."

All of them bowed to Master Shail, knowing the words he spoke were true. The honor of the cloak would always be about them, ensuring their lives truly belonged to them.

"When the ocean was young, the Realm sent Wooders to seek newborn babes with no surviving father or mother, no family, to call their own. They protect them and bring them to the capital, to give them to the Spears.

"They are trained, fed, and loved. They are clothed, educated, and given the abilities needed to serve the Realm. They are not slaves, but watchers, they are not evil, but judges, they are not corrupt, they are Spears."

A great cheer erupted along the walls of the practice square as shadows became forms, and forms turned to hooded shapes, and hooded shapes turned to cloaked beings, and the cloaked beings pulled back their hoods to reveal the faces of Spears.

Each Spear came forward and took the hand of the child in front of them. They moved them aside, and spoke the words of the oath to them. The young learned the words. Each Spear teaching the young the ancient litany that would bind them together, an oath which would give them power to use the knowledge their instructors would be giving to them.

They learned the words, keeping them in their minds by repeating them to their instructor. It had never been written down, nor would it be. It would always be passed from one generation of Spears to the next, letting them hear it from one who has taken the oath. It was the ancient way, the only way they knew how to do it.

"I am a Spear, I am the justice, and I will protect the Realm and those who live within it. My life will be given for the protection of the people, never to attack, but only to defend against those who mean them harm. I will give everything to the Realm when asked; even my life to save a citizen. I will never yield, but always stand fast, as one who stands between the darkness and the light. This I vow as a Spear of the Realm."

The children chanted the words to their mentors, feeling them burn in their souls. The desire to fulfill the words empowered them, making the meaning shine brightly in their hearts.

"It is time!" called out Master Shail, as he heard the young Spears had committed the words to memory. "Come with me now Spears, the temple awaits!"

***

They marched to the temple at the western end. The parade brought out many, who watched as the Spears marched to take their oaths. In their ranks walked a Wooder with a drum that he beat with a stick. It was the ceremonial drum of the Walk of the Oath. It was little more than a small barrel with cured cow hide stretched across it, but it made a good resounding thud when pounded.

The Clutch walked in time with the beat of the drum, proudly wearing their cloaks, their spears across their backs. The march was a mile in distance to the temple of the five Gods, and they did it with pride. When they reached the temple they walked up the stairs, entering two at time.

The priest greeted them as they entered. He was dressed in the robes of a high priest, cloth made of the same fibers as the cloaks of the Spears. The shades across the lower part represented the colors of the Gods. Black for the first God that gave them the stars, Yellow for the second God that gave them the sun. A splash of brown for the third God that gave them the earth, a slash of blue for the fourth God that gave them the sea. The last was white, and it was the predominant color of the robe, for it represented the fifth God, the one that gave them their souls. Of all the Gods, it was he that would always be worshiped with the most passion, for without him, no one would have been born.

Chail stood beside the priest, dressed in his robe, a spear and bone strapped to his back. On his side he carried his sword and ceremonial dirk encrusted with small diamonds and rubies. On the pommel was mounted a large opal, glowing with a fire deep inside. On his back, beside the spear, was a large curved sword. It had a large hilt, made to be wielded with either one or two hands. The hilt was wrapped in soft leather.

The priest suffered the weapons in the sanctity of the holy temple but once a year, when the Spears took their oath. It meant a lot of money to his treasury, so he smiled, thinking of the pouch filled with silver he would collect after this day was done. Once the procession entered the temple, he turned and closed the doors, making his way to the pulpit. His fingers snapped as he climbed the last steps and an acolyte came forward with a cup of wine. It was the cheapest wine he could find, a sour red that smelled more of vinegar than anything else.

He started to speak the ancient language, those words passed down to him from the priests before. The words they say must never be written, only remembered. He had not written them down, but the priest before him had given him a rare book bound using anthropodermic bibliopegy methods, binding using human skin. It was old, older than any book he ever knew before, and would ever know again.

He had studied it for a month to refresh his memory, knowing he would be called upon to officiate again this year. So he had studied the ceremony, learned it, and memorized it. Of course, it would be perfect, as it had been for years. He took pride in his work, for he would be paid well for doing it again this year.

He started saying the words as the Spears sat themselves in the pews. He did not know the meaning of the words, just that he had to say them at the right speed, using the correct pronunciation. So he looked at each child in turn, saying what he needed to. He finished the first part of the ceremony, and raised the cup of wine to the sky, as if to invoke the blessing of the five gods upon their congregation. He then brought it down to his lips, holding his breath, and made the liquid in it touch his lips.

He handed the goblet back to the acolyte, pointing to the children. The priest once again uttered the words he had memorized. He did it at such a speed as to allow the acolyte to drip a little wine on the forehead of each child. It worked out perfectly. Once all present were anointed, the cup was handed back to him, and he turned, facing the brazier on the alter. He tipped the cup and emptied the wine on it, along with the crushed yellow rock he had prepared for the ceremony. The powder burned in a flash of light, surprising the young Spears.

The cup went back to the acolyte, who took it to the small table to the side alters side. The ceremony was complete and he was now able to stop reciting the ancient words.

"May the five be with you during this time of your Oath."

"And also with you," the Spears present echoed.

"The words have been spoken to you, have you learned them as you ought?"

"We have, your worship."

"Then speak the ancient truths, and keep them safe in your hearts as the five look down on our proceedings."

The children made the holy sign and held their hands out in front of them, palms up, and spoke as one.

"I am a Spear, I am the justice, and I will protect the Realm and those who live within it. My life will be given for the protection of the people, never to attack, but only to defend against those who mean them harm. I will give everything to the Realm when asked; even my life should it save another. I will never yield, but always stand fast, as one who stands between the darkness and the light. This I vow as a Spear of the Realm."

The priest switched back to the ancient tongue and bestowed an ancient blessing upon them. On completing, he bade all present to rise.

"You are now oath sworn Spears. May all the love of the five be with you," he spoke to them.

"And also with you," the children replied.

And with that, the ceremony was completed.


## Year 10

They had been running for six hours without stopping. Master Chail had given them to the Wooders to learn basic aid skills. The start of the training involved a long run, and surviving in the wild for several days.

So they ran, drinking from water skins and chewing on dried meat when they hungered. Running was tiring, but Master Chail told them they could run for three days without stopping, if they really wanted to; that would not be needed today. Their run led them to a clearing on the side of the trail, shielded nicely with tall oak trees. The Wooders had picked the location, knowing it would supply shelter on three sides of their camp.

The group slowed. Not because they were tired, but because the Wooders were not running fast. Soon they stopped.

"We'll make camp here," one of the Wooders told the children. "Set up tents, and get ready to find wood for a fire."

When they finished setting up camp, the Wooders sent half the children to pick up firewood, and the rest to hunt small game. They explained they needed to stretch out the food they carried in case game became sparse. Conserving their supplies made sense to the children, so they split off to carry out the tasks requested.

Thomasyn, Bethany and Jon found themselves directed to collect firewood, a task that Thomasyn did not appreciate.

"Why send your three best hunters out to collect firewood?" Thomasyn mumbled as they looked for firewood. "It just doesn't make sense."

"When does anything the Wooders do make sense?" Jon replied.

"You two, all you do is complain about what we are asked to do. How about helping me with the wood? I will not be doing all the work," Bethany said as she stood looking at them, her arms full of fallen tree limbs.

The boys stopped arguing. They felt guilty when they looked at her, standing there with her arms full of dead tree limbs she had picked up. They helped her gather more wood for the fire. Picking up enough wood took little time, and they walked back to camp laden with their fruits of their effort.

The Wooder looked at the bundles carried by the trio. His eyes rolled and head shook slightly, as if he expected more from them. He opened his pack, pulled out a small axe, and looked at Bethany, axe extended.

"You had better cut those branches into smaller pieces. We will need twice as much to cook food for everyone."

Bethany cut the wood as the boys held the pieces in place, and once they finished cutting, they started the fire.

"I don't think we're going to eat much tonight," Thomasyn said. Jon just grumbled, poking a small stick into the ground.

The Wooders did not join them, content with cleaning up the campsite.

More children returned from gathering wood. They had enough to last through the night. The children responsible for hunting had not returned.

Two hours passed. The Wooders became concerned. They decided to split the children in groups of four, each one taking the small charges to search. Bethany, Jon and Thomasyn stayed in one group with the elder accompanying them.

"We will travel into the forest there." He pointed to the darkest part of the forest. "And search inward. You Spears will lead, and we will keep in line from behind, marking the path we take. Retracing will be easy with the marks in place, and we can know how to mark without injury to the forest. Hopefully the spirit of the forest is not restless."

"The spirit of the forest?" Bethany asked, wonder in her eyes.

"Yes. This area near the sea is full of spirits. Some enter the forest and become lost, roaming without purpose, till they find a wondering soul. If the children have encountered any of them..." The older Wooder shuddered, fear in his wide eyes as he talked to his wards. "The song of the wondering souls can capture the mind of one who hears it."

"But Master Chail told me those were just stories," Thomasyn said. "He told me they were a way to keep children from wondering at night."

"We will see, and you can make your own choice whether they are or not," the Wooder said. "That is, when the children go missing."

The sun was low on the horizon, but the shadows still stood short and the group moved forward without needing torches. As they moved through the forest, shadows disappeared and the sky was shut out by the leaves. Thomasyn reached up and could touch branches, and measured the trees to be under twenty feet, being stunted by the salt air coming in from the sea just a mere twelve miles south of them. Gnarled and twisted tree limbs bearing little fruit reached out to snag at their clothing. The squawking of birds flying away from their meal of carrion distracted them. Bethany felt a chill as they walked in the gloom, and darkness approached.

They walked through the woods, taking care not to let the branches snag their cloaks. Watching for any signs of their lost comrades as they moved forward, without their weapons out, for the older Wooder had warned them angering the spirit of the forest. Again, Thomasyn thought, the old superstitions are coming out.

Long shadows appeared to their right as they walked deeper into the woods, and glimpses skyward through the leaves told them they did not have long. Jon heard noises ahead, deep rumblings from a distance, like a gurgling sound of a drowning man with a deep voice. He motioned Bethany and Thomasyn to stand still. First, they could not decipher from the sounds all around, but then it became clear. It was the sound of people talking. They did not know the language. It was a strange, guttural sound. Sharp snaps could be heard in the voices.

The older Wooder warned the children with a hand signal. He wanted them to be cautious. They nodded. Thomasyn motioned for the Wooders to hold fast, allowing the children, the Spears, to investigate.

Bethany, Jon, and Thomasyn pulled their hoods over their heads and closed their eyes for a few seconds. They breathed deeply. The cloaks became one with them. They blended with the forest, disappearing from the sight of the Wooder, who nodded with approval at the skill they displayed at such a young age.

The children moved forward, crouching low. All the training, the ability to move, to not be seen, they drew on it. Hugging the tree trunks. Staying in the shadows. Their foot falls were gentle. Thomasyn felt a foot under his foot. He curled his toes slightly, forming a bridge over the twig. He made no sound. No movement could be seen.

They did see each other, but just barely. Each Spear knows what to look for. The slight outline in the dark, something in the corner of the eye. Yes, they knew where each other was in the forest.

A soft glow appeared in the distance, and they continued forward, with caution at the forefront of their minds. Light crept through the tree trunks, wavering and throwing ominous shadows about. They changed their approach, using the shadows cast by that light to hide themselves.

Bethany noticed the clearing first. She motioned for the others to slow even more, to ensure they stayed hidden. Jon noticed a few moments after that the trees became thinner.

Thomasyn did not notice any break in the forest, but he did notice thinning to his left, telling him he was on the edge of a clearing. His training told him what to do, and he did it. With a quick signal to his two partners, he turned into the thinning forest, making sure he was able to see what they saw. The three stopped just before the trees broke into a clearing, staying in the shadows. Bethany bit her lip and her eyes went wide.

They saw three giants. They stood over eight feet tall, with limbs as thick as Jon was wide. Each had sparse hair on their heads, but great tuffs covered their backs, chests and arms. They wore leather armor over their bodies. The guttural language spoken by the three rumbled through the air like the sound of thunder. Bethany noticed four of their group lay next to the fire, arms and legs tied together with hemp.

The largest of the giants pointed a finger the size of Thomasyn's forearm at the bound children, letting out a spurt of words and laughter. His hands came together, and he shook them, making the others laugh.

Thomasyn looked away and spied a Spear to his right, looking at him. He signed a question, asking if the child was alright. No, came the reply, injured. He asked how many had escaped. His brother Spear responded seven. Thomasyn knew that was the number missing when he added the three captives. A fury of hand gestures, other children injured and unable to assist.

He relayed the information to Jon, who relayed it to Bethany. At first Jon and Bethany signalled they wanted to leave, but Thomasyn messaged no. He had a plan.

———

The three positioned themselves along the circumference of the clearing. The plan was simple: Thomasyn would throw the first spear to take out the largest giant. When the other two pursued him, Jon and Bethany would take them out. Simple, easy and would finish off the problem fast. His friends watched as Thomasyn readied a spear. He accepted the impending action in his mind; they had captured three Spears, and injured eight others. The justification was easy. A very quick decision. The third law has been violated. And they were an invading force in the Realm. They could have been here for a long time, gathering information or just to kill. He validated his actions, knowing the path the giants took showed they would have attacked anyone in the forest if they found them. He would throw to kill.

He prepared himself and looked to the clearing, seeing a makeshift spit over their fire. The larger one stood over one of the children, a knife in his hand, and evil in his thoughts.

He fixed the spear and readied his arm. He took a quick step out, one arm raised for aim, the other for throwing. With a twist of his body, he propelled the spear, turning his wrist like Master Chail. The spear leapt forward with little arc, hitting the neck of the knife wielding giant. The sharp point punctured below the chin, collapsing the giant's windpipe. The spear continued through the neck, hitting the spine and crunching bones.

The look in the giant's eyes told a tale. His body stopped responding to his mind. He folded forward at the waist, legs collapsing under him. The knife fell.

Thomasyn watched as the body of the giant fell, the life leaking from him. He saw the others stand and see the fate of their companion. The weapon had passed through the giant and imbedding itself in a tree. Shocked, they turned, looking at the forest over the fire. Then they saw him, Thomasyn, standing there. A Spear without a spear to throw.

They reached back and picked up swords as long as Thomasyn was tall. The blades, covered in brown dried blood, were curved with no guards. In a quick few strides, they were heading for the edge of the clearing. Their eyes screaming out in rage, bodies propelled forward in desire for revenge, for blood.

They moved swiftly, and without thinking, for they forgot to pick up their armour. Their only protection was thick skin and leather leggings.

Both Jon and Bethany stepped from their cover and threw their spears the way Thomasyn had. They estimated the speed and direction of the giants, tracking with their outstretched arms. The points entered the bodies of the remaining giants, puncturing their hearts.

The giants folded, heads slamming to the ground with a thump.

The three friends entered the clearing, followed by the other eight Spears who either limped or held their arms. The sight told the others why no assist could be given in the attack.

"I will get the Wooders," Bethany said, turning back to the forest.

"Yes. Jon, help me untie the others. We need to make this area secure."

As they approached the bound children, they saw they lay on the bones of man and beast. Jon pulled out his dirk, and cut the legs and arms free, and Jon freed the other two. They stood them up and moved them off the bones to where the giants had been sitting.

Bethany entered the clearing, followed by two of the Wooders. They moved about the children, tending them. Shortly, the rest of the group arrived, Spears and Wooders alike. The Spears grouped and inspected the camp and its surrounding forest while the Wooders tended the injured.

"I guess this will be the advanced teaching. Okay children; let me show you how to find healing herbs wherever you are..."

It was a slow march back to the city, and it took three days. The injured needed assistance in making the trip, so the other children created litters to carry them. The Wooders assisted as best they could, tending the injured, and carrying the litters when the children needed help.

Chail had been waiting for them in the barracks along with Tess. The children filed in and headed for their bunks while the most senior of the Wooders spoke with Chail.

"Master Chail," the Wooder spoke. "I must tell you about the encounter we had in the southern forest outside of Realm Hest."

Chial looked at the children. Some bandaged, and others helping them. He surmised something bad had happened, but was not sure what it was.

"We encountered three giants in the forest," continued the Wooder. "They had captured three of the children and injured eight others. Jon found them while scouting. He is good at knowing what presence is around him."

Chail nodded, understanding what was being said.

"I saw what happened to the giants." The Wooder stopped for a second, his eyes glazed over a little as he remembered the scene. "It was hard to imagine it was the children who had done it, not older than ten years. The head of one of them had been all but severed from its body. I had never seen such a perfect strike, and on the neck of all things!"

"Yes, Thomasyn is one of the best we have," Chail said, smiling as he thought about the achievement, and his mind wished the child was his own. Alas, he would contend himself with the satisfaction the child performed with excellence.

"I would say he is, but I do not mean to understate the skills of Jon and Bethany. Thomasyn's target was not moving very quickly. Jon and Bethany's, well, their targets were at a dead run when they threw! Truly amazing!"

"Did you see how they reacted to the giants?"

"No, they were ahead of us when we came across them. They cloaked themselves masterfully. The approach was one of perfect stealth. It is a testament to their trainer, Master Chail. You must be proud of them."

"I truly am," Chail said, looking at all the children asleep in their cots.

---

"They are all burning up," Tess said to Chail. "I have never seen anything like this before. What could it be?"

Chail looked at Bethany as she shivered in her cot. They had her bundled up in the hope to break the fever, just like they did with the other twenty-seven children. Each showed different signs of the sickness, but Bethany was the first one who contracted it.

"What are those red marks on her neck?" Chail asked.

"They appear to be lesions of some type," the Wooder said.

Chail and Tess turned in surprise. The Wooder was looking over their shoulders as she spoke.

"If you would like, I will examine the child and let you know. If you don't mind," she said.

Chail stood, stepping aside for the Wooder to assess the child. She sat on the side of the bed and put the back of her hand against Bethany's forehead to check for fever. She nodded to herself as if knowing already what ailed the children, pulled the blankets down, and lifted Bethany's shirt. On her stomach, some of the lesions looked deep red and filled with puss, while others had formed scabs.

Humming to herself, the Wooder covered Bethany up, and went to another child, performing the same examination. She repeated this until all the children were examined.

"You are to stay here with the children," the Wooder said to Tess and Chail. "I will return shortly." The Wooder turned and walked out of the barracks.

Over the next ten minutes, several other Wooders came into the barracks to check on the children. They looked at the lesions, tested the children's temperature, and walked out. Tess worried about all the traffic coming in and out with the children sick as they were.

Finally, the Master Wooder came into the barracks and headed straight for Chail and Tess. He had a somber look on his face and carried a large sack.

"You will both have to stay here for at least seven days," The Master Wooder stopped and looked directly at Chail. "They have the pox, an infection that can spread. It is bad for adults who did not have it when they were young, and if they did, it could reoccur from exposure, which is what has happened to you. I have a salve to help keep the itching down if you develop lesions, and allow them to heal. Do not expose anyone else to this, for it will infect others, and could spread to the rest of the children.

"Make them drink lots of water. It's important since they will not eat much. They may be over this after six days, but if either of you get the pox, it may take two weeks for you to get over it."

---

It had been seven days, and all the children made it through the pox. Chail and Tess did not show any signs of being at risk, so the Wooders cleared them.

Individual training commenced. Each child was assigned a Wooder for the healing trials. This week, they knew they would be given the chance to leave the city for long runs and allowed to visit the small villages scattered about the countryside. Bethany ran out the gates of the city early with Cole, a Wooder in training. His looping gait told her that they would be running for a long time. Bethany did not worry, she was familiar with running a day without stopping. Even after the illness had ravaged the barracks, she was still in good shape.

They ran till the city was far in the distance, along the same path the children had initially run as a group, for it was the only way out of the city.

Bethany easily kept up with Cole at the start, though she had been told that the Wooders spent a lot of time training for long distance running. It was something that was needed beyond the healing skills, for they did not fight, officially, that is. Although they would protect themselves, if needed.

Bethany remembered her training during the run, but bodies needed time to heal, and hers had not completely healed from its ordeal. She stopped several times during the run, her bladder filling and causing her the need to make water. Cole stopped when she did, the natural instincts of a Wooder telling him something was wrong with his charge. During the stops, Bethany's bowels loosened, letting more water escape. She started to feel uncomfortable, her bottom reddening from the constant cleaning. At first, Cole did not worry about the stops. He just waited for her to finish and they continued on their journey. After her fifth stop, he decided to address the issue after hearing Bethany struggling and the way she walked back from the bushes, looking saddle sore and a bole legged.

Cole was more concerned about his charge than anything, wanting to make sure she was able to continue.

"Your body's expelling water. Not just making it, but pushing it out of you. We need to fix that," Cole said, looking about the field that they had stopped in. "Do you feel poorly in the stomach?"

"No, just sore on the bottom. I have been making water from it all day since we started running."

"Have you been drinking a lot of water?"

"Yes," Bethany said.

Cole checked the water in her water skins, noticing that she had drank more than usual. He nodded, and went walking through the field with his head down, stooping occasionally to pick something. After a few minutes, he came back with dandelions, both the heads and some leaves. Cole brought them to her, holding them out.

"The flower, eat it. Eat all of the peddles, as much as you can get in you," he said to her. "It will help stop the water from escaping you from your bottom and help you keep more of it in you. The leaves will help you keep the energy in your body. Eat it as best you can. I know the leaves are bitter, but it is good for you. I need to find more." And he left her there with a healing bouquet.

Cole returned a few minutes later, holding purple flowers in front of him. He approached Bethany and held them out.

"Your head probably hurts also, right?" he asked.

"Yes, it does."

"Eat these. After a little while it will settle the ache, and you will be better. We will wait here for a little while to let them work in your body, and then we have to run again."

Bethany nodded and ate her purple flowers.

***

Jon ran, keeping pace with the Wooder Juliette. She was a tall girl, the age of fourteen, and she had very long legs. He had to push himself, but he did keep up.

After running for an hour, Jon stopped and emptied his stomach. It quickly came up to Jon that he did not know what was happening at first. His stomach empty, Jon looked up and Juliette stood there, looking at him. She saw what had happened.

"Wash your mouth. Is your stomach still feeling bad?" Juliette did not wait for him to respond. "Wait for a moment while I find something for you."

"Yes, it is. I... I'll wait here," Jon said.

"It is from the pox. Your body has not fully recovered," she said. "I will find something for that." She walked away from him.

After a few minutes, she came back with some green leaves in hand. She came towards him and he doubled over to try to empty his stomach again, although nothing came out. Jon wiped his sleeve against his mouth, hoping that would help, but it did not. He looked up at her, hoping. His eyes showed the strain he felt in his stomach from all the heaving.

"Here, take these leaves. You will need to chew them and swallow, but not the leaves themselves," she said. "You have to have your stomach settle first before you swallow the leaves. Just the juice for now."

He took the leaves. One of the leaves he crumpled up and popped it in his mouth. Jon chewed it and felt a coolness wash over him. His mouth salivated, and he swallowed, making sure he did not swallow the leaf.

Juliette started a small fire and put a clay cup over it filled with water. She also crumpled several of the leaves in the cup and waited. Jon did not know what she was doing, but he did feel better since he started to chew the leaf.

A few minutes later, Juliette handed him the cup wrapped in a cloth to protect her hands as well as his. The smell of the boiled leaves was pungent, making a strong odour. Jon took the cup and held it in his hands.

"Let it cool a little, but breathe in the odour of the tea. Once it has cooled down enough, you will need to drink it, all of it. The water needs to still be hot when you drink," Juliette said.

Jon nodded. Juliette turned and walked away again, hunting for something else. Jon lost sight of her after a few minutes and sipped the water. It had the same taste as the leaves, but intensified. Juliette returned after he had finished the tea and handed him some green leaves with yellow around the edges. "You need to chew these leaves and swallow them while we are running. It will keep your stomach quiet," she told him.

He took the leaves and started to chew one of them. His eyes opened wide as his tongue came alive with the flavour of the juice. It washed away the rest of the sick from his throat as he swallowed.

"Lemon?" he asked.

"No, but close. Lemon thyme. It will settle your stomach and clear the sour from your mouth," she said. "Now we need to run."

Jon stood, and they both turned, making their legs pump as they started to run.

Thomasyn followed Gillian out of the city and over the same path as the others. Once they had traveled a league, she turned into the forest, picking a path slightly different from the others. Gillian had a special stop to do and needed to travel this way to get to it.

During the early parts of the run, Thomasyn was coughing slightly. He had suffered a lot from the pox, and his throat was still sore from it. The coughing became extremely harsh sounding, causing Gillian to slow and eventually stop.

"Is your throat sore?" she asked him.

"Yes," he said and coughed again.

"I see. There's something that can help you." Gillian walked over to one of the trees.

She examined the leaves and bark; nodding with approval. She took out her knife and cut into the tree, removing a piece of bark. Gillian returned to Thomasyn and pulled out her clay cup and a linen cloth. She stripped out the inner bark and put it into the cloth, tying it up. In the cup, she put water and the bundle she had just created.

Gillian gathered some twigs, lit them, and heated the potion into a tea. She handed it to Thomasyn once it was hot, and he drank it slowly, feeling the relief.

"We can stop here for the day. Let the tea take its effect on you. We can run tomorrow. We have a full week to complete this training, and our destination is not that far away."

Bethany ran but kept falling behind until Cole slowed to a walk. Thankful for the respite, she felt a need to empty her bowels. The flowers Cole gave her helped, but she had been warned it would take time to work through her system. Bethany noticed she did not need to stop as often, and less water was escaping her when she did.

This time Bethany's bowels emptied more solid than the last, and no water rushed out of her. She was happy and reported it to Cole, who nodded.

"We are near the first village I would like to stop at," he said, pointing into the distance.

Bethany followed the line from his arm and realized that they had come close to the southern waters. The ocean stretched out on the horizon as far as her eye could see. Close to the shoreline was a village, with fields and small huts as homes. Her vision could not make out the village; she imagined it had a number of huts. Bethany could see fields that had been cultivated near the village and away from the water.

"Come! We have two hours of running still ahead of us to reach the village before nightfall."

***

"We stop here for the night," Juliette said to Jon. He was feeling a lot better. The lemony leaf had worked as it was supposed to.

"A small camp and a little fire. We can eat some of the food we brought with us."

Jon looked forward to eating. He had been only chewing on the leaves he had been given, and needed something substantial now that his stomach had settled.

They found a clearing that was flat, putting their bed rolls down and setting some rocks in a circle for a fire. Jon looked at the supplies Juliette had packed and almost lost his stomach again.

"What are those?" he asked.

"Vegetables," she said.

"What about meat?" he asked.

"None for tonight. We will have meat when we get to the village, if they have any."

"Oh, well, how about you get the fire going and I will bring the meal," he said, as he moved away, drawing out his spear.

***

"Have you hunted before?" Gillian asked.

"A little, but nothing this small." Thomasyn smiled back at her.

He noticed movement in the brush and watched it closely. The movement was something small, but enough to feed them both. Thomasyn flipped the spear around, aimed and threw it butt end first at the target. After it had left his hand, he quickly followed the spear to see what it was he had hit.

He came back to Gillian carrying a quail. Thomasyn grinned at her as he handed it over.

"What do you want me to do with this?" she asked.

"I caught it. You clean and cook it. Need help?"

# TEN

Bethany and Cole ran right up to the first buildings in the small village before they slowed to a walk. The sun was sinking under the horizon, and Bethany was glad they had slowed.

"What a pair we must be," she said, catching her breath.

"Why would you say that?" Cole asked. She looked at him. He was not even breathing hard. Bethany decided she had better put forward a better effort, and show the Wooder she was made of sterner stuff.

They advanced in the village, watching the people going about their daily business of fetching water, haggling over the price of goods, and cleaning fish they caught from the ocean. The huts in the village appeared constructed out of straw and planks, held together by some dark substance the villagers stuck on the outside.

She moved her head back and forth, looking at the huts and people. Several children worked alongside adults, cleaning fish and doing chores. When she saw a woman scolding and hitting the child as punishment, she broke away from Cole to confront the woman.

"Where are you going, Bethany?" Cole called to her. She stopped and turned her head to look at him.

"Setting out the law," she said, and turned back to move towards the woman.

"Wait," he called out. She stopped and turned back to Cole. He was coming up to her. "She's not breaking the law; she's punishing her child for some reason. See, no one is bothering her." Cole motioned with his arm towards the other people going about their business. "She can do this when the child misbehaves or does something wrong."

Cole put his hand on Bethany's shoulder. "A parent is responsible for their child's behaviour, so they must also be empowered to punish them for doing something wrong. We don't know what the child has done to deserve punishment, nor should we interfere." He turned and saw the child crying and hugging his mother. "Look, the punishments done, and the child is asking forgiveness for doing something wrong. There is no law broken here, only a teaching."

"But she was hitting him!" Bethany said. "It's a violation of the second law. Do no harm."

"She punished him," Cole corrected her. "It's not breaking the law to teach your child right from wrong. That child did not grow up as you did. He may have done something like stole from someone, or not do his chores. We don't know. Bethany, we do not interfere with such things."

Bethany looked at the child held in the woman's embrace, even though she kept verbally scolding him. She felt it was wrong, but not knowing the reasoning behind, as Cole mentioned, gave her pause. The strikes did not seem powerful to her, for the child did not fall or stumble backwards, so she shook her head, muttering under her breath.

Cole led her away, towards the centre of town, looking for something in particular. He seemed to be searching the front of the buildings, but he did not find what he was searching for.

A man came up to them, reaching out for Cole, whose back was turned to him. The man was old, shaky, and smelled as if he had not bathed for a long time. Bethany saw him when he reached out to touch Cole with a gnarled hand. Her breath caught in her throat, and she pushed his hand away, standing defensively between the two men.

The old man cowered back as if threatened by a blow, which, if Bethany's stance portrayed anything, she was ready to deliver. Cole stopped and turned at the commotion.

"Bethany!" he said. "Don't hurt the man for the sake of the five! He probably just needs something."

Bethany relaxed, dropping her hands down and unclenching her fists. She looked sideways at the man, but addressed Cole.

"He was about to grab you! Right in plain sight of everyone," she said, defending her actions.

"Nnnnnnoooo!" the old man exclaimed. "I am in need of a Wooders help. I am ill..."

"Not ill enough to remember manners," Bethany said. "You don't grab people from behind; you come up beside them and ask for help."

"My apologies, young Spear, I meant no harm. I was concerned I would not be able to reach him before he left the village," the old man coward. "My need is great, Master Wooder."

"I am not a master, just a Wooder with a Spear in flight," Cole said to the old man. "But I fear your need may be beyond my skill. What is it you need?"

"It's my wife, Master... I mean, Wooder, she is coughing all the time. She can hardly catch her breath sometimes."

"Take me to her," Cole said.

The old man turned and moved toward a hut. Cole followed and looked back briefly to say, "Are you coming, Bethany?"

<hr>

Jon started a fire and fed it a few small fallen branches to keep it going. Juliette had started pulling the fur off the jackrabbit, and it was almost completely skinned by the time Jon had the fire burning.

The spit was made from small green branches, and Jon took care to keep an eye on it. The large rabbit cooked quickly, and the two ate till nothing was left. They talked about the training each had taken so far, and what had become of their friends over the years.

"I was told almost all the Wooders started as Spears," Juliette said. "We are the same as you, fatherless and motherless. The Realm is our parent, and we have to serve it. I actually made it through to year five as a Spear, but I was taken out due to a failed test."

"The poison test. I almost didn't make it through that one, as well," Jon said.

"Yes, the poison test. I was so sick, they did not think I would make it. I did push through, though, and made it through the training for a Wooder. It is hard, as well, but different in a way. We don't have to have great physical strength or a constitution that will not quit. We just have to be able to survive and learn. As you are tested and trained in killing, we are tested and trained in healing. You learn to approach in shadows, and we learn to use the shadows to hide. You learned to fight, and we, how to set bones."

Jon nodded as he listened to her, paying attention to the way she explained the training. His nose told him that something was wrong, and he then noticed the remaining of the rabbit was still over the fire. The bones had blackened along with what flesh was left of the animal. He looked at Juliette with a question in his eyes.

"Yes, just dump the body in the fire to burn it. If we don't, we'll have visitors in the camp looking for food," Juliette said.

Jon dumped the carcass in the glowing coals, ensuring it would burn to ash. He poked at the fire a little with the remains of the spit to get it burning a little better and threw another piece of wood on.

The light of the day was fading as the sun started to sink. Juliette pulled out her bedroll, and spread it on the ground, pulling a blanket over her body.

"You will need to sleep so we can get to where we need to tomorrow," she said.

Jon followed her advice, pulled out his bedroll, and curled up on it with his blanket over him.

---

Thomasyn did not make Gillian do all the work, but he did play it up till they arrived back at their camp.

Gillian had been picking the feathers off the bird and saving them as Thomasyn had requested.

"If you could just finish the bird, I will get the fire going,"

Thomasyn told her, as he picked up what fallen branches he could find. It was easy for there was a lot of branches on the ground.

After a few minutes, he had the fire burning, ready for the bird. Gillian had taken off all the feathers and removed the guts, putting the lungs, liver, heart, and kidneys into a bundle of leaves. The bird she stuffed with different flower peddles, and handed it over to Thomasyn who put it on a spit to cook.

"You are good with that spear," Gillian said to him, pointing. "I tried to throw one last year, but just could not figure it out."

"I didn't know Wooders used weapons," Thomasyn said.

"Well, just a few. Mostly we are shown how to protect ourselves a little, but not to attack. We are taught how to talk to people first, and find out why they do the things they do."

"We are taught how to listen and judge. It takes a lot of listening," Thomasyn confessed. "I sometimes grow tired of the lessons. I want to just go into the world and be a Spear like I have been trained to."

They waited for the bird to cook, and when it was done they shared a meal. Gillian took the leaf packet from the side of the fire and inspected it. She tossed it from hand to hand, cooling the bundle. She smelled it and seemed satisfied. The wrapping made its way into her pack and she smiled.

"What is that?" Thomasyn asked.

"It is a poultice, a bundle to boil and drink. If mixed with the correct herbs, it will help heal a number of ailments. It can stop the pain of the joints and the loosening of the bowels. With this, a man can lay with a woman, and bring forth a child on the first coupling," she said.

Thomasyn just looked at her with that comment. "Coupling?" he asked.

"Oh. Well, I guess that you've not been told about that yet. You are still young. It is how men and women make children. They lay together and couple. Your teacher will explain it better in a year or two."

Thomasyn had always been taught to wait for any teaching. If something is deemed not to be ready for them, they waited till it was. So when Gillian said he would be told in the future what it meant, he took it as a given. He would learn.

The light of the day was failing, the night coming in and the forest growing dark. They prepared their bedding and sat around the fire. Thomasyn kept it burning with wood picked from the ground.

"I think we should sleep. We have a lot of forest to walk through," Gillian said to Thomasyn.

"Then we should sleep," he said, and lay down to do just that.

***

"It is the bad cough," Cole said to the old man. "I can give her something to help, possibly giving her enough strength to fight it, but the art of breaking it from her is not known to any of us."

The old man just looked at him with blank eyes, his jaws chewing together with nothing in his mouth.

"So you can heal her?" he asked again, voice full of hope.

"Not heal, help. But it is not something that is a sure thing. Her body must also help fight it."

"So she can fight it," the old man said. "She's strong, ya know. Twelve children we had together. All strong, but one that died coming out of her. She's strong, that one. Love of My Life." The old man took the woman's hand and pet it lovingly.

Cole put his hand on the old man's shoulder, making him focus on him.

"I will give her the medicine. I will also give you something to give her tomorrow. I need water in a pot on the fire. Can you do that for me?"

"Yes, pot on a fire with water. We have it over there," he said, pointing to the fire pit with a large metal pot hanging from a set of hooks.

Cole looked at the pot. It contained water, but it was not clear, and smelled brackish. He shook his head.

"We cannot use this. It is salty. Can you dump it?" Cole asked.

The old man shook his head. "'Tis too heavy for me. The young lad comes by to fill it from the well. No idea why it's salty. He is a good boy, and fast, as well."

Cole understood the meaning. The boy had probably taken a run off, taking in salt water as well as fresh from a large water hole close to the shoreline.

"We can't use it. Bethany, can you take this pot and dump it? Use the well we passed to fill it, but make sure the water is fresh, not salty."

"Yes, Wooder Cole," she said, coming forward and taking a rag to wrap around the handle. She lifted it, went out the door, dumped it, and headed to the well.

The village folks had started to gather in the centre of town. Bethany walked past them, drawing up water from the well before returning to the hut.

Cole had stoked the fire and added more wood to make it higher and hotter. The old man was talking.

"You're using all the wood. I will need to get someone to split some more for me soon," he said. "When the winter comes, I need to have a lot, or ma complains desperately about how her bones ache."

"If we do not boil the water, you will not have the pleasure of hearing her complain this winter," Cole said.

Bethany took the pot and put it on the hooks over the fire. She looked at Cole who nodded a thank you to her, before turning his attention to the pot. He tested the water and nodded again. No salt.

Bethany went back out of the hut to look at the ocean. It was almost completely dark out now, and she could just make out the line of the water against the sky in the distance. It was getting cooler, more than it had been earlier that afternoon. It seemed as if the air flowed from the land towards the sea in front of her. Her long, auburn hair floated in the breeze, shielding her face from view at times. Bethany smelled the potion that Cole was making and wrinkled her nose at the stench.

She moved, walking towards the common fire the village folk had built. It was large, like a beacon to the water. Its flames struggled to overcome the breeze of the evening that pushed against them. The whole of the village seemed to be gathered around the fire, listening to a man in a dark robe as he talked to them with exaggerated movements of his hands.

As Bethany moved closer, she could make out the words he was saying and distinguish the man's features easier. The man's voice was almost hypnotizing, but she focused on the words, studying the man.

"...and beautiful, and we will call this earth. The fourth God looked at his brothers and spread his body on the earth, filling it with trees and animals, filling the big depths with water and the high peaks with snow. My body will supply life to the earth, so life will abound; I do this for the love of you all."

He was an older man, maybe in his mid-fifties. Bushy eyebrows did little to hide small eyes. A large, hooked nose exaggerated just how out of place his eyes appeared.

"The fifth God looked at his brothers with pride. He came to the earth and saw the day with the light and the night with the sparkles. He moved upon the land and saw the trees and plants that grew. He cried, and the tears created fish in the sea, beasts in the fields, and man. He cried till man came forth and his tears carried his soul into them."

His chin was a sculpture all by itself, with a definite cleft in the centre. He looked like a powerful man, standing well over six feet, shoulders broader than average. When he spoke, Bethany could see he had his own teeth, a very impressive feat for someone who lived in a small village.

"He faded away, saying to his brothers, 'The men will walk your earth, under your stars, and sun, and among your trees, and flowers to appreciate what you have done. They will love us and remember us and cherish us. I give them a soul so they can be forever with us,' and he faded away into the children he created."

Bethany looked at the man's clothing, a simple rough-spun cloth stitched together. Sandals adorned his feet, with straps frayed at the end.

"The bothers wept for their loss and created the lesser races of the elves and the dwarfs and the gnomes and the giants, and they all disappeared into their creations.

"Thus we are all gods," he said, finishing it by lowering his head to the children around the fire, and looked directly at them. He finished by seeing Bethany, her hair now whipping across her face as she approached. The cloak was about her with the hood down, allowing all to see her for what she was, a young girl, not yet a woman, and a Spear.

"But that is the old story of the gods," the old man said. "We are told to believe they were benevolent beings that will always take care of us, tend to us, and make sure we survive the world made from them." He stood straight, raising his arms to the air.

"But they told us lies. How many times has a God been good to us? They look down and send locus to our fields. We must harvest early the food we grow because we would lose it. They send storms to sink the ships our children are on! The snow comes early or leaves late, bringing hardship to the land. But still, we are told to believe in them, to trust they will look over us. The man that swims to shore is told the Gods must be looking over him! But what about his drowned friends? Did the Gods deem them unworthy to save? Was it not the man's strong arms which saved him?

"I beseech you to look into your own lives, and tell me when the gods actually helped you?" he asked, pointing a finger at the crowd and sweeping it around.

"My cow gave birth because of the Gods..." a voice came from the crowd.

"But was that not because you bought a new bull, Samuel?" the man responded.

"My crops were better this year than last," another voice spoke out.

"But you planted twice as much!" the old man said in retort. "Everything we receive, we receive from ourselves! We are the gods!" He raised his arms to the heavens.

Bethany just shook her head and started to walk away.

"Spear!" he cried out. "You are one of the believers. Tell me I am not true! Prove to me the gods are real!"

She stopped, slowly turned, and looked at him, her hair moving across her face. Even at her young age, the villagers respected her for what she was. Bethany did not smile, did not flinch, she just unslung her spear and bone. She placed the spear in the bone and lifted it in her hand, balancing it, feeling the familiar weight of it in her hands.

"If I throw this at you, will it hit or miss? If it misses, am I a poor thrower, or did the Gods interfere with it? Who can tell? If I hit you, is it because I am a good thrower, or did the Gods make my aim true as a punishment? Would you be able to tell? Should I throw the spear and let the Gods decide? Or should I just leave you standing there, shaking at the thought of being dead?" She looked at him and used her free hand to push the hair out of her eyes.

"Or maybe if I just put this away." She slung the spear and bone over her back again. "We can say the Gods told me to spare you. It is up to you to decide what you believe in, not someone else." And she walked away from them towards the old man's hut.

---

The fire slowly died as Jon and Juliette slept. A slight breeze fanned the fading embers till only ash was left, allowing darkness to be the only companion of the two sleeping beneath the stars.

Jon's sleep was restless, his dreams full of strange shapes and noises. He dreamed of the forest, all bent and tangled above him. He ran through it, slowly at first, but faster as he tried to escape the dread of something chasing him. The branches reaching out for him made his legs pump up and down, but for some reason, he kept slowing, as if his strides were shortened with every breath.

The presence of an adversary stalking him weighed heavily on Jon's mind as he went between the trunks, looking desperately for an escape. He had all but given up when a sudden memory of a weapon made itself known. His spear was still on his back. Jon pulled if from its looped holder, feeling the familiar weight in his hands. The smooth oaken wood of the shaft eased the strain on his mind. It was a comfort, reminding him who he was.

He stopped running and turned, the presence of something still approaching him screamed out in his mind. Jon could not discern anything, but he knew something was out there, stalking him, following. He backed up again. Jon's heart leaped and pounded in his ears.

It was close. He could see the shadow deep in the trees moving towards him. Jon set his spear in the bone and pulled his arm back, ready to loosen the weapon when the earth shook...

"Jon," a voice said in his ear, and he opened his eyes. Juliette was shaking him.

"Wha... What happened?"

"You were tossing and turning. I wasn't going to wake you, but you started thrashing about," Juliette said, standing back from him. "Get up, we have to go."

Jon sat up to see the day had just started to crest the horizon. He wiped the sleep from his eyes and noticed the spear was by his side, not on the pack where he had set it the night before.

"We don't have far to go," she said.

Jon stood and straightened his clothes. He looked about, feeling the rumbling in his stomach, reminding him he ate very little last night.

Juliette heard his stomach growl, saw some barriers and they walked over to them, eating their fill.

"These are good," he said to her, eating with furiousness. The juice squirted into his mouth and made him smile.

Once they had finished their meal, he quickly packed the bedding in his pack. Juliette indicated the direction they needed to travel in, and they started to run once again.

Thomasyn woke up before Gillian opened her eyes. He tended to the fire and put more logs on it. His stomach grumbled, reminding him he had only eaten breakfast and dinner yesterday. He then decided to find something that would settle his stomach before they started their day's travels.

The sun started to show by showering rays of light to lighten the earth. Thomasyn's eyes could just make out forms as he searched the close brush for something they could eat for breakfast. The Spear scanned left and right, forward a little and back. Thomasyn almost missed the small, dark berries that clumped in a small clearing. Blueberries! He moved to the small field and bent, picking the treasures from the small bushes and eating. It was a full field of them in front of him, and Thomasyn picked as quickly as he could. Before long, his square cloth was teeming with the small treasures.

Thomasyn stood, turned, and made his way back to the camp.

Gillian was up and stoking the fire with a stick. She looked up at him with a smile that turned into a grin as he handed over half of his find.

"These are the best," she said, eating a few of them at a time. The juice burst in her mouth, and the flavour of the small berries wrapped around her tongue, coating her throat. "I can't believe you found these."

"It is easy if you know what to look for. I'll clear the fire if you fold the packs." Thomason stood, wiping the juice of berries from his hands.

"Sure. I like that." Gillian put the rest of the berries in her mouth.

Thomasyn used the end of his spear to loosen the dirt and put it on the fire, using his foot to smother it. Once done, he emptied his water skin over it. Thomasyn grabbed Gillian's and did the same. The fire quenched, he headed to a nearby stream to fill the skins again.

Gillian folded up the bedrolls, and put them in their packs to ensure they were secure. She pulled her pack on and waited for Thomasyn to return.

"Ready?" she asked him.

"Yes. Are we walking the rest of the way?"

"Well, if we walk it will be easy for us, but we will not get to the village till dark. If we run, we will be there in a few hours. Probably in time to have lunch with a family, I know. Want to run?"

Thomasyn smiled. "It would be nice to have someone make us lunch," he said, stretching a little to limber up for a run.

She smiled back. "Then this way, my Spear." Gillian started to run North West through the forest, ducking under branches as she went.

---

The old woman had another fit of coughing that woke Bethany up from her slumber. She rolled over and saw Cole holding a cup to the woman's mouth, encouraging her to swallow. The old man was over to another side of the hut, snoring away as if nothing was happening. He had told Cole he could remember to give his wife the potion, but when the man tried, he forgot how much to put in the cup, and at one time, he almost drank it himself.

The woman was nice enough. She had some fresh bread and sharp cheese she shared with them, along with some cured fish. Bethany did not especially like the fish, but the cheese had a very sharp taste of sweetness to it, and when it hit her pallet, the taste surprised her. The woman kept cutting pieces for Bethany as she quickly nibbled them. The bread was crusty and nice. Bethany had never tasted bread this pleasant in her life.

Cole had eaten sparingly, for he knew this represented a great wealth to the old couple. He promised he would help out as much as he could, which meant Bethany would be doing some work for them.

The first part of her job was to take the covers and blankets from the bedding and wash them. She had done it in the dark, leaving the laundry out to dry in the wind as best as it could. When she returned, Bethany put fresh sheets and blankets on the beds for them all. Cole commented on how happy he was when she had finished.

They had talked for a long time after that, listening to the old man's stories of how he used to fish the ocean, and salt the catch to preserve it. He was a good man, with the charisma of making another person smile.

When his wife was not looking, he handed Bethany a small brown ball wrapped in paper. She looked at it, not knowing what to do with it. She watched in wonder as he pulled out another one, took the paper off it and put it in his mouth. She did the same and the reward of sweetness burst in her mouth. Her eyes opened wide, and she looked at the old man, who smiled and winked at her, putting his finger to his lips to tell her to keep the little treat quiet.

The treat lasted an hour in her mouth. She sucked and enjoyed the flavour. After when it dissolved fully, Bethany only had the memory of sweetness to remember the rest of her life.

When the old man had finished his sweet, he started to talk. His voice seemed to change, only grating when his excitement peaked. The man's memory from long ago was either sharp or spotty, depending on the subject he remembered. He spoke well and seemed to have knowledge that ranged back many years.

"I remember the Spears of old, long before you were pulled from your mother's belly, young Spear. They numbered many, and patrolled the shoreline in boats with great sails. It was well before the great Dwarf war, when the miners from up north revolted against their king and killed him. His name was Rav... Ran... Rangor! Yes, Rangor of the

Dwarfs. He worked his people to the bone, he did. Hardly gave them any of the coin he was paid for mining the mountains. That was under King Savoy's grandfather. The King saw the uprising and the people that had been hurt in the villages. You see, the Dwarfs are a torrent of problems when they get going. Especially when they drink great quantities of the ale they make.

"I remember for ten years we did not see a Spear come through the village, and then news came down they had killed almost all the Dwarfs! The King had sent at least five thousand Spears against at least fifty thousand Dwarfs, and killed almost every one of them! The problem was, many of the Spears had been killed also, along with the great number of the Wooders who had gone with them. Only about a thousand Spears returned at the most, and many people say it was actually less than five hundred." The old man paused for a second, stretching out a leg.

"Most were given titles for their sacrifice, and allowed to step down from being Spears, but more refused, saying they would rather serve than leave.

"They said once a Spear, always a Spear."

He sat there for a while, looking into the fire and remembering.

"The fishing back then was better than anything here now. These kids think they can fish, but you get an old salt like me on the water and I'll show you the fish. Mark my words, I'll show them to ya."

He rambled on for another half hour.

"The time is late, we need to let your wife sleep, and I think my Spear friend there is falling asleep where she sits," Cole said.

"I'm okay, Cole, I can hear more," Bethany said.

"No, Bethany, I think we both need rest. I will tend the old woman and you sleep. We have a lot of running to do tomorrow, so close your eyes."

Bethany looked at him and tried to stifle a yawn, unsuccessfully. Her need for slumber was quickly catching up with her as the night wore on. With a nod, she went to the patch of straw her blanket covered, and laid down to sleep.

But sleep did not come quickly to her. She smelt the fire burning in the hut, and the rankness of the clothes she wore. Bethany tossed and turned from the constant noise of the wind through the huts and the surf on the beach nearby. It kept up until her body finally gave up caring, and she drifted into a fitful rest.

---

Jon and Juliette had been running for over two hours through sparse trees and grass-grown fields. Juliette had found the path she wanted to use, and followed it diligently. The path was little more than an animal path, with some small clearings where large creatures had rested. He followed her without question or thought, just putting one foot in front of the other like he was trained to do during long distances.

The fields of grass changed slowly, becoming devoid of trees except those a great distance to the south. The smell of the damp forest was replaced with sweet flowers and grass. Jon took small drinks from his water skin as needed, feeling he should conserve just in case they ran longer than expected.

He caught sight of the village as they crested a hill. It was in the valley below, with fields being cultivated and a small stronghold of stone close by the settlement. Juliette pointed, and Jon nodded. They were in sight of their destination.

Upon closer inspection, Jon noticed several people working in fields and tending livestock. They seemed to take no interest in them until they had approached very close to the village. As the people looked up, Juliette slowed to a walk and Jon kept pace beside her.

One child ran from the village towards the stronghold and disappeared inside. After several minutes, he emerged again with three large men dressed in chain mail. Jon took no real interest in them, save they seemed to be coming out to meet them. The huts grabbed his attention for they seemed strange, built with timber and straw with large stones at their base.

The three men walked to the edge of the village, waiting for Jon and Juliette to come within hailing distance. The sun was nearing mid-day, and Jon was feeling hungry again, since he had only eaten a small amount of berries that morning.

One of the men called out to them, and Juliette changed her

approach to meet the men. Jon kept moving along, studying the three of them as they approached.

The man in the middle was standing forward of the other two and appeared to be in charge. A tall man, he stood at least half a foot over his companions. A bushy black and grey beard covered his face, and bushy eyebrows complimented his brow. The man's shoulders showed he must practice with his sword and shield every day, for they stood out large on his body. The rest of him was covered in chain mail, so Jon could not tell much more of him from this distance.

His companions were not slouches either, both being large of frame with great, prominent beards. Each scowled as they approached, as if they felt the two intruders were bearers of bad news.

"Hail!" said Juliette, holding up her hand in greeting.

"Hail!" the large man called back to her. His voice was a booming deep base warning of a chasm underneath. He did not scowl from what Jon could tell, but he could not see much beyond the amount of hair that covered the man's face. He noticed the large great sword on the man's back. It had a pommel that would support two hands, even the great hands of the man who carried it. The pommel was wrapped in soft leather, with a fist carved in the end. The guards had many dings in them, as if they stopped many a sword from getting to the wielder.

"We are travelling through, but have seen your village to stop and offer any aid that may be needed in these troubled times," Juliette said, looking closely at the man and his fellows.

"We have no need for healing, Wooder. No Spear helps us, nor do the elves attack us. We are peaceful and take care of our own," the man's companion said.

"Hush, David, these two have been travelling for hours, I would guess. Look how they sweat but have not been breathing hard. They are well trained and welcomed."

David spat on the ground and frowned under his beard.

"They are nothing but the king's hand and voice. I say bade them farewell and be done with them," David said.

"You must forgive my brother. He is harsh and does not understand why he was not picked for a Spear when he was born," the man said. "My name is Orin. We are from the house Dreaden, in the home of fields. We pay homage to the Spear and Wooder for joining us today. May I offer you food and shelter?"

At the sound of food, Jon perked up and smiled. Juliette seemed a little more cautious at the invitation.

"I thank you, sir, for the invitation. We are moving through to the next village, but would welcome some bread and cheese if you have any. We have been running since this morn," Juliette said. "We are to be there today, but we do not have a set time of day to be there."

"You may call me Orin, if it pleases you. Your lives have been spent training. It is now time to enjoy it," he said as he stepped aside and motioned to the small stronghold. "I will welcome you. Please join us."

Jon looked at Juliette and saw that she was about to refuse the offer. His stomach wanted food. Since they offered it, he stepped inside.

"I believe that turning down such a generous offer would be very poor manners. We accept your offer. Please lead the way."

Juliette's head turned to Jon, her eyes furrowed and brow pulled together, but would not refuse what he said. As the three men turned and started to walk towards the stronghold, Juliette punched Jon on the arm, not hard, but enough to tell him she was not pleased.

"What was that for?" he asked in a hushed tone.

"For accepting to eat with them. Be careful to only eat what they eat," she replied in a whisper.

They followed the men to the stronghold. It was a small stone building with a great room inside, which could hold thirty-odd men at the tables. A stair led to the upper level. On one of the tables sat bread and cheese, with some cooked meat.

The men sat at the one table with the food, together on the one side of the table, motioning Jon and Juliette to sit on the other side. It looked as if they had been in the middle of their own meal when they had been called out.

Jon sat and reached out for the bread, but stopped and looked at Juliette. She shook her head slightly, but Orin noticed. He reached forward and pulled off a chunk of the bread, then cheese, and finally a piece of meat. He put them together and stuffed them in his mouth. Orin chewed and swallowed. He then picked up a pitcher and poured water into the cups in front of them and his own, from which he picked up and drank. He looked at Juliette with a raised eyebrow. She nodded and indicated for Jon to go ahead and eat.

Jon wasted no time at all. He pulled a chunk of bread, cheese and meat from the platter and ate as if he had not eaten for several days. Juliette took smaller pieces and ate with more control.

"You two must have been out in the forests for a long time," David said, watching them eat. He drank from a flagon; it contained dark mead that left foam on his whiskers. When finished drinking, he stuffed his mouth with meat and cheese.

The other man slowly tore pieces off a bread ball and soaked it in the drippings of the meat before putting them in his mouth. He was large and fat, the hair on top of his head was thinning. What hair he had was long and stringy, getting into his mouth as he ate. He pulled the hair out of his mouth when he noticed it.

"So, you are going to San's village are you?" Orin asked.

Juliette looked up from the food she had been eating, and nodded to him, trying not to talk with her mouth full. She swallowed and answered him directly.

"Yes, I have friends there, and they usually have a need for a Wooder at this time of year. Do you know San?" she asked.

"No, I never met the man. He usually sends one of his bastards over to us asking for seed every summer. It's like he doesn't know how to save for the summer. We usually give them some and move him on his way," Orin said.

Juliette nodded as if she understood what he was talking about, and why. He smiled and nodded towards the food, picking up some meat and toasting to her with it. She smiled back a reserved smile, and took a little bit of the meat for herself. It was greasy and well done, but good. She chewed and swallowed, then returned to her bread and cheese.

Jon kept eating, stuffing more meat into his mouth. He was starting to feel full from all the grease, but did not stop, not knowing when he would be able to feast like this again. Grease was running down his chin while he ate, and Juliette reached out with a small cloth to clean it.

Orin and his other brother laughed at this, but David did not. His scowl deepened as it happened.

"So you let a girl clean you, do you, Spear?" he asked.

Jon looked at him, redness colouring his cheeks. He went to say something, but Juliette stopped him, and spoke in his stead.

"I would have thought guests would be treated a little kinder than this. If your intention is to anger the Spear, even if he is young, I will warn you it is not good to pull the tail of a tiger, even if a cage separates you from it," Juliette said. She thought for a second while the men stared at her. The decision made, she stood, and motioning Jon to do the same.

"We thank you for your kindness, but we must go forward to the village we meant to stop at. I am sorry if we offended you by stopping here," and she turned to go.

"No, don't go," Orin said, a smile creeping under his furry face. "We could use your knowledge to help heal the ill my brother has."

Juliette stopped. It made her pause, the need of another. Her teaching from the first time she became a Wooder, she would offer aid to those that needed or asked for her help. She turned and faced Orin again, wanting to ask that question of him but finding it hard to decide what his reason for asking it was.

"What ill is troubling your brother that I could possibly help heal?" she asked.

"Why can you not tell? Look at him, his head has no hair!" he laughed, and his brothers joined him, slapping the table with their hands.

# ELEVEN

Thomasyn and Gillian ran through the forest, ducking under branches and sidestepping tree trunks. Thomasyn would run in front of Gillian, slow down to keep pace, and then Gillian would run faster to get in front of him. It was a game they played to pass the time to their destination.

As Gillian had guessed, it took them just over two hours of running to get to the village. They slowed to a walk as they broke through the forest, not needing to run any more. It was in a field, close to the edge of the forest. Thomasyn was surprised at the size, for he had been told the village only harbored a few residents. Instead, the village had a lot of people and was located at the intersection of several roads.

As they approached, Thomasyn saw children playing in the fields and between the huts. They laughed, ran, jumped, and chased one another. He thought there was something wrong. The children were wasting their lives by not studying or practicing.

They approached, and a tall man dressed as a Wooder came out to greet them. Within a short distance of them, he spread his arms in greetings. He wore the same cloak and hood as Gillian did, but his was worn and frayed at the edges.

"Welcome to Hallow Woods, my friends. If you are in need, we can supply. If you want to trade, we can trade. How can we help you?" he asked.

Gillian and Thomasyn came up to the man, and Gillian spread her arms and a smile lightened her eyes.

"We come to share your love, old man. Now give me a hug, before I forget how much you love me." She hugged the man like a bear.

"Gillian! My sweet child. You have returned," the old man cried out to her, and returned her embrace.

Thomasyn approached, and noticed under the hood, the man had no eyes. There were only empty sockets looking blankly forward.

"Oh, my sweet child," the man said, stepping back from her finally and reaching out a hand to touch her face. She took his hand and guided it to her cheek, leaning her head sideways to his touch. "But you have grown so much over the last year. I am surprised!"

"I am now sixteen years, and a woman grown. I have missed you, old man. I still cannot believe they stuck you out here. Your skills are wasted in a village, when you could help heal hundreds back in the capital."

"It's the eyes. They're no longer, and it's the reason I'm here. These people need a Wooder, just as much as any city or village does, and they're a trade center. I can use my skills on any and all that pass through. But enough of me, you have another with you. Is it your apprentice Wooder that comes with you?"

"No, my old master, I am not that far along yet. It is a Spear who travels with me. Thomasyn, please come here," she said. "Master Aimond, I would like to introduce you to Thomasyn Saye, a Spear in Flight. I've been charged with teaching him some healing lore. Thomasyn, this is Master Aimond, my most favourite teacher in the Realm. He was my Master for several years till they sent him out there."

Thomasyn stuck out his hand in the traditional way for the other man to grasp, and blushed, realizing the old man could not see what he was doing.

"Ha!" Aimond cried. "I bet he has his hand out does he not!" He smacked his lips together and smiled. Leaning forward he whispered, "I bet you feel damn silly there, don't you, young Spear." Master Aimond straightened. "Well, don't worry, I won't tell anyone if you don't." He stuck his hand out for Thomasyn to grasp.

"I don't understand," Thomasyn said.

"What is that, young Spear?" Aimond asked

"Well, when Elana lost one eye, she was not able to serve as a Spear, or Wooder, but you have lost both. Why are you allowed to serve?" Thomasyn asked.

"Hush, Thomasyn, mind your manners," Gillian said.

Master Aimond just laughed, reaching out his hand towards Thomasyn's face to feel his features. Thomasyn did not flinch, knowing from his teachings it was how a blind person recognized people.

"That is a long story, and long stories deserve a good meal for the saying. Come, you must be hungry after such a long run. I have food on the table, and the story is one that can be told over it," he said as he felt Thomasyn's face. "Such a strong face you have there. Okay." He dropped his hand. "Come with me and I will tell you the story of the old man who lost his eyes."

He turned and led them to the village proper, walking with confident steps. Gillian walked beside him, her arm around his as she leaned in on him. His path led them into the village, passed the first line of huts and then he stopped for a second, and turned slightly before proceeding forward.

Thomasyn looked on in wonder, not knowing how the man knew where he was, till he spotted a stone that was buried in the ground. He moved his foot forward and felt a definite impression with broken ridges.

"My marker stone, young Spear. It tells me where I am in the village. There is another one up ahead about thirty paces. The villagers put them in the ground to help me know where I am. You will find a number of them throughout the village, at different spots and in different shapes."

They walked and came across a large hut. When he approached, he reached out his hand to touch and feel along the wall to the door. He pushed it aside.

The inside of the hut was surprisingly bright, with several openings in the roof. There were several straw beds with linen draped over them, but only one was occupied. An older woman was sprawled on the bed, wearing a heavy wool blanket over her. Deep circles coloured the underside of her eyes, and her movements, though sure, were slow. Her breath rattled as phlegm moved in her lungs, however, they were not obscured.

"Mind old Meredith. She is here to get clear of the bad cough. Please, come sit by the fire," he said.

They saw the bronze pot near the fire, and Aimond moved the vessel to a plank of wood on the ground. He then went to the back of the hut and returned with bread balls and cheese. The small plank on the ground became a table when he put the bread balls down on it along with the cheese, motioning the two to sit with him near the fire on the dirt floor.

"Come and share food. It is good when the broth is hot. I will need you to help a little, Gillian," he said.

She stood and ripped the tops off the bread, making bowls out of them. She scooped out thick broth, filling all the bowls. Once filled, she handed one to Thomasyn, Aimond and took the last for herself and sat beside her old mentor.

They used the ripped bowl top to soak up the broth and eat. The cheese was similarly picked at during the meal, a quiet repast they enjoyed in silence till Aimond spoke.

"I promised you a story, did I not, young Spear?" Aimond turned his head in the direction of Thomasyn. "Well, let me tell you about a young man, training as a Spear."

Thomasyn raised his chin, looking at the man and seeing something in the face. The chin, though not square, had strength with an air of defiance. It was a strength he had seen in a number of his trainers, and the air felt the same as during a lightning storm. Thomasyn recognized the air of command when he felt it.

"About forty years ago, when he was training. His age only five, working hard and learning the laws, running every day and learning to kill. He had always passed the tests they put him through, and nothing bothered him.

"It was the poison test they administer. A mix of toxins put together and fed to the Spears. Small amounts at first, and larger later on. It causes discomfort and sometimes sickness, but if a child is really ill from it they are not strong enough of body to be a Spear. Even at the age of eight they are fed more of the poisons, their bodies having a tolerance after having taken it for so many years.

"But I am not really telling the story when I talk of your training. The child could not keep the food down, and was forced to realize he did not have the ability to take testing any further, and accepted being a Wooder, a healer. He started his training immediately.

"Using his mind in a different way, and only training in long distance running, caused him distress at first. He studied and extended his knowledge in the healing arts, mending instead of breaking. He studied the body, how to mend what was broken, and healing herbs as well as how to mix them.

"When he was fifteen, he was accepted into the ranks of the Wooders, a full year before the usual age. He trained and readied to help those around him. He ventured forth and found the world. His journeys took him from one shore to another, through the mountains in the north and the sandy sea of the east. And finally, he came across a child being born in a brothel, to a young girl he knew would not survive. He watched, and waited, hoping against hope she would survive the birth, knowing he could do nothing to help. She did survive, for a time. And she was able to hold her child for a few minutes and feed it. She loved it with all her heart while the lifeblood ran from between her legs. When she died, she heard the Wooder tell her of all the wonderful things her child would be able to do as a Spear.

"So she passed away with a calm soul, understanding her child will be one of the chosen ones; a leader, a soldier, and a weapon for the good of all. The Wooder took the child to the Realm to learn. He did not just leave the child to be trained, he stayed and watched the child. He followed how the child grew during the training, becoming one of the elite, a leader among leaders.

"The Wooder stayed, and trained other Wooders, teaching them how to find the ones who would need them before it was too late. Then tragedy struck, the child was no longer allowed to be a Spear. He watched as the young one was brought to the Wooders, and he helped with the training. He took the child under his wing, helping with the learning of the skills needed to be a Wooder.

"So the one who once was the student became the teacher, an

instructor of Wooders. And during one day as they wandered the world together, a man delusional with hate threw an evil potion at them. The vial struck the teacher and splashed, taking his eyes and scarring his student. But even then, it was not enough of a loss to dissuade the teacher from teaching, and that is what he has been doing till this day."

He reached and took down his hood so Thomaysn could see his face better. The scars showed pot marks like rivers across his eyebrows. They ran over the bridge of the nose as well. He noticed the eyelids had sunken in the eyeholes, giving a skull like look to his face. Aimond then reached across and took the neck hole of Gillian's skiff, gently pulling it aside for Thomasyn to see the ugly scars on her shoulder.

"As you can tell, the student was Gillian, and because of my teachings, she was able to help me live through the incident. I live because she is a good healer, and a Wooder, and knows her art well. The council allows me to practice still, for I have a talent of healing even without my eyes."

He pulled his hood back over his head and Gillian shrugged her skiff back over her shoulder. She was blushing at having her shoulder exposed, but said not a word.

"I didn't know," Thomasyn said, looking at Gillian with a newfound respect.

***

Her sleep was restless and she tossed and turned on the blanket. Bethany dreamed of swimming in the ocean, with great creatures raising out of its depths to watch her. Her clothes were making her sink slowly, and she kicked her feet, trying to surface again. It was a perpetual struggle she had to suffer through in order to break the surface and breathe the salty air.

She sat up with a start, as she flailed her arms, trying to swim as she woke. Bethany's eyes opened and her arms came down as she realized where she was. It was the old man's hut. The dull light from the fire pit cast shadows on the hut wall, making her imagination leap before she should make sense of the whole vision.

Bethany swept the blanket off and rose. Her bladder complained, and she knew she had to make water immediately. With her mind still waking she began to move silently as she left the hut.

Stepping out into the cold night air, she noticed rays of sunshine, like the fingers of the sun, had started to stretch across the sky, grabbing hold and trying to lift the shining orb from its slumber under the horizon. Light clouds peppered the sky, telling her that they will have a good day for their run.

Bethany turned to find a private place, but did not see anything close. She realized moving away from the huts was the only way she could have privacy.

She was just about to step into the field when she caught a movement from the corner of her eye. Bethany stopped and pulled her hood over her head, using the training, making herself still, and the cloak making her invisible to anyone looking.

She scanned the village for any moving shadows, her bladder screaming at her in earnest. Bethany ignored it as best she could, pulling her knees together and putting the pain out of her mind. The movement caught the corner of her eye again, and this time she heard a scraping noise.

Bethany could not handle it anymore and broke her cover to run to the side of another hut. Once there, and in the shadows, she pulled down her britches and emptied her bladder. Once done, she pulled up her clothes and looked around.

At first she did not see anything, and then Bethany caught the shadow moving. The shadow was using the huts to make its movement as unseen as possible. It hugged the small buildings and moved slowly. She watched the shadow move cautiously; look, sniff the air, and crouch in the shadows again. It did not seem to be a man, but it did not look unnatural.

Bethany watched as it started to move from the shadows again, but this time it was light enough for her to see. The creature had a thin and elongated face, with a nose and chin stretched to points. Its hair was straggly and long, coated with grease. Eyes were larger than a person's, and bulged out under thick brows that stretched back to its hair. The arms were skinny, with coarse hairs all over them. It wore what she guessed was a leather jerkin but the light was too dim to tell. Red dye coloured its clothes, and on a rope belt hung a crude axe.

The thing seemed feral in its movements and manner. It carried what looked to Bethany like raw meat in one hand. The creature moved to the side of the hut and started to drool. With a movement that surprised her, it lifted the meat and took a bite. That was when Bethany realized it was not just a piece of meat, but the leg of a person. She shivered, and remembered the first law.

With a fluid motion she reached for her spear, unslung the weapon and threw towards the creature, butt end first. Her throw struck the side of the creatures head, knocking him to the ground unconscious.

---

"Why are we waiting?" Jon asked.

"Because I say we wait," Juliette said.

They had left the town with the sound of laughter at their backs, which made them angry. Juliette had insisted they walk through the town, and not directly to the woods. Now they were hidden in the long grass, watching the village and waiting. Juliette told him it was needed, so he did it, wondering what they waited for.

It took several hours, but it happened. David walked out of the stronghold towards the huts, and disappeared into one of them. After a few minutes he came out dragging a woman by the arm. She was struggling, trying to break free till he turned and struck her across the face. The woman spun and dropped to her knees, with her hand on her cheek. He pulled her to her feet and dragged her over to the stronghold.

Juliette looked over at Jon and pointed to the stronghold.

"That is what I was waiting for," she said, and stood.

He stood also, removing his spear from its holder and hefting it in his hand.

"A Spear delivers justice when the law is broken," he said, and started to run.

It took him very little time to get to the front doors, but he did not charge in, he waited. Juliette followed him as he flattened himself against the wall.

"What are you waiting for?" she whispered.

"This will be done my way, now. I am the Spear," he whispered back and stared down her argumentative glare.

His head turned sharply as the woman let out a muffled scream. Jon looked at Juliette for a second and then ran through the doorway into the eating hall.

David was not in the hall, only the two other brothers, sitting there, eating and talking. They looked up as Jon entered, surprised for a brief second. They soon gathered their wits and stood up in a rush, drawing their swords.

Jon threw his spear with all his weight behind it. The weapon struck the bald one in the stomach, piercing the ring mail easily and dropping him to the floor. Jon pulled out his short sword and took a fighting stance, waiting for Orin to come towards him.

"I am going to gut you, child," he said, pulling out his sword and walking around the table. "I will gut you and hang your empty middle for the village to see. And once that is done, I will find that Wooder you came with and do her like a woman should be done, on her knees, like a dog takes a bitch."

At that moment, Juliette walked into the room, standing back and watching.

"Oh, you brought her with you," he said, now only a few paces away. "That will make it easy. I always want a woman after killing."

Jon did not react, he let his training take control, and he waited. It is always the first move your opponent makes that will tell you if you will beat him, he thought, remembering the teachings of Master Chail. The man in front of him stood there, also waiting, examining the child in front of him. He figured Jon did not know what he was going to do. He attacked.

With a great rush forward he swung his blade from high left to lower right, looking to cleave Jon in half. It would have worked if Jon had waited the weapon to hit him, but he did not. He stepped back and aside sharply, and let the sword strike the ground. Jon just looked at him, shaking his head. Orin recovered and stalked forward toward Jon.

Jon backed up and Orin followed him, hunting him like a cat hunts a mouse. The man felt he was going to be the victor, for the child was backing away.

He lunged again, this time extending his arm to skewer the young boy, but instead he struck air, as Jon had seen the move coming and stepped sideways out of its path. He flipped the flat of his blade upwards and struck the blade with enough force to make it ring.

Orin swore and pulled back, only to lunge again where Jon stood, but again the child was no longer there but moving to the side again as the blade sailed past him. He twisted and ran past the man, pricking him with the point of his sword as he went. Orin howled in pain and frustration from the blow. It did not kill, nor was it meant to. No, the blow was delivered to cause his opponent to become reckless and foolish. He knew the man would be angry with pain from the sting he inflicted, and he was right.

The small prick he placed on the man's bicep caused him to swing wildly with a backhand slice. He forgot momentarily his opponent was approximately two feet shorter than a regular opponent. The swing went wild and over Jon's head.

Jon was now with his back to the main part of the hall, backing slowly away again.

"Damn you, boy," Orin cursed, he was approaching Jon like an animal that had been bit, with a little more caution. When Jon backed to the bench Orin lunged again, but this time with more forethought, not overextending himself, and ready to swing a counter if Jon went sideways. Jon jumped up and back, over the bench and onto the table. He kicked a flagon of ale at Orin and jumped down to the other side.

Orin jumped on the table to follow him, only to get the tip of Jon's sword in his right shin. The man jumped back and was again incensed with anger.

"Enough, boy, stand and fight!" he yelled.

Jon looked at him and stood his ground as Orin came around the table. He stood in a fighting pose, waiting for Orin to come at him again. When he was in striking distance, Orin did not attack, not this time. He stood there, red faced and angry. He gripped his sword, inching forward to engage.

Orin tapped his blade against Jon's, making them ting. He knew the tactic from Master Chail, and just returned the tap in rhythm, waiting for a tell that would say the man was going to attack again. It did not come in the usual five strikes, nor did it come in the next five. On the twelfth strike it happened, and he was ready for it.

Orin did not return his sword to the tap position, he raised it quickly in an effort to slice down. But Jon was ready for him yet again and rushed forward, drawing his sword under Orin's arm and cutting into the flesh, slicing the artery. Orin's arm came down, blood erupted from his body and down in rivers to the floor. He did not scream, he only looked at the blood as it leaked from his body in shocked surprise.

Jon did not wait for the man's body to fall, he rushed up the stairs, two at a time, to see if he could save the woman they had taken.

He reached the top of the stairs to see the woman crying on a bed, the body of David unclothed beside it. In her hand was a large candlestick, covered with blood. She held the makeshift weapon in one hand as her other one clenched a sheet to her chest.

Juliette was up the stairs behind Jon, moving towards the woman quickly and taking the candlestick from her grasp. She looked at the woman and brushed the hair away from her face, soothing her.

"You are safe now," she said.

"I... I... he was trying to take me, but the noise from down there and... I touched the... I swung and hit him... He stopped and laid on me till I pushed him away," she cried, almost hysterically.

Jon turned and went back down the steps to the hall. He walked to the table and started to eat his fill of the meat and cheese.

***

Thomasyn made himself busy as Gillian helped Aimond with the old woman. He went to draw water, and then helped others with their water as well. He listened to the gossip the women and men spoke to each other, and answered questions the curious children asked, for they were curious of how a Spear spent his days.

He humored them, explaining the different tasks Spears did along with the training. He also told them about injuries that happened during training, and how some of the children had suffered.

He returned to the hut late, just in time for an evening meal.

"So, where have you been all afternoon?" Gillian asked.

"I helped draw water for those in need, and talked to the children, answering their questions," Thomasyn said. "They had lots of questions."

They ate, mostly in silence, until Aimond started to talk. He was a skilled storyteller, and Thomasyn enjoyed listening to the old man as he spoke.

"You may not know of the Hobs, Thomasyn, but they are ghastly creatures. Long chins and noses with pointed ears. A lot of children are told that Hobs can steal them from a bed before the parents know what happened.

"Of course, you being a Spear, do not have to worry. You get to sleep in secure barracks, far away from the woods. But the common folk, they are the ones who suffer. They have to live this way, in huts or small homes near the wild. The dangers abound, and the Hobs have always taken advantage of it.

"One night, similar to tonight, the Hobs attempted to steal as many children as they could. It was a daring attack by Kindra, the Queen of the Hobs at the time. She was a piece of work if there ever was one.

"Her chin was pointier than all the others, and her nose hooked down to almost touch it. Ugly brown blotches of green spattered about her skin and whiskers on the sides of her chin hid all but the largest boils, many of them on her face.

"She walked up and down her castle cave, day and night, craving the flesh of children. The sweetness of the skin, silkiness of the liver and tartness of the kidneys. Yes, she lived in a castle, built in a cave for the lore of shaping stone is what they know, how to dig out caverns from the very rock. They are so good at tunneling, they rival the dwarfs in their ability. They do not crave gold or silver, nor do they crave gems. Flesh and bone of children, they lust after. The Hobs use every bit of their victims from tanning the skin for clothes, to using the guts for bow strings.

"But she decided she wanted a feast in order to draw a mate from the clans far and wide so she could bring forth babies into the world, and they could overthrow the world of man. But that was not going to be, for they forgot the prying eyes of the sages of the Realm.

"The sages of old could hear the minds of those who meant ill to the Realm, and they heard Kindra's ravenous musing loudly for weeks and months.

"The sages brought their discovery to King Basson, who ordered the Spear Danton to action. A main force of over five hundred of the Spears marched out of the city, and started their run. They ran and ran, day and night, to get to the village the sages said would be the target of the Hobs.

"But they arrived too late, for the Hobs had taken the children, and left no one else alive. Horror fell upon them, seeing that they had failed, for they were Spears, trained and bred to protect.

"Their commander, Danton fell into a blood rage vowing to find and destroy the Hobs and teach them what the true meaning of killing was.

"So he drew up his Spears and followed the Hobs into the forest. For days they tracked their movements, till they came upon the Hob's caves. Leaving one hundred of his men to guard the exits, Danton took the remaining four hundred deep into the heart of the Hobs city and killed all, male and female, young and old. Whether they fought, cowered, or slept, Danton killed as his rage empowered him; he embraced it fully in his heart.

"They say rage is the one thing that can kill a Spear, and vengeance overwhelmed him. For though he had killed many, he turned and counted only two dozen of his own Spears left. No longer a force of hundreds. Victory, the bittersweet spoils of revenge, cost the souls of those he commanded. He wept for them, and swore vengeance by licking the blood of the enemy from his blades.

"And when Danton found the castle of the Queen, he called her forth, and what he saw shocked him.

"For Danton did not see the face of legends and nightmares, instead he saw a beauty with long hair and enormous green eyes. He fell in love with her face, her clear skin. His fellows could not understand, for they saw what she was, and when they looked upon Danton they no longer saw their beloved leader, but the ever crafty face of a Hobs.

You see, the blood of the Hobs had taken his mind. He fell to his knees and forsook his vows. He renounced the Spears and swore to be with her."

Aimond stopped his recital of the story and listened. He smiled, knowing Thomasyn had fallen asleep and without ceremony, the old Wooder walked over to his cot, laid down and drifted off.

———

Bethany picked up her spear and kicked the axe out of the way. She inspected the body, flipping it on its back. The creature carried many weapons, from small knives, to a few daggers, and a cruel looking small sword.

She relieved the thing of the weapons and turned it back on its stomach. Bethany's hands moved quickly as she tied her captive up, tethering feet to the rope binding its hands. She frisked it again, checking for anything she may have missed. Her thoughts went to Master Chail who told her to always double or triple check work to ensure nothing was missed.

It was good she checked, several small pieces of sharp metal had been stitched to the creatures clothing, sharp enough to cut the cloth she used. Bethany found fragments of bone, sharpened to points hidden in the clothing, as well.

"What are you?" she asked, more to herself.

"He's a Hobs," a voice came from behind her.

Bethany spun while pulling a dirk from her belt. The sun just started to rise above the horizon, and the morning rays caught her eye, making her squint. The speaker was to the left of the sun, casting his face in shadows. She brought her hand up to shield her eyes but not fast enough; something struck her and she lost consciousness.

The man bent down and scooped up Bethany, holding her gently in his arms. His fingers worked quickly, pulling at her cloak to remove it and trussing it together in a makeshift binding to hold her.

"You dishonour me," he said, looking at the Hobs in bindings.

"My King, she surprised me," the Hobs said.

"No, you got greedy, and decided to take a snack from your hunting in the forest," he accused. The creature grimaced in fear. "I should leave you here with her, to be found with the rest of them."

The Hob's eyes went wide with fear as it pleaded. "No! They will kill me most assuredly. I need to be way! I will tell the Queen you helped me. She will be good to you again."

The man squatted beside the Hobs, looking at the creature with pity. "I don't need your help with my queen, I will get her back on my own." He reached out, taking a dirk from Bethany's belt and drawing it across the Hob's throat.

The creature gurgled as its own blood filled his lungs. The look of shock in its eyes told the man the Hobs actually thought he had a chance to survive the encounter.

He stayed there, hunched over the body, watching the life drain out of it. He knew he would have to move soon but wanted to see. The man reached out and turned over Bethany. He studied her face and sighed.

"So young. Was I ever that young when I went out with a Wooder," he whispered, more to himself.

His finger traced the line of Bethany's jaw, and he remembered a distant memory from a lifetime ago. His hand stopped and he watched her breath go in and out of her body at a steady pace. She will survive, the idea ran through his mind, and then he made a decision. He flipped her over carefully and untied her arms.

Standing, he dropped the dirk beside her and wandered off away from the rising sun for it hurt his eyes so much. He decided he would have to stop spending so much time underground in the castle.

***

Juliette was able to talk the girl into coming down the stairs. It was not an easy accomplishment, knowing how upset she had been.

When the girl saw the bodies of the bald man and Orin, she started to scream, putting her hands to the sides of her face.

Juliette tried to calm her, holding the girl in her arms. She turned her to face Jon as he was eating at the table.

"What are you doing?" she called to him, accusingly.

"I'm hungry," he said, stuffing another piece of meat into his mouth.

"You could have covered them up or something," she said to him. "And if you wanted to eat, you could have cleaned up first, and then sat down."

"So, I save the girl, and have to clean up also? Not much of a life for a Spear." He kept eating, pulling a piece of meat off the roast and grabbing another small bread ball. He looked at it, and then looked at her. He shook his head and put the bread down. Getting up, he moved over to the bodies and grabbed the bald one by the feet, pulling him out of the stronghold and beside the door. He returned and grabbed the feet of the other body, of Orin's body, and pulled it outside as well.

"They were heavy," he said when he returned. Jon looked around and saw a bucket filled with water. He cleaned his hands.

The girl stopped crying and Juliette walked her to the table, convincing her to eat a little of the food and drink some water. She made sure the girl was not injured and went over to Jon.

"Is that the first time you ever killed someone?" she asked.

"No. A few years ago I killed a giant with Bethany and Thomasyn. They had tried to kill some of our troop so we hunted them and killed them. It was Spear justice," he said.

She looked at him, taking in everything he said and appreciating the words, wondering about his feelings. Jon was talking without emotion, saying what he knew but with no feeling in his voice.

Juliette watched him and wondered if the training was worth it, the numbing of the children to be the way they are. She knew they were well taken care of, not suffering, and even loved, but it was something that worried her.

She looked over at the girl who ate as if she had not dined for three or four days.

"She has been starving while those three stuffed themselves," Jon said. The girl they saved looked up, taking bites from her food and swallowing without chewing. "I think they have been doing this to the village for a while"

Juliette turned to him and nodded. She made up her mind and headed out the door of the stronghold, followed closely by Jon.

"Everyone!" she called out. "Hail, everyone." Heads started to come out of huts and people came forward. Juliette waited for the group to gather before she started to talk.

"I am Juliette, and this young Spear is Jon. He has passed judgment on the three men that have been ill to your village. They have paid the price, and are no longer alive to do what they have been doing. Enter the stronghold and take back your food, for you deserve to have what is yours again."

The village folk stared aghast, then they saw the bodies of the two men. Some of them started to cry and others moved towards them, heading for the stronghold.

Jon looked at Juliette and winked.

"That is our sign," he said, taking her hand and leading her back out of town to where they left their packs.

---

"He does tell a lot of stories," Gillian said.

"Yes, but they are good stories." Thomasyn stretched. "I love listening to them for I hardly get to hear anything like them."

Gillian looked at him for a second, his sandy brown hair was more ruffled than usual. She clasped her hands on her lap and thought about Thomasyn's words.

"So they don't tell you any stories anymore?" she asked.

"Well, not that much anymore, usually we are studying."

That struck a chord in Gillian's heart. She stood and motioned Thomasyn to follow her.

"Stories are one of the best ways to teach the young about the past." They exited the hut and walked towards the well. "It helps us understand one another and teach about the past."

As they walked to the well, they heard the parents talk to their children, telling stories about how the harvest was many years ago. They kept walking past the well, down to the first field, watching the people working, talking, and laughing. Thomasyn observed for a few minutes at the interaction between parent and child. He started to realize what he had been missing all these years out of his life.

Gillian turned to him for a few seconds and reached out her hand. He took it and held tight. She felt a lump in her throat at the sign of tenderness from one so removed from emotion.

"Look, just because your mother and father are not alive, does not mean you don't have a family," Gillian said. "In fact, you have a mother and father."

Thomasyn looked up at her, a question in his eyes.

"Look, if something happens, who do you go to?" she asked.

"I go to Master Chail," he said. "Well, depending on what happened. If it's a problem with training I go to him. But if it's anything else I go to Nanny Tess."

"Well then, they are your parents."

"But we have many in our training group."

"And families have many people in them. There are brothers and sisters, aunts and uncles, cousins and nephews. In fact, most families aren't as well looked after as we are." She turned and faced him, placing a hand on his shoulder. "Think of it, Thomasyn, you and I are rich with family. We have hundreds of brothers and sisters, cousins and nephews. Every Spear is your brother or sister, every Wooder is your cousin or nephew, and every trainer is your uncle or aunt. A rich family life, if I say so myself."

It took a while to sink in, but Thomasyn did understand what she was trying to tell him. His world was much richer than the people he protected. In fact, it was much richer even than the Kings.

"We have to go soon; we have a lot more traveling to do. We actually have to meet up with everyone at the next town," Gillian said.

"Everyone?"

"Yes, everyone from your group of Spears and my group of Wooders. It is usually kept secret from the Spears while we train, but we have a gathering to do in Salman, the next largest town to the Realm's castle. Feel up for a run?"

A SCREAM WOKE BETHANY FROM THE DARKNESS. HER EYES

opened, and she tasted dirt in her mouth along with a salty stickiness. She groaned and pushed herself over onto her back.

A woman had come up to her and knelt, touching Bethany on the arm.

"Are you alright? Are you hurt?" she asked, brushing dirt and blood from Bethany's face.

"I'm not hurt," she said. It was a lie; she felt the bruise even now as it swelled up on the side of her head.

"You came with the Wooder. I can get him–"

"No, I'm good. I just need you to help me stand... oh."

Bethany tried to get to a sitting position, but the dizziness made her stop. She took a deep breath and pushed beyond it, using her arms to prop herself up. Her head spun, but she still looked around. The vision of the Hobs laying on its side, throat slit, surprised her, but not as much as seeing her dirk as the weapon that did it. Her spear and other weapons lay over to the side, just out of reach.

The sun was up but not high in the sky, making her think she had only been unconscious for a little while. Her mind recalled the vision, a man in the light, and she realized he was the one who knocked her unconscious.

"There was a man, in a cloak. Did you see him?" she asked the woman.

"No, I just came out to dump the chamber pot when I saw you. I wanted to make sure you were okay. You gave me such a fright when you moved." The woman looked around to see a couple of people staring. "Are you sure I can't get the Wooder for you? He's just over in the next hut with the old man."

"I think that would be a good idea," she said, feeling a little sick.

The woman hurried away for what seemed to be hours, but she returned after only a minute.

Cole rushed to her side, looking more concerned than she thought he should be.

"Are you alright?" he asked her, kneeling down.

"I'm good." She felt her forehead.

"No, you're not. Your eyes look foggy and you have a slight fever. I would say that you're probably sick to your stomach."

"I think I got a little of the blood in me," Bethany admitted.

"Hobs blood?" Cole asked rhetorically. "Not good. We have to be in the other town soon. Well, one way to cure that," he looked at the woman. "Can you get me some sea water?"

"Certainly," she said, and rushed off.

"I don't know how much you took in, how long do you think it's been since you took it in?"

"Maybe ten, no, twenty minutes ago, no more than thirty." Her head was really starting to swim and her stomach ached. Pins and needles raced in her belly as she sucked in her breath.

Cole took her hand and rolled the fingertips between his. He felt her forehead again and swore an oath to the five Gods while shaking his head.

The woman returned, carrying a small bucket of water. She put in down next to Cole.

"Is she in trouble?" the woman asked.

"Yes. Hobs blood is poisonous. We have to force as much out of her as possible," Cole explained. He took out a small pouch and emptied it in the bucket. He stirred it with his hand and scooped up the water and dripped it in Bethany's mouth. "This is going to taste bad, but you have to drink it. Drink as much as I give you."

She almost gagged. The taste of the salt along with a wooden chalk caught in her throat. She forced it down. He scooped more, and more, and more until her stomach reacted. She vomited. The whole of her insides felt like it was going to explode upwards and out of her mouth.

Cole pushed her onto her hands and knees. Her body expelled all it had in it, and he rubbed her back. Bethany's stomach tried to flee from her body. She kept retching even after nothing came out. She was astonished at the amount that had come out of her. She must have taken in half of the creature to have so much in her.

Cole stopped rubbing her back and slowly sat her on her haunches. He produced a small rag and wiped the blood and vomit from her face.

"Here, chew on this," he said, handing her a few leaves. They tasted familiar to her, like she had tasted them before. "Don't eat them, just chew. Let their essence settle into your stomach."

She did as he told her, and after a few minutes, she felt much better.

# TWELVE

They ran for several hours before Juliette called a stop. The land they traveled across was covered in short brush, and she could see the ocean when they broke out over the last hill. They were close to the city.

Jon saw the two others running across a field not far away. He waved to them, and the two changed their direction. Jon pointed them out to Juliette.

"We'll wait for them," she said to Jon, and opened her water skin, taking a drink. When Gillian and Thomasyn joined them, the two women rejoiced in the meeting.

"Thomasyn!" Jon called out. "You should have seen what happened."

Jon explained hurriedly about the encounter at the stronghold. He embellished concerning the fight with the bald man.

Gillian and Juliette hugged. Their expression of love made Thomasyn understand her words about family even more.

They stood idle for a few minutes before they started the last leg of their journey. In the distance, they saw the city of Salman, resting near the shore. Its mass of small buildings outside of the walls peppered the landscape, marking the farms that fed the people.

As they walked the rest of the distance, the group came across fields of grain, a golden sea of colour. The other fields stood green with tall stems of corn, and pastures were filled with livestock.

They skirted the sides of the fields, making their way to the well-travelled road connecting the city with the Realm.

"Why did we not just take the road?" Jon asked Juliette.

"It is more the journey than the destination, Jon," she replied. "That's the whole point of this test, to see if you appreciate the journey in life."

Approaching the city, they saw more of their fellow Spears coming as well. Jennifer, William, Fredrick, Paulette, Joseph, all part of their clutch. They travelled in the same direction toward the town. Each had a special story to tell the others when they met, all but Thomasyn, who kept the knowledge he gained close to his heart. He knew if Gillian wanted the others to know, she would tell them herself.

Thomasyn noticed that the Wooders who had taken the Spears were all from the same foresting. Each greeted the others with a familiarity the Spears did not share. The men clasped hands, giving back slapping hugs, and the women hugged each other softly. The casual and overly familiar greetings between the men and women Wooders astonished both Thomasyn and Jon. It was disturbing for the young Spears to watch.

"Why are you not kissing the boys?" Thomasyn asked of Gillian.

"It is something that is only done with those that have coupled. I have not coupled yet," she said to him.

"Coupled?" he asked.

"Been together. Juliette has been with a few, and she kisses those men, the others she just hugs. I have not... been with anyone."

"But why?" Thomasyn asked, not understanding. "You're just as beautiful as the other girls, maybe even more so," he said.

She smiled and lowered her head, blushing at his comment.

"You saw the scars," she whispered. "Not many men would think that attractive."

"But that is just on your skin. It doesn't mean you're not pretty. If you ask me, I think they are the stupid ones for not wanting to, what did you call it, couple with you."

"He is intelligent," Juliette said. "You know that Jorie wanted to couple with you even after the accident. Paul wanted to be with you, also. It's not because you didn't have a chance."

"It's because I don't want anyone to look at me differently," she finished. Her eyes looked to the sky. What could it have been like had she accepted one of the men's advances?

"I can ask one of them if they want to couple with you, if you like," Thomasyn suggested. "And if you want, I could couple with you. It just involves holding hands and kissing a little, right? I think you're pretty, and that would be okay, I guess."

Gillian and Juliette laughed, finding the words Thomasyn said to be some of the kindest they had heard from a Spear. Gillian took his hand, and though she stood a good foot over him, she bent down and hugged him, giving him a kiss on the lips. When she pulled away she saw the great big smile only a young boy could have when he felt the love of another come without reservation.

"Is everyone supposed to come to the city with us?" Jon asked.

"Yes, your clutch is supposed to make it today," Juliette said.

"What is it for?" Thomasyn asked.

"You'll find out." Gillian smiled at him.

As they travelled the rest of the way to the city, they were greeted with cheers from the villagers, as if they knew something special was about to take place.

The bridge to the inner city was down, with two guards standing outside it. They waved the Spears and Wooders through without even taking notice of them. It was something they knew in advance, something that happened every year at the same time.

The group walked toward the centre of the city, towards a large structure of stone. The stones started to show their ornate designs, and the perfection of their placement. There were archways of perfectly hewn granite, arching above statues of marble. Each statue appeared to represent a different city in the Realm.

They marched to the first opening, and saw the structure was a coliseum, with a great wall stretching fifty feet in the air all around. An odour came from the structure, and they were reminded of the training grounds.

As they approached, the group encountered a large double door which allowed them entrance to the interior. There stood Master Chail, dressed in his armour of office. A helm on his head was decorated with a horsehair plum and inscribed with designs representing different regions of the Realm. It shone with such ferocity that looking at it when the sun hit it would blind. Over his chest was a great coat of ring mail, shining as intensely as the helm. Over arms and legs he wore chaffs of hard leather, fastened with the ornate cloths of the Spears. Chail wore the cloak of a Spear, sparkling white as if encrusted with diamonds.

He wore a spear on his back, with an ornate sword at his side. The sword was a work of art, the pommel wrapped in soft leather. The end of the grip had the point of a spear formed out of silver. The scabbard was made of leather stitched with silver thread.

Master Chail stood smiling at his Spears as they entered the coliseum, counting as they came. His mind worked endlessly as he searched for the one face he did not see, Bethany. The corner of his mouth twitched a little, realizing she had not been in the main group as they entered the coliseum. The main doors were closing now. Chail looked up to the crowd to find Tess; concern clouded her face.

The cheering of the crowd covered the sound of the large doors closing. Master Chail scanned the faces again, locating Jon and Thomasyn, Sandra and Phillip and all the other Spears. Bethany was not by the side of her closest friends. He scanned the children again, his eyes flickering with concern.

Then he saw Bethany entering the arena from another door.

He peered, realizing something was wrong. She stood with a guard and moved slowly, as if trudging through mud. Chail's concern became obvious to Tess, who watched him. Her fear for what was about to happen was growing in her eyes, as well.

Realizing the importance of the day's events, Chail forced his concerns to the side. He looked out at the audience that had gathered, spreading his arms wide to them and bellowing in his loud baritone voice, "Citizens of Salman, I am pleased to announce the passing of the torch between the Spears of the Realm!"

A great cheer rose from the watchers. They roared and hooted to the children gathered in the arena, clapping their hands together in welcome. Master Chail let them continue for a count of twenty, and raised his hands again for quiet.

"Today, these fine Spears in Flight will take their first steps to becoming Protectors of the Realm. They have travelled for two days to be with us here, learning from the Wooders in the old ways of healing. They join us here today in order to take the very important step to being full-fledged Spears of the Realm.

"Today they have proved their value and have shown they are worthy of being accepted as protectors of the Realm"

The crowd cheered and clapped at the presentation as members of the Spears standing at the back of the arena came forward to the children with cloth of grey. They banded the cloth around the wrists of each child, tying them so they showed an ornate decoration embroidered in them. Others presented belts of leather to replace their old cloth belts. The leather belts were inlaid with branding of the year and silver studs marking each achievement.

"And now, we will honour our newest protectors!"

The children, now bearing the badge of a newly accepted Spear of the Realm, walked forward, proceeding to the dais. They climbed the steps and stood beside him, and he greeted each, congratulating them on being accepted. When he saw the lump on Bethany's head his eyebrow rose with a question, but she shook it off as if it was nothing.

As the last of the children stepped up on the dais, the great doors at the other end of the coliseum opened to admit the entertainment. It began with tumblers, men and women on stilts juggling torches and knives, large lumbering elephants and fools with bells. The crowd gaped at the tumblers, clapped at the jugglers, cheered the elephants and laughed at the fools.

It was like this every year after the parade of the Spears. The town would hold a grand festival to celebrate. Chail believed it was just a reason to drink and eat. At the last ceremony, he had left before the end. But this time, they were his Spears. He would stay with them through the end.

The children had not seen anything like the entertainment before. They cheered with the crowd as the tumblers and jugglers showed how well practiced they were. They laughed at the fools as they jumped and slapped each other, yelling and making the only thing they could out of each other, fools.

Once the entertainment had finished and filed out of the coliseum, Chail ushered the children together.

"This day is one of celebration. You are each given two silver points to spend as you will. Be warned though, one silver is a large amount of money to be walking around with, let alone two. Be mindful of the price of things that are being sold. Don't just buy it when someone offers it, but listen to what they offer to others before rushing in to purchase. Count all your change carefully to ensure you get back what is due you."

The young Spears took the silver, putting it into their wrist bands as Master Chail showed them.

"Remember, mind your money," he said again, as they left for the city proper.

Bethany, Jon and Thomasyn left as a group, talking about their adventures over the last two days.

"Two big men! Almost giants when you're next to them," Jon said.

"Jon, everyone is a giant standing next to you," Bethany laughed.

"No! I mean they stood over six feet each. Even the bald one was tall. And their brother was huge, as well."

"You have to stop spinning the long tales, Jon, you know people don't stand that tall," Thomasyn remarked.

"Then they must have had giant blood in them. Is there not a story about giants taking women and giving them babies with their blood in them?" Jon asked.

"Meat pies! Fresh baked meat pies!" came a cry from the side. The three looked over to see a man pushing a cart out a door laden with small pies. Jon looked at his friends and nodded.

"Two copper points," they heard the man say to a woman. She handed him four coins and took two of the small pies, juggling one with finger tips and one in her hand cloth.

"Are they good?" Jon asked of the woman.

"Are they good?" the cart pusher repeated. "Of course they are good! Best in Salman! Just ask anyone. Spicy and hot from the oven just now. My wife makes them with onions and garlic," he said, looking at Jon as if he had just insulted him. "You see, watch her eat."

The woman did eat the one pie, and then started on the other. The juice from it dripped down her chin, but it did not take long for her to catch it with the cloth as she walked away eating.

"I want one," Jon said to the man, holding out one of his silvers.

"Oh, my young Spear, I am yet to have change for such. I only have what the woman just gave me," he said, holding out the four copper points to prove it.

"So how much will my coin buy then?" Jon asked.

"Well, that would buy almost all on the cart!" the man said, looking at the shiny coin in Jon's hand.

"But that would be forty pies?"

"Forty eight!" the merchant said to him. "I had fifty, but the woman took two"

"We will come back," Jon said, looking disappointed. "I only have silver and would eat one, or maybe two myself."

The man looked at Jon and saw the disappointment in his eyes.

"You are the young Spears that passed today, right?" he asked, and the children nodded. "Then I will give you each two pies. But promise me, you will come and pay for them at the door when you have change," he said. The three smiled and nodded. He gave them each two pies. "Remember, back at that door when you have change."

The three promised to return with the change when they had it.

"Hot pies! Fresh baked!" the man bellowed, and he pushed the cart down the street.

Jon watched him leave and went to the door.

"We don't have the change he needs yet," Bethany said.

"Who says I need change?" Jon said. "Anyway, for all the food we get when we travel, I think it would be nice to return the kindness."

A plump older woman answered the door. She looked down at him.

"He was nice and the pies are good," Jon said, holding out a silver piece to her.

The woman's eyes went wide as she slowly reached out for the silver.

"How much change?" she asked.

"We had six pies, but I really liked them. We would have paid twelve copper points, but I think twenty would be better."

The woman looked at him, wondering if the young Spear was making fun of her. She decided he was not.

"Can you wait here for a little bit while I get change?"

Jon nodded, and she went inside. He looked in the shop and saw the wood ovens and a lot of baked goods. His mouth watered though he already had enough to eat. The woman shuffled about for a few seconds and then came back to the door. She counted out the change he had requested and looked at the three. She saw the bruise on the side of Bethany's face and that did it.

"Wait here a second," she said, turning and going back into the kitchen. She fussed about for a second and returned. In her hands, she had several squares, blue ones and red ones.

"Here, I figure if you paid so much for the meat pies, you should each get a treat for being good." And she handed a blue and red square to each of them. "And I want to see what you think of them. They are special today, just for your day."

The three young Spears smelled the squares and bit them. Their eyes opened wide with the explosion of taste in their mouths.

"The blue ones are blueberries from the Northern hills. They say the land makes them so sweet the hills weep when they are picked. The red ones are the heart berries from the Western lands. The tartness of them should make your lips pucker."

"Oh, these as so good," Bethany said, licking her fingers. "You used honey on them, right?"

"Oh, you don't ask a cook for her special ingredients," she said to Bethany. "But yes, honey and the juice of a grass from the southern island afar," she whispered to them.

"These are wonderful. I thank you," Thomasyn said.

The young Spears said their goodbyes and walked further on down the street, following the push of the crowd. It was a lot to take in, being on their own for the first time in a big city. They walked and finished their small tarts, enjoying the city.

## Year Eleven

"Come on Bethany, keep up," Thomasyn called back to her. He did not know why Bethany had been falling behind. It was only the start of the day.

"I don't feel well," she called to him.

It was their third day running and the young Spears had been extending their trek more and more. They knew once they hit the five days running mark, Master Chail would approve the use of horses for short outings. He always told them that no matter how fast a horse runs, you can always run further and longer than they can. It is just one of those small truths they experienced firsthand.

"Well, try, you're falling behind. You know what Master Chail can be like."

She pushed herself harder. Bethany did not want to tell them what she felt happening between her legs, of the tying up of her insides. She knew what her body was doing; Nanny Tess had warned her, and the other girls, about the changes they would be going through. The biggest shock was her chest, and the building up of what she was told were her breasts.

Nanny Tess had told her she could start binding her chest with cloth to make herself more comfortable soon. It was still a little too early in her growth to do it now. Soon her body will be ready to make babies, if she wanted to, but Bethany did not think that would be a good idea. Not yet, anyway. She could not think of any of the boys in her group climbing on top of her the way she had been told they could. Just the thought of one of them naked was enough to make her shiver. She told the girls she thinks boys have strange looking parts between their legs, and those parts always make her laugh and point.

She kept running, hoping the wetness would not be bad for the next couple of days. Bethany had cloth to protect her clothes, but they only went so far, and she really did not want to test it.

This was the first time her body had started to expel the blood, and it was not pleasant. Nanny Tess had talked as if it was a magical time when it happened, the signal of womanhood. But all Bethany could think of was the cramps she felt and the stickiness that came with it.

She still had not let any of the boy's touch her, and she really did not want to touch any of them. She knew in the future she would have a child and a husband to spend her time with. That is something she did look forward to, the change that would make her want to have children.

No, not really. It is something that would have to happen. She would need to have children, and they would not be Spears.

"Why are you slowing down?" Thomasyn asked. He had slowed also, falling back to run beside her. Bethany had not even noticed it, but he was now beside her, running in a casual way.

"I have to make water," she lied. He could tell it was a lie, he could always tell. But Bethany was sure Master Chail had not had the talk with the boys yet about the truth behind how babies were made.

"Well, then maybe you should stop and make your water. I'll wait for you, and we can catch up with the others once you're done."

"No! Euch! You keep running. I'll catch up soon," Bethany told him, and she slowed to a walk, changing her path towards some bushes that lined the road they ran on.

They had been running on the road for the last couple of months. Master Chail said it was to help improve their impression of the distance between cities and villages. She just thought he wanted them to use the road to hone their hunting skills when foraging for food. Game was easy to find when you travelled through the forest.

She looked around to make sure no one was near and dropped her britches. The bleeding was light, no more than a little dribble, but they told how bad it could be. Anne had hers first, and it was bad. It was as if someone had cut the girl, and the cut would not heal. That was when Nanny Tess had talked to all the girls.

The boys had wanted to come with them, thinking it was a lesson. That is until Nanny Tess had made them leave with the threat of extra work to do.

She had first tended Anne and told the girls about the flowering they would be going through. That magical time.

Bethany used a little water from her skin to wet a cloth and clean up between her legs. She folded another cloth the way Nanny Tess had shown her and tied it in place. She pulled up her britches and came out from behind the bushes, putting her clean up cloth into her pack.

"Are you hurt?" the shocked sound of Thomasyn came as he saw the blood on the cleanup cloth she had used.

Bethany stopped and looked at him. Of course, he would have ignored her request to be left alone and wait for her. Of all the times for him to be a good friend.

"No. Oh, just let me be," Bethany said, and she started to run in the direction the group went.

Thomasyn followed her, catching up quickly.

"I saw blood on the cloth. Are you okay?"

"Yes, I'm fine." Just becoming a woman.

"But the blood. Where did it come from?" Thomasyn persisted. He was curious and concerned for her. If she was injured he wanted to help her.

"Why don't you ask Master Chail about it," she snapped at him, and redoubled her efforts to catch up with the group, leaving him running at his usual pace, mouth hanging open.

"What did I say?"

---

THEY STOPPED FOR THE DAY AS THE LIGHT STARTED TO wane, picking a section of the road with a small clearing for them to camp for the night. The young Spears broke their formation and laid out their packs.

Everyone knew what was needed. One group broke off and started looking for firewood, while the small hunting group picked up bows and made their way into the brush. As usual, the hunting group was Jon, Bethany and Thomasyn.

"How long do you think we'll be out this time?" Jon asked, looking through the thicket.

"How should I know?" Bethany snapped back. Her stomach was feeling like a tight vice, and the knowledge she would have to change her cloth soon weighed heavily on her mind.

"What's got into you?" Thomasyn asked, looking over at her. "You keep biting at us for some reason. What's wrong? Have we done anything?"

Bethany bit her tongue. She just wanted to get back to camp and clean up, but the hunting was necessary to feed their group of twenty-seven souls. Two trainers had accompanied the group of twenty-five, so they had to make sure their hunt was successful.

"Oh, rabbit or bird? I heard they have wild turkeys here. Or maybe we can find a deer that would feed everyone," Jon said.

"And take forever to clean and cook. The guts would attract all sorts of animals, and the carcass would do the same with all the bones. Best to get the small birds and rabbits if we can. Anne will have a lot of the vegetables collected by then, maybe even some potatoes for cooking on the fire," Thomasyn said. "Besides, the birds will be easier to find than deer."

"And if you two keep talking, you'll scare everything around us off, and we won't find anything," Bethany shot back at the two in a hushed voice. Her bow was raised, and an arrow notched. She stomped her foot at the brush and four grouse broke cover in front of her. Bethany took aim and let lose her arrow. It flew straight and true, catching a bird in flight. Both Jon and Thomasyn pulled their arrows back and loosened them at a bird, each striking their targets.

"There should be more up ahead." Bethany pointed with her chin as she pulled another arrow. They crept forward to the spot their birds had fallen. They found the kills and pulled the arrows out of them. Jon volunteered to carry the birds until they caught their fill.

Another few yards and more birds lit to the air. Three more arrows let loose and down came three more birds.

"How many do you think we need?" Jon asked in a hushed tone.

"Three, no six more, to be sure. One for the trainers and eleven should fill the rest of us," Bethany said quietly, scanning the brush for further prey.

The friends felled three more quickly. Jon commented they must be in the middle of a bird breeding ground only to be hushed once again by Bethany. He did not like the way she told him to be quiet and was about to say something, then they came upon the site.

Up ahead of them, the brush cleared. In the centre of the clearing, they saw a fire pit; ash covered mostly burnt logs. It was a large pit, at least seven feet wide. Bethany saw it first, the charred remains of three villagers in the pit, their bodies contorted and black as coal, with a wisp of ash covering them.

Bethany sucked in a breath as Jon and Thomasyn approached the pit. They saw scattered about small stones in the clearing, as if they had been thrown haphazardly around. The pit had large river stones as the border, making the three of them wonder where they had come from.

Jon leaned forward as he went down on one knee and examined the body close to the edge of the fire pit. It looked like a full-grown man, and in good shape from the size of his shoulders.

"Something is not right here," Bethany said, looking from around, her eyebrows furrowed and mouth drawn tight. "I think we need to get the others here now."

The sun was almost completely down, and the three had turned to retrace their steps back to camp, when the sound of voices sent shivers up and down their spines, an eerie tone grinding and clashing off-key. The sudden sound of trees crashing caused them to jump, and they pulled arrows from their quivers, notching swiftly.

"We should go," Thomasyn said. "Whatever did this may be coming back, and it must be big to take three men out. We can return with the others if need be, but not until it is light."

"Agreed," Bethany said.

"Yes, we have enough birds." Jon was already moving backward, but slowed and scooped up a few of the loose stones, putting them in his belt.

As they made their way back, several birds flew into the air, and they claimed six of them on their way. They jogged back at a good pace.

Once they entered the camp, they sought out the trainers who had accompanied them on this outing.

They found Master Bethan and Falon near the fire, talking to the group who had finished their tasks. Falon looked up at the three to admire their catch.

"We need to get Anne to clean those birds for the fire," Bethan said.

"We found something in the woods back there," Thomasyn said. "There was a clearing and a fire pit–"

"–and three bodies in the pit," Jon interrupted.

The two trainers looked at each other for what appeared, to the young Spears, an eternity.

"Did you see any river stones?" Bethan asked.

"Yes! Here." Jon held out four of the stones he had picked up.

Bethan took them, examining the markings closely. He turned them over; he noticed each one had a strange marking on all sides.

"Have you seen anything like this Falon?" Bethan asked, tossing two of the stones to his companion.

Falon frowned and caught the stones easily. He turned them over and his brow furrowed, making large creases in his forehead. His eyes went wide, and he tossed the stones into the fire, and made a hex sign with his hand that circled his heart and nose before he spit at the fire.

"Witches!" he hissed. "Throw those stones in the fire or they will track to us."

Bethan threw his two stones in the fire.

"Girls, are any of you bleeding?" he asked, not being diplomatic about it.

Two girls besides Bethany blushed.

"Three. That is not good. We have to move quickly! Pack up everything, we're starting a night run immediately," Bethan said.

"What is it?" Falon asked.

"Witches hone in on three girls with the monthly bleed. If they are young, they will attack viciously with spells and hexes to capture the magic of their bodies. Our only hope is to be a league from here as soon as we can. Two hours of running should do it. Have the birds cleaned on the run, but we have to run. Now!"

The Spears broke camp quickly, and the fire was smothered. The packs went on backs and the group started to run on the road. Some of them carried torches to light the way and fend off the growing darkness.

---

The ground rumbled as three forms floated into the clearing. One large, bulky shape pulled off its hood and sniffed the air. Its large bulbous nose quivered, and the veins pulsed, sending lines across the scar riddled face.

"I smell blood," it said, turning the hideous head back towards the others.

Hoods came off the other two as they sniffed the air. The skin on their faces stretched over skulls. Lips parted and drool ran out of their mouths.

"Yes, one with blood," the smaller figure said.

They stood there for a few seconds, allowing the failing light to engulf them. The largest one, the first to smell blood, looked around the clearing, spying the movement of their charms. It swooped to the fire pit and examined the charred body closely.

"It is done," echoed an eerie voice. "The body is ready to harvest for the brew."

"But the blood!" the voice of the smaller one cried in earnest. "If there are more than just the one..."

"Enough!" the large one bellowed. "Three will be needed. If they are not three, we will be found..."

"We have been found," the third said, pointing to the ground. "Charms have been taken. The ritual is desecrated. Revenge is needed for this before our strength fails us. Leave the body; it is no good with the charms taken."

The large one screamed a hissing sound and looked at the others.

"I want my brew!" its breath wheezed out.

"Not now. We hunt them and take them. If they have more bleeding, they will be found."

The three figures pulled up their hoods and moved silently out of the clearing, following the path of the three young Spears.

---

"Move faster!" Falon called, as he made his charges push more than they had in the past. Before, they always rested for the night, not using the last vestiges of energy they would usually keep in reserve.

They had moved fast in breaking camp, not knowing why the rush was so important. The two trainers had just told them they would not be resting now; they needed to put distance between them and the clearing they had found.

The boys did not know what it meant to be bleeding, as Master Falon had called it. They wanted to ask questions, but only had time to do what they had been told to do and run.

They had formed the group in a running circle, putting the girls who had been identified as bleeding in the centre. All were told to make sure they stayed close, and not to let them slip behind.

"We need to get at least two leagues away," was all Falon would say. So they ran.

The night set in and the moon was split with half its face in darkness. Their feet pounded on the road as they pushed, trying to keep pace with each other. They ran and looked behind them as if to ward off what may come, but nothing did.

Once they had run for an hour, Master Falon allowed the group to slow, believing they had reached at least a safe distance. It was then they noticed something following them.

The call went forward, and both Falon and Bethan looked back.

"It is too late. They have followed us. Form a protective circle now!" Falon called out.

All the young Spears stopped and drew out their weapons, holding them point outwards, their backs to the centre of the circle. Falon and Bethan stood outside of it, looking at the perfect protection circle the group formed surrounding the girls. The appreciation of this group grew as they saw the way they worked as a team, not as individuals.

"If they approach, you will protect. They will be after the three and they must not have them," Falon spoke. "They are witches and will kill them for their unspoiled blood at this time. They would use it to make a brew to grow their power. We must be strong. If they come within length, poke your point in them fast, and do not linger, for they are likely to grab it if you do."

They waited, watching as the three images approached quickly. Jon knew this was not a test, but a real encounter like the giants had been a few years ago. He tensed a little, feeling the wood of the spear shaft in his hands.

The air seemed to chill as the three approached, making everyone's breath mist. The smell of rotten flesh engulfed them as the apparitions halted a few feet away, just out of spear thrust. The largest one pulled back its hood and smelled the air.

"Three! We want the three!" it said in a deep voice. When it spoke, the rank odour of decay rolled forth from a gaping mouth filled with broken teeth.

"You shall not get any, not the bleeding ones and not the others. Be gone evil, you are not welcome here. In the name of the five, you are not welcome!" Falon bellowed at them, his spear strapped to his back and the great sword he favoured held in front of him.

Bethan was ashen from the sight, wondering how such creatures had escaped his knowledge. He looked as the young Spears held fast, not breaking formation. He slowly inched towards Falon and whispered to him.

"What do we need to do?" he asked.

"We need to break their covenant, pry them apart from one another, and they lose their power," he replied.

"Can they be killed if need be?"

"Yes, but only a perfect hit in the heart will do it, and their bodies will be twisted under the cloaks."

Before the two knew what was happening, a torch sailed over their heads and hit the large witch in front of them. The creature watched in horror as the flames licked its cloak and spread up. The witch screamed in frustration as it first tried to pat down the flames, but to no avail. It pulled the cloak off its body and threw it to the ground in disgust.

All eyes stared at the creature. It was naked and twisted. Its spine must have been contorted over the years of its life, bending back and forth, forward and back. The legs that supported it seemed strong but misshapen, shins bowed out and thighs bowed in. Its manhood hung disfigured between its legs as it moved away from the burning cloak. The body was not only twisted and slumped, but it appeared to have faces molded into it. As the body moved, the eyes of the faces opened in terror, and the mouths gaped in silent screams.

"Now!" Thomasyn shouted, and three of the young Spears threw with deadly accuracy. One aimed for the left side of the creature's chest, the other aimed at the right and the last to the centre. The spears flew swift and true, puncturing the creature at the same time.

The air grew electric as the three witches shrieked. A rending sound erupted as the creature tore at the spears puncturing its body. The other two stood watching in horror. It looked at the group and rolled its head back, grabbing at two of the spears, but could not pull the weapons from its chest.

A last gasp of breath gurgled from the witch's body as it fell forward, driving the spears the rest of the way. The other two gyrated in pain and collapsed on the spot. The atmosphere immediately lifted to a warm breeze filling the area.

"Their covenant is broken, they are no more," Falon said, as he watched the three girls walk forward to retrieve their spears.

# THIRTEEN



Thomasyn stood looking at all the tubs steaming with hot water. His body had changed a lot over the last year, hair sprouting on his chest as well as between his legs and lower body. It itched, causing him to scratch at times, which made a certain part of his body react another way.

Now, standing there in the bathing room, he looked down at himself and saw it pointing up at him. He could just let it stay that way, but he could not make water. He would usually just let it stand up, swollen and hard, and it would go back down after a while. Sometimes he woke in the night to see it like this, and sometimes his bed was sticky wet, and not from his body's water. A dire concern, but Master Chail said it was natural.

He heard someone coming and jumped in one of the tubs. The water was nearly scalding, but he liked the heat. He immersed himself; the heat loosened his muscles, and he started to use the brush with the hard-caked soap.

"...but that is what she said we should do. Kiss and see what happens," a voice came from the hallway. The voice broke with adolescence from the hall. It was Bastion, a boy in his group. Bastion was always around Anne, even though Anne was usually around Jon. He lowered himself further into the water, staying under the lip of the large tub.

"And what did you do?" Jacob squeaked.

"What do you think I did? I kissed her. She even touched me," he said, exaggerating with his lips as he came in the bathing room. Jacob was walking with Bastion, along with Tannis. The three boys stripped, getting ready to climb in tubs as well.

"This hair is strange. I have it under my arms now. What about you?" Tannis said.

"Yes, but it's not bothering me," Jacob said.

"I have lots, see?" Bastion stood up and lifted his arms.

The boys started to laugh and Bastion looked down to see his private pointing up at him. He smiled and swung his hips around, pointing at it.

"See my spear? It's big and strong and I put it where I want to," he sang out, thrusting his hips. "See the hair? I have lots of it. Soon I will have a lot on my chest as well," he boasted.

Thomasyn knew not every part of a boy's body would get hair. Master Chail told the boys about that, as well, and Bastion's chest was as hairless as a newborn. The rest of him sprouted it in great waves, especially around his "spear".

Jacob stood as Tannis walked from behind a tub. Tannis was not excited as the others, but he did have a little hair. The three boys stood there for a few seconds and then picked their tubs.

Thomasyn stayed low in his tub, not making a sound. He did not enjoy the company of the three, but he did not truly dislike them either. They had a loudness to them he did not really care for. They never stopped talking.

He knew the bragging was a lie. Knowing this did not help. Anne would not kiss such a fool, because she only had eyes for Jon. Thomasyn remained low in the water while the others finished bathing, stepped out of their tubs, dried and left in an extremely loud ruckus.

Thomasyn stood and finished scrubbing himself clean, noticing that he was no longer excited. The towel beside the tub was very soft to the touch, and his body was dry in no time.

He thought back to the talk Master Chail had with the boys, and how uncomfortable the trainer had seemed. His explanation of what their bodies were going through had been confusing, and they did not truly understand the references. All they knew was a boy, or man as Master Chail told it, put himself in the girl, or woman, and planted seed.

The thought of planting while putting himself in a girl made him curious about what Master Chail really meant. He wondered if that was why all the small folk planted all the time. Just to make sure they had children? It would explain why they had so many. He just did not understand why it was put in the woman when the man plants it in the field.

But that was not his worry. Tomorrow would be the day Master Chail and Nanny Tess would marry.

They had announced they would be married soon because they loved each other. They had not married earlier, believing the children needed their utmost attention. But the children were almost adults now, and soon would be sent out with other Spears, assuming the duties of protecting the Realm. It would be a glorious day when it happened, and Thomasyn was looking forward to it.

He walked out of the bathing room and towards the barracks. A partition was built two years ago to separate the large room. One side held the girls and one side was for the boys. During the day, they pulled the partition aside to allow them to walk amongst each other.

Now the partition was closed. Thomasyn could hear the girls talking and giggling, he did not understand why. He approached quietly, his curiosity aroused, trying to be as stealthy as possible.

When he reached the partition, he knelt down to listen, but it did not help much for they were at the far end. Thomasyn could only hear a little bit of the words being said, so he leaned a little more against the partition.

He heard talk about the dress Nanny Tess would wear, and the food they would be serving to all the Spears. Thomasyn already knew they would be at the wedding. Master Chail had asked Master Gaion to stand with him during the joining. Nanny Tess had asked Sister Lila.

It would be a short ceremony, joinings always were. The feast afterword would be the stuff of legends. Master Chail was high enough of station to warrant the King and Queen's attendance, so the repast would be very elegant. Afterword, there would be dancing with the girls. Thomasyn looked forward to it, even though most of the girls in the troop were a quarter of a foot taller than most of the boys.

His only concern was if he would be able to dance with Bethany. She had been very friendly with him of late, more than just the ordinary friendship they shared when they were younger. Sandra had been trying to be friendly with him also, but after the problem when they were seven, he had tried to shy away from her, especially when he discovered what they had actually been doing.

The memory brought up thoughts of Michael, and the vengeance they took out on Master Dress. The trainer was the reason Michael was dead, and the Spears had taken Master Dress's life for payment of such. No, being close to Sandra had too many memories.

The tapping of a foot interrupted his melancholy. He looked up to see Bethany. She was standing there in her small clothes, hands on hips, as she glared down at him. She had grown over the last year, filling out both in height and other areas. It was her chest most of the boys saw first when she came in a room, rather than her spear and sword. Even in her fighting uniform, you could not mistake her for anything but a girl.

He blushed and stood up, wiping his knees with his hands.

"I thought I heard something..."

"Yes, us. We were having a private talk when your elephant feet hit the floor. It is rude to listen in on private talks, you know."

"Sorry. I just wanted to know what was happening."

"Well, next time just barge in, why don't you, and we can all laugh at your little spear," she scowled at him "Boys!" She walked away.

---

THE SUN CRESTED OVER THE HORIZON, THE NIGHT CHILL receded, and a mist rose. Men and women in the capital of the Realm started their day. Cooks lit kitchen fires, moved pots about, and began to get ready.

One such kitchen started to get ready for the order they had received the week earlier. The cooks broke off chunks of yeast and mixed them in sugar water in order to prepare a mix. Large cups of flour ground just a few days prior were piled into mountains and lard was melted slowly with salt.

In another section of the city, a butcher awoke and washed his hands. He needed to get the meat cut and ready for the ovens just a few doors down.

The butcher was old, near his seventieth birthday, and he still insisted on sharpening his own knives. His children had been in the shop for an hour and they had already removed the meat from the hanging area for his inspection. It was an honour to him, being picked for this celebration, and he was not going to let his customer down.

When he had finished washing and dressing, he walked down the stairs on his creaking knees, taking each step slowly in order to keep his feet under him. His foot touched the floor of the shop and he raised his pale blue eyes to see his sons. Each had picked two sides of beef and placed them on the butchers table. They had picked the best of what they had in the basement, but would not do anything without his approval.

The butcher moved from one son's offering to the other, smelling the meat and running his fingers over the flesh to tell how tender it was. He nodded and pulled out his knife, along with a sharpening stone. The stone was worn in the centre from the constant drawing of the knife-edge against it. His practiced hand held the stone for the edge of the blade as he pushed it down. He drew the knife in circles, making the stone hone the edge.

He passed the knife over the stone with no sense of urgency and then tested the edge of the blade. It was sharp, as sharp as it would get. He nodded with satisfaction.

His eldest son flipped the first side of beef over to expose the outside. The old butcher ran his fingers along the bones and started to cut the meat. He was an expert at his craft. In fact, there was no one else in the Realm who matched his skill. The knife followed the bone, whittled around connective tissue, and within seconds, the loin was free. A smile crossed the old man's face. Yes, that will do.

The fish market was opening as several of the small crafts hit the beach not a mile away from the city. The fleet had been out all night for the catch.

Men ran in the water with wicker baskets. They approached the boats, water up to their waists, holding their baskets to the crews, who filled and handed them to their monger. Each boat had their own workers who would put the fish in barrels of seawater to keep them fresh.

One monger who had an order for sea bass, made a deal with the mongers beside him. He would forgo all fish but this one type, and they would supply him with those he needed.

He filled his barrels and thanked his fellows for their help, and made his way to the city to supply the order for the feast.

The young Spears started to wake up for the day. It had taken many of them a long time to fall asleep the night before, and now they felt it. They rubbed their eyes, stretched their arms, and yawned. Some tried to shake the sleepiness out of their heads, turning one way and then another.

A member of the kitchen staff entered the barracks with a bucket of tea and a push tray of cups. She ladled cup after cup of the black tea, and handed them to the children to help them wake up. She then shuffled them off to wash and clean.

The boys went to one bathing room and the girls to another. They had only started to separate three years ago, just a year before one of the girls had bloomed.

The bathing room baths had been filled with hot water and a scrubbing soap for each. They all bathed, scrubbing themselves clean. Once clean, they returned to their barracks to find new uniforms laying on each bunk for them.

The boys found pants to wear and the girls, skirts. A change had been done to each of the uniforms to include a special design approved by the King, that of a spear standing on end to symbolize the uniqueness of their clutch.

As they marvelled at the new uniforms, two members of the kitchen staff brought in push carts with bread and cheese for breakfast. The young Spears ate their fill, knowing they could be waiting a long time for their evening meal.

The morning was not as structured as it usually was. They did not have training, they did not have drills, and they did not have classes. No, they had been ordered to just pay attention to two of the most important people in their lives, Master Chail and Nanny Tess. These two important people would be joining their lives together after being in love for over ten years.

The girls shuffled out of their side of the barracks to see the boys waiting for them. Each one knew who they had been matched with for the procession, so they moved about each other, finding their partners.

Thomasyn waited for Bethany to come to him, and Jon waited for Anne. And when they did, the boys held out their arms as escorts, the way they had been told to. The girls took their arms and together they perambulated to the two tents set up outside in the training square.

---

He woke slowly, the way he liked. A small beam of light entered his bedchamber, telling him what time it was, and giving enough light to see the small chamber.

His arms pulled the heavy wool blanket off his body and swung his legs out of the bed, onto the floor. Cold greeted his feet and caused him to pull up quickly. He gasped at the shock. *Where is my damn acolyte and why is the floor cold?* He thought.

"Jason!" he screamed. "Jason! Get in here!"

He heard a crash. Something hit the floor and the slap of Jason's feet running up the hall towards him. He waited and was rewarded by the door to his chambers flinging open. The boy he had taken in to train stood there, out of breath.

"You will have to start exercising if you cannot run here to answer my call," he scolded the boy.

"Yes, Chanter of the Word," Jason said, gasping for his breath.

"Why is the floor cold? Why has it not been heated from below?" he asked, perturbed he needed to ask.

"I... It... It was the edict, Chanter. All joining ceremonies are to be performed with the start of the cold. I remember you read it to me a number of times this year," the boy explained, worried.

"For the ones being joined, you idiot. Were you dropped on your head when your mother pushed you out? Get to the basement and light the fires." His feet wavered over the floor and the boy turned. "Stop. It is too late for that now. My feet are cold and my mood tuned sour. Fetch me some sweet bread and hot tea to take the chill out of my bones."

The boy looked at him and saw the look on the Chanter's face. He had seen that before, the day a serving woman had scoffed at a soiled bedchamber. The Chanter had been incensed, striking out and knocking one of her teeth from her mouth. He sent her away, never to return.

"What are you doing there? Go get my breakfast."

The boy shook his head and ran off.

The Chanter put his feet back on the floor and scowled again, lifting them just as quickly. He looked around and saw the slippers he usually wore, and stretched out his legs to get them. When his toes found them he slipped them on and stood. His night shirt draped down to his ankles, covering his bony body.

He looked at his bed and saw the yellow stain from the night, and smelled the odour of his own urine. As he looked down on himself he noticed the same stain on the front of his night shirt.

"Am I that old that I cannot hold my water through the night?" he asked himself. Of course, he was old, almost at his ninetieth name day, and he realized soon, one night, his eyes would not open again. He would have to find someone to take over the head of the order. But who? The boy? No, he was just a whisperer, and hardly knowledgeable, like some of the ones before him. No, he would have to find a replacement from somewhere else. Maybe from another church in the out country, or maybe even Salman.

He shivered again and wondered what was taking the boy so long.

"Boy! Where is my breakfast!" he yelled as he crossed to the dresser and changed his nightshirt.

The boy came back, and faster than most would have. He carried a tray, and on it was a cup of steaming tea with a half loaf of sweet bread covered in butter, steam still rising from it.

"Just out of the oven and the boiling pot. Please mind the tea. I wouldn't want it to burn you," the boy said.

The Chanter took the cup and used it to warm his hands, his bony hands with the flesh no longer soft or subtle, but worn, cracked and smooth. His mouth worked up and down for a second while he contemplated the day ahead of them, but he could not focus.

"Have them draw a bath and make it warm. My bones are chilled and I need to be presentable today." He sniffed at the tea, shuffling his feet forward. As he passed the boy, he reached out and snatched the sweet loaf from the tray and stuffed it in his mouth. It was hot and sweet and perfect. A swig of the tea melted the treat and he swallowed.

"And get me the other half of that sweet bread."

***

Milon woke before her husband, stretching her arms and legs. The bulk of her body made it difficult to get out of the bed without waking Savoy, but not impossible.

She heaved her body to the edge of the bed and put her feet on the floor. Milon rolled a little forward and then back till her feet touched the floor, and her body lifted from the bed. Milon walked over to the clothes horse and took the large robe, putting it around herself.

The door opened, and a chambermaid entered, curtsying quickly and moving to the bed to collect the chamber pot. Milon ignored her, consumed in her search for something to eat. It was her custom to search out some sweet breads in the morning to take the poor taste out of her mouth.

"Me, Lady." It was the voice of Tullie, the head servant who tended the royal couple. "You are up early again, I see. Do you have a need I can supply?"

"No, Tullie, just heading to the kitchen."

"As you will, me Lady," he said, and made way for her to pass.

She smiled, for Tullie was her favourite. He always took care of her, making sure she was happy and fed. It was why she had gained so much weight over the last few years.

Milon's feet moved one in front of the other with a quickening pace as the odour of fresh baked breads enticed her. The way was longer than she wanted, but worth the trip. Once outside the kitchen, Milon took a breath and pushed open the doors.

Four cooks moved about, shoving raw dough in the ovens, and pulling out beautiful breads and tarts. She watched as they worked and waited till what she wanted was ready. Her father had always told her to make sure she took the time to enjoy life and food. He had died at the old age of seventy, and well over three hundred pounds. He was a well-loved king, for he did not tax the people heavily and he allowed the Spears to dispense justice without hindrance. Her husband was not like that.

It was a marriage of need, not love. And to make matters worse, her husband was mean to most, and a very cold man in bed. Savoy's idea of making children involved climbing on top of her and putting himself in her for only a few seconds. He loathed touching, especially in public. But he did give her three children who she raised herself, teaching them the proper love a woman needs. She believed, for the most part, she had been successful.

Lemon squares finally came out of one of the ovens. Her hands clapped in delight as the large sheet of them was put out to cool before cutting. They steamed on the table as the fragrance filled the room. By far her favourite way to have breakfast.

The baker saw she watched the large square with a hunger in her eyes. He knew the queen had a kind heart and wanted to make sure she was rewarded for such. He came over and sliced the blocks, moving five pieces aside and motioning to them.

"My Queen," he said with a smile.

She looked at him, mouthing a thank you, and he winked at her as he walked back to the ovens.

She scooped one and started to munch on it, loving the taste. Her desire for more swelled as she finished another one, then she took another, and then another. Before she knew it she had eaten the five and was feeling quite full.

It was time to wake the bastard of a husband now and get ready for the day.

---

"I am a little uncomfortable in this dress uniform," Chail said, pulling at the collar of the sir coat. The new uniform had been commissioned by his wife to be Tess, and he was still uncomfortable about her picking out what he was to wear. Chail looked over at the rest of the ornate equipment he was supposed to wear and cringed a little.

"Are all the children going to dress like this as well?" he asked.

"Mostly," Con said, as he adjusted his own collar.

The sir coat was only the first of the uncomfortable items they both wore. A sash went across their shoulders and around their waists, and the pants seemed to be very tight making Con feel exposed due to his lack of manhood.

"I will say this, your bride has a way of making one feel very ill endowed," Con said, looking at how the pants fit his body. "She was married once. Am I not correct?"

"Yes, but he died before she lost her child. Do you not remember interviewing her for the position of wet nurse?" Chail asked.

"I interview many women every month. Some I accept and some I reject. Most I reject," he said, thinking back on that day. He did remember it. She had been shy, her child having passed away just a few days after his birth. Tess had entered the selection process the day after and tried not to become attached to anyone, but that did not happen. She fell in love with the children, and then afterwards, Chail.

Con remembered her. He remembered every woman that came for the interview process, but he did not need to tell Chail that.

"I may have a brief recollection of her," he admitted the understatement.

"I am sure you do."

"Well, of course I do, but I don't know what that has to do with anything," Con said. "We are all grown people. She needed a position, and we needed her services. And after that service was fulfilled, the children needed her once again. It is fortunate they loved her, as well."

"I think this group of Spears loves us all."

"You have that opinion, but I hold no illusions on how they feel about me. Neither indifferent nor loved. It is something I will have to live with."

"You are loved, Con. Don't let yourself be fooled. The children love you in their own way."

"But I do not fool myself. I have no misconceptions. They see me but once a year to measure their progress and insure they are well. They have more contact with the Wooders than with me."

"They notice you more than you know. By the five! How does this thing fit me?"

<hr>

"Well, young ladies, what do you think?" Tess asked the girls as she spun around in her dress. She was ready. Finally ready to marry the man she met over ten years ago. She had not thought love would happen again after she lost her first husband and her only child.

"I think it makes you look beautiful," Bethany said.

"Yes," Anne agreed. "You look very lovely in that dress."

The dress had an off white colour, with a sash across the front. It clung in the right areas, just like she had ordered it, and now she was using it to marry Chail and the twenty-seven children he had adopted when he took the position.

The girls were all nodding approval. They loved Nanny Tess and wanted to make sure she felt accepted, even if she was old in their eyes. She had reached an old age of thirty-six, with very little problems due to her position with the Spears. Her ready access to the Wooders kept her healthy, and the children kept her active, and that kept her happy. That and Chail.

The time was drawing near for the ceremony, and she knew they had to get to the temple; that was why she dressed early. But her concerns were unfounded–she had a lot of time left.

She stood there while the girls fussed about to make sure she was ready. They moved about, paying attention to the little things like her hair, the dress, seeing if a flower was right.

They are blooming, she thought, watching the girls move about. She wished the children could stay with them, but they would be assigned new roles soon. She only had one more year to be around these wonderful people and then they would be assigned to full-fledged Spears for one on one training. It will be hard to say goodbye to them when the time comes, went through her mind while she watched them move about.

"Okay, girls, I think we are ready," she said, straightening up. "It is time for me to get joined."

THE PARADE THROUGH THE CITY FOLLOWED THE SAME route they had taken just a few years ago, when the Spears spoke their vows. All the boys followed Chail as the people of the city parted, as tradition dictated.

It was a slow and tedious walk for Chail, who was anxious to join with Tess. He had to control the pace in order not to look as if he was running. His chest was out with pride, though the sir coat restricted his breathing. The sun was at its zenith, beating down upon them all, and making it easy to forget it was fall. And when they reached the steps of the temple, Chail looked up to the top of the spires, to see all of them had been marked with gold and blue cloths bearing elaborate designs of spear heads.

Chail knew they had not been ordered by Tess, so it must have been done by another. The only person who had the ability to do it would be the King, and Chail was very impressed the ruler would do such for them.

Standing there, Chail looking at the temple for a short time, mentally going over his words. Tess had requested they write their own vows, so it would be special, and just for them. All the children wore the same dress uniform, down to the final details of the wooden buttons which held their shirts together.

He decided he had stalled long enough, and the nervous groom must make way for the anxious husband. Chail looked back at the children, who smiled and nodded their approval. Once done, Chail climbed the steps to the doors of the temple and entered it, holding his breath.

———

SHE STOOD THERE, WAITING TO ENTER THE TEMPLE, DRESSED and ready to marry. The girls waited around her for the signal to enter the main chamber; the rapping, which said everyone was ready.

Her face had been scrubbed and powdered, making it appear paler than it actually was. The red berries had coloured her lips, leaving a sweet taste in her mouth, making it water. Her stomach was rumbling, and the worry showed slightly across her forehead.

Candles were lit in the room, making sure all could see, for no windows adorned the walls. The smell of the burning wax was a little sickly, but she was able to put up with it, just like the thoughts raging through her mind. She wondered if he really did love her, or if she was just a way of filling time. If Chail would be gentle with her, or not. She knew he was kind to her, but that was only because they were always in public, with Spears usually around them.

The soft rap came on the door, telling her that they were ready for her to come out. It was time for the joining, the ceremony that would make them man and wife. She blushed and looked at the girls as they waited patiently, looking for her to tell them what to do.

"This is it," she said. "The five will guide us through this day." She walked towards the door and opened it to the main part of the temple.

———

ALL WERE STANDING, LOOKING DOWN THE AISLE. ONE MAN stood there at the end expectedly, hoping she would be with him. This was one time he had no real control over what happened, so he could only wait and hope she did follow through. His fear mounted as he wondered if she had changed her mind, but the thoughts were short-lived.

The door swung open, allowing the girls to walk out in procession. They moved forward, walking down the aisle, looking as pretty as any young woman could.

Once they had taken the customary positions, Tess came down the aisle, looking stunning in her dress. Chail felt a lump in his throat when he saw her, the essence of her, as she started to walk towards him. It would be a simple ceremony, and then they would be as one.

---

The Chanter spoke loudly for all to hear, explaining about the joining of the two together in order to make one. Through the ceremony, Chail and Tess watched each other, waiting for their cue to say their words and swear their vows.

"And you will now speak your vows to each other in the presence of these witnesses and the five," the Chanter said.

They looked at each other, nodding and speaking at the same time, just as they had rehearsed.

"We share our lives from this point forward, not forsaking the love we have had or have. We vow to be man and woman, husband and wife, mates from this time till we join with the five. We swear this in front of witnesses and the five represented by all here."

"And with that, you are now joined. Two that are one, two lives will now move forward together, and not apart."

The Chanter spoke the words and clapped his hands together five times to signify the completion of the ceremony.

The two newly joined turned to the witnesses and walked to the doors, smiling happily, making their way to the feast.

# FOURTEEN



"Thomasyn, Bethany, Jon! Front and centre," Chail called out, standing at the door of the barracks.

He stood looking down at the only occupied bunks remaining. It was hard to say goodbye to the children, but something told him it would even be worse with his three best students. These three stayed together through all the early years until now, when the last of the assignments would be given to them as Spears in Flight. He did not want to give them out; no, he wanted to keep these three here with him and Tess. They had grown up with him, and he loved them dearly.

Tess was watching from the hall, wiping tears away from her eyes as her favourite children came forward to talk to their master. They each looked at him with love and respect. Respect earned after long days of training them, listening to them and teaching them. Love, because he had been one of the few constants in their lives, and had been there for them during their initiation to the Spears.

Yes, there had been others, but none as much as Chail. He was the leader of the group who trained them. Chail was a father to them. He loved them, and he would not let anything harm them, and they knew it. Today, this would hurt him more than he wanted to admit. Today he would have to send them forth for the final training assignment for a Spear. Today they join a garrison.

Pushing the children out into the world would be the worst experience. There will be shock, having only been exposed to the capital and Salman. The world is a much more different place than they have grown up in. But that's why Seasoned Spears would be assigned to them for the final training, to handle anything the children would be unfamiliar with. The Spears would be able to help them judge what is right, and what shades of grey lay between them and the darkness. With luck, he would see them again in another year, after they have travelled and learned.

Chail watched as the three approached. Their easy gait did not hint at the speed at which the new Spears could move if needed.

He felt pride as Thomasyn smiled at him; he did not return it, but examined all three of the children closely. They carried themselves with honour, and an air of confidence surrounded them, having not yet experienced the pain of failure. It was the arrogance of youth.

"Yes, Master Chail," Thomasyn said, as the trio stopped in front of him.

"I have your assignments," he said with a smile. "It will be an interesting assignment, to say the least. You three are to travel to the Teeth of the World, to Mountain City. You are to oversee the justice of the Dwarfs for the next year, with the Spears already assigned there. The journey is long and will take several weeks, if not a month, of travel.

"I want you to be mindful of the journey you are about to undertake. It can be a treacherous trip," Chail said, looking sternly at the young Spears.

"We will, Master Chail," the three of them responded as one.

Jon looked over Chail's shoulder; he was almost as tall as his old teacher. He saw Tess standing at the end of the hall, teary-eyed. Jon smiled and winked at her, then looked back at Chail who was staring at him.

"Sorry, Master Chail," Jon said, making his face deadpan again.

"You will be traveling with Masters Garion and Shail. You will be safe with them. Mind what they say, you can still learn much from them. You will be allowed horses in order to make the travel easier."

"But we don't need–" Bethany started.

"I didn't ask what you needed. You will have horses. You will have to take care of them. The horses are not just for you to ride; they are for the city garrison. Be fortunate, for you could have been assigned to take carts and supplies, and that would have slowed you tremendously."

"Yes, Master Chail," they said again in unison.

"So, what are you waiting for? Pack and saddle up for the journey," he bellowed at them.

GARION STOOD UP IN HIS STIRRUPS, LOOKING TOWARDS THE stables. His nose wrinkled from the smell of the horse. He really did not like being a deliveryman, though it was part of his job as a Spear; to take what was needed and deliver it to others.

He was looking forward to the trip, though. It will be the first time in years he had travelled so far north. Garion was hoping to see the four dwarf brothers of the Halton Pass mine.

The last time he had seen them was over ten years ago, a long time for a man, and a heartbeat to a dwarf. The week they had spent together, he was shown how they mined the jewels and precious metals from the mountain. During that time, they had shown him not only how to dig, but to smell the metal, and taste the dirt that held jewels, as well as how to drink. They could swallow more than a man twice their size without stopping. It seemed that neither mead nor wine could quench their thirst.

He had tried to keep up, only to fall behind in the tankards of ale he had ordered. The first morning he woke and felt as if his head was twice the size it actually was. The day after he had lost his stomach midway through the drinking and feasting, making the dwarf brothers laugh. They had teased him for hours as he tried yet again to pour the same amount of ale down his throat.

They not only drank, but they ate. They ate so much he swore he gained many pounds in just a few days. The dwarfs would eat just about anything they could get their hands on; cooked meat, potatoes, greens, grubs, moss, and lichen. The lichen was what finally did Garion in.

"Move it, you Spears!" he called out to the young ones.

"You are so concerned with when we are leaving. Why must you rush the young ones? They have not been on horseback much in their 14 years," Shail said.

"I grow tired of having these walls about me. Men were meant to be out in the open, with the life of the Five around them. This is no way for people to live, so closely packed together they cannot tell who I am from a simple smell," Garion said.

Bethany was the first out of the stables, astride a beautiful chestnut mare. She sat in the saddle with perfect form, riding the beauty towards the two masters, who watched with shocked surprise. It was as if she had been born on the horse, guiding the horse effortlessly with gentle nudges from her knees.

Jon and Thomasyn came out next, both astride their stallions, as naturally gifted as Bethany, moving them with calm precision. They were talking and laughing with each other as they made their way to the two masters.

The two masters led them out of the city to the road that would take them off the peninsula. It would take at least a week to make it to the mainland.

The two warned the young Spears about what they could run into; giants, bears and maybe Hobs. Bethany was surprised they had not been told about her encounter with a Hobs. She let them know about it, and how it had almost cost her the parade of Spears.

"It is fortunate you had a seasoned Wooder with you. Most who take in Hobs blood die without knowing why," Shail said.

"And others transform in one way or another to a Hobs, as well," Garion commented. "Have you heard about the tale of the Lost Spear?" Bethany and Jon shook their heads.

"Is that the story of Spear Danton? Wooder Aimond told it to me a few years back when I visited him," Thomasyn said.

"Then you know the story. Wooder Aimond tells it well. He'd developed a bard's heart after the accident that claimed his sight. Well, by all means, tell it as you remember." Bethany and Jon echoed

Garion's request, and Thomasyn started the telling as they left the city.

Thomasyn felt as if he would not do it justice, but after chiding by Jon and Bethany, he surrendered to their requests, and tried to tell the story as best as he could. He spoke elegantly, retelling to the best of his ability, and when he was finished, the other two looked at him, their eyes wide with surprise.

"You never told me that story," Bethany accused.

"I bet you heard stories also, and you never told me," he said in return.

"Well, you could have at least told me about that one," Jon said, looking dejected.

"As close to telling it as I have ever heard," Shail said. "It is indeed a true story. Danton was a Spear, the best of them. He lost his way, but there is no knowledge of why he changed. Was it because of lust or was it because he drank the blood of one of the Hobs? It is unknown. All we know is because of him; the edict ordering Spears to never marry or have children was struck down. Before, they had to stay celibate."

It was not until the end of the story that they took in the surroundings and found the city streets had given way to a well-travelled dirt road. Garion just nodded. "It is the mark of a good story, to make it hard to realize how far you have gone during the telling," Garion said. "I could tell another one if you like."

The three young ones nodded at this, expecting maybe another story about the Hobs.

"It was from a long time ago, when the king of the land at the time wanted to make the riches of the land his own. He decided the Dwarven people would be able to help him, so he sent messages to the King of the Dwarfs, asking if they would mine the mountains for him.

"The Dwarf king was a shrewd and proud man, thinking he was smarter than all others in the world." Garion looked over to the children, and they returned his gaze, expectantly. "He accepted the Realm King's emissary with kindness, putting a feast together that would show him the best of their world. He plied him with food and mead, pushing more and more in the man till he could not stand any more.

"When the man almost toppled over from drink, the King of the Dwarfs showed him a contract for digging the Teeth of the World. He put his seal on it and turned it to the emissary, who signed it and affixed the King of the Realm's seal." Garion smiled at the children, widening his eyes to show the amusement the Dwarf King would have shown. "The King of the Dwarfs cried out in triumph and yelled 'See!' to the emissary 'See! I have won from you! I will be rich and your king will have nothing but the smalls.'

"The Dwarf King danced around the feasting table. He pranced and danced and went parading about. And once he had done parading for several minutes, he puffed, his breath having left him. He came to the emissary and sat across from him, his lips spilling forth froth into his great beard at the exertion.

"He smiled, though you could barely tell it from the whiskers, and he gloated even more 'See! It says he may only have the jewels that are less than a thumb! A thumb!' and he held out his thumb, showing how small it was. 'He will have no riches and I will have them all.'

"The emissary sobered quickly, and could not imagine how he would save his king's riches. He thought, and he thought, sitting there and wondering. He read it and read it and could not see any way around the wording of 'The King of the Realm will only be allowed gems under the size of a thumb.' It was then it struck him, it did not say whose thumb." Garion paused, waiting for the children to edge him on.

"Who's thumb did they think it was?" Jon asked.

"Hush, I want to hear the story," Bethany chided him.

"So the emissary took the agreement back to the King of the Realm, and humbly presented it to the King. He smiled and spoke of the agreement he had been struck, and how the King would be rich! 'But how could I be rich with such an agreement?' the King asked of the emissary 'The thumb of a dwarf is small and blunt. I will only have the small jewels and the Dwarf King will have all the big jewels.'

"The emissary just smiled at the King, knowing he was making the same assumption the Dwarf King had made. He waited for a second and agreed with his king. 'Yes, your Majesty, if we assume the Dwarf King's thumb is the one we use to measure against. But I charge you to find it in the agreement where it is his thumb we need to use. In fact, the agreement goes out of its way to not mention whose thumb will be used. Tell me, my King, how big is the thumb of one of the five Gods?' he asked, smiling at his King.

"The King thought of that for a few seconds, and a smile crossed his face. He stood and embraced his emissary, kissing him on each cheek. 'They say the King is smart, but I say he is wise, for the King will always have the wisdom to use the smartest man to do what he is not able to do.' The King sat back on his throne and spoke to the emissary 'You have done well. The Dwarfs also believe in the Five Gods, as do all civilized men. They will not be able to argue this for when one is not mentioned it is one of the Five. The hand of the third brother made the world, and he pushed his thumb into the earth to make the great sea. So to get anything, they will have to have something bigger than the great sea.'

"So with the King's assent to the Dwarf Kings stipulation, the Dwarf King directed his people to start digging. And when, after a year, the Dwarf King had not received any of the jewels that his people had mined, he questioned why. 'I am owed any jewels which are larger than my thumb,' he bellowed, but the jewels were not forthcoming. So the King travelled to the city of the Realm demanding his payment for the use of his people. 'I want my jewels!' the Dwarf King bellowed, looking at the King of the Realm. 'But your people have not dug anything larger than the thumb you mentioned from the mountains,' said the King of the Realm. 'I will show you,' he said, and took the Dwarf King to the treasury.

"When the King opened the treasury to the Dwarf King, his eyes opened wide, and he looked accusingly at the King of the Realm. 'You are cheating me!' he said to the King of the Realm. 'How do you prove that?' the King of the Realm asked the Dwarf King. 'Here,' the Dwarf King said, shoving an emerald in the King of the Realm's hand. 'That is bigger than my thumb!' he said.

"The King looked at it and turned it around in his hand. He looked at the Dwarf King, speaking 'This is a beautiful stone, I admit, and it is large to say the least, but it is not big enough for you!' he said, smiling down at the Dwarf King. 'But it is bigger than my thumb!' yelled the

Dwarf king, holding up his hand, thumb extended to prove he was right.

"The King of the Realm just smiled and produced a copy of the agreement. 'According to this contract, it is not your thumb which is used to measure if a jewel is the size needed for payment. No, it says larger than a thumb! And according to law, if a name is not used to measure, it is considered one of the five would be used. The creator of the world's thumb is still larger than a jewel one hundred times the size of this jewel, so dig and dig, my Dwarf King, dig until you find the jewel of the sea.'

"And that is why no one will make an agreement without a name on it." Garion smiled at the young Spears. "So, can you remember that one also?"

The three smiled and said they enjoyed the story, which made the old man chuckle. And for the rest of the day, they travelled in silence, committing the story to memory. Every once in a while they would retell the story to one another, making sure they had it right, and by the end of the day, the three of them could recite it from memory.

That night, they camped near the first forest, setting up camp at the edge. They still travelled on the peninsula, and the smell of the salt air came across the land.

"It is from the water," Garion said to them, as he finished building the fire. "We will be safe here, but we need to eat."

"I'll go," Jon said, picking up his bow and heading off to the forest.

When he returned, he had a pheasant and a smile.

"He was just twenty feet in, waiting for me," he said.

"Well, let's clean it and get cooking," Garion said.

***

THE NEXT DAY, THE GROUP STAYED CLOSE TO THE INNER shore, preferring to avoid the villages. Past experiences have proven the villagers were always eager to celebrate newly promoted Spears when the travelers stopped to replenish their supplies. Approaching one such village, Garion stopped, then pointed and explained.

"That is the Town of Lands. It is the first village we will stop at, for they have the ability to supply us for the next leg of our journey," Garion said.

"Master Garion?" Jon asked. "Are the Dwarfs still mining the mountains looking for a jewel larger than the thumb of the five?"

Garion laughed, smiling at the thought. "It was a great many years ago. No, they had negotiated a better position with the king not long after. They are rewarded with almost half of what they take out of the mountain. Now, a fair deal for both."

The Town of Lands was a large city, spanning a huge expanse of land. It hugged the shoreline and docks spread out in the water. There were a large number of ships, from merchant to pleasure and military. Garion pointed them out to the young Spears explaining what they were.

The older Spears were right; as they approached the town, folk started to gather. The word spread; newly passed Spears were visiting the town. Soon, it seemed the whole of the town was surrounding them in order to look at the new protectors. Children reached out and touched them while men and women asked for their help. It was confusing, for there should have been a small detachment of Spears in the town.

There were so many hands that Garion and Shail used their mounts to push their way through the crowd, making their way to the building marked as the Court of Spears. It was in this building they would find the men and women assigned to the town as their protectors.

The surprised crowd parted for them as they approached the building, which appeared to be abandoned.

Garion tied the reins of his horse to a post without moving his eyes off the building, he pushed open the door, peering into the darkness of the building, allowing the light of the mid-day sun to penetrate enough to show him something had happened there.

He entered the building and looked for the duty board. His knowledge of how a Court of Spears was run told him anything of importance would be there, and it was.

On one desk was a message concerning the finding of strange occurrences taking place four days' travel from the town. His eyes read further and found the Spears had left the Court in order to investigate, two weeks ago. He wondered what could have happened to them and why no one returned.

"Master Garion, what happened?" It was Bethany, looking in from the doorway of the building.

"I don't know, Bethany, but I intend to find out."

He moved about the room, looking for anything that would tell him what had happened. His eyes went from one part of the room to the other. Six chairs and six desks, six hooks and six holders.

He found the report on the third desk, filled out by the senior Spear of the court. Garion picked it up and read aloud.

"Report by Dynson Paul, lead Spear for the Town of Lands. It is the seventh day of the summer period. Pearson Tan, a farmer from the northern region a full ten leagues distance, had walked almost two days to file this report. He reported ten of his cattle have disappeared in two days, their whereabouts unknown. The fencing around his grazing area has not been disturbed. My fellow Spears and I have agreed to investigate."

Garion put the report back down on the desk and looked at Shail. The other Spear had a furrowed brow as he tried to decide what should be done about it.

"We should investigate while we are here," Garion said to Shail. "But first, we have to hold court for the town."

---

Holding court involved listening to the disputes of the people. Some argued about having been cheated in a trade deal, and others had complaints about theft. The Spears heard them all and called witnesses forth. Most disputes were resolved quickly, while three of them had to be put off for a period while witnesses were found, and the accused called out.

They had overseen a total of twenty disputes and fifteen robbery complaints by the end of the day. Shail requested the remaining people hold their complaints until they returned from the investigation. It was not something he wanted to do, for it meant holding off on the justice needing to be dispensed, but he had to.

Garion agreed with a grumble, and the people agreed and let them be. The first order he gave the Spears was a good night's sleep and food, for the next day would be a hard ride.

And when the morning came, they rose from the beds refreshed. After a quick cleaning, the Spears ate and readied themselves for the journey ahead.

When they exited the building, they saw their horses were brushed and fed. Extra packs had been put on each, giving them supplies to get through the traveling ahead. They mounted and proceeded to ride in the direction of the farmer's home.

The ride was hard, changing between walking and running with the horses. It caused the animals strain, but it was necessary to travel the ten leagues before evening set in. And when they came upon the home, it was just starting to get dark. Approaching the hovel, a large bundling of logs and straw were giving shelter to what appeared to be a deserted home.

"Do you hear that?" Thomasyn asked.

"Hear what?" Jon said.

"Yes, I do. Or should I say I don't hear anything," Bethany said. Both Garion and Shail nodded.

"What is it?" Jon asked.

"Nothing," Thomasyn said.

"Nothing?" Jon exclaimed.

"Exactly. Nothing. No sound from the birds, no sound of animals. Nothing."

Entering the home, they found the bedding and cooking area clean and void of any personal items.

Garion noticed strange marks near one of the beds, but did not know what they were. It could have been an animal, or a person leaving their mark, but it was not something done with a blade, for the marks were not straight but ragged, as if done by a fingernail, or claw.

Exiting the home, they walked towards the shelter built for animals and found it empty. Blood splattered the ground and hay. They all agreed the blood must be that of animals, but why?

When they left the shelter, they noticed darkness had settled over the land, leaving only a slight glow over the hill in the distance.

The soft glow came from the distance, and the Spears decided they would investigate it. The two Masters would go forward, with the three young ones following behind.

They moved quickly, jumping over the fence and silently running through the field. When the Spears reached the end, all of them jumped the fence, landing on the other side just before the forest. It took two strides to reach the woods, and they quickly moved through the trees. The forest grew close together, making it difficult to move swiftly.

After making their way for almost an hour, the trees started to thin out. The light was coming from the forest in front of them, so the group slowed to a careful walk. Soon, the Spears came to the end.

Stretched out in front of them was a clearing that was not clear. The forest ended at the crest of a hill and stretched out in front of them were tents and fires. Moving among the tents were thousands of Hobs, going to spits over fires, pulling off meat and eating. The closest fires did not have food animals, but the bodies of two adults and five children. The Hobs had always had a desire for human flesh, and it appeared the family who lived at the farm had paid for that desire.

It was not just a tribe; it was an invasion army. The thousands stretched out before them, clad in leather and chain, and were ready for war.

Garion looked at Shail, who just stood there, looking out upon the army gathered in the field. The three young Spears came up, and each one took a sharp intake of breath.

Shail shook his head as he saw a tall Hobs walking amongst the force with a spear of the Realm slung on his back. Bethany recognized him.

"That was the one who knocked me out a few years back," she said.

Shail looked at the figure she pointed out. "It is Danton, the Spear of years ago, and that is an invasion army. I think we're in trouble."

# THANK YOU

For reading the first book of the Spear series. Please take the time to either write a review or leave a star rating of the work.

Reviews and ratings are the life blood of the Independent Author and Small Press publishers. Each 5 or 2 star rating and written review tells other readers it is worth at least looking at the work. Please feel free to leave an honest review where you purchased this work.

# About Douglas Owen

Douglas Owen is a writer of fantasy, urban fantasy, science fiction, horror, and crime fiction . His short stories have been published by Cedar Cave Books and Mash Stories.

Doug wrote an article series called A Written View for Self Publisher Magazine, Indyfest Magazine, and Indtale Magazine. He also spent two years as a circulation manager for Indyfest and Self Publisher Magazines.

He is an active member of The Writers' Community of York Region, and spent several years as their Special Events Coordinator, and once ran the communities special Book Shelf event, bringing authors and publishers to the forefront of the region.

Doug lives in Goodwood, Ontario with his wife and three cats who make sure he does not sleep past 5:00 on any given day.

Visit Doug on his website for updates- https://douglasowen.ca

Follow Doug on Facebook https://facebook.com/AuthorDouglasOwen